She heard his footsteps coming down the hall and him shouting, 'It's me Sylvia, where are you?'

'In the kitchen wiping coffee off my blouse.'

'What made you spill your coffee?'

'You, banging on the door like that. Is there a fire?'

'Fire? No.'

'You should really have waited for me to answer the door you know.'

'Well, I knew they were both out, so I thought I'd come and cadge a coffee with my Sylvia.'

'Nevertheless, I work here, Willie, it's not my house, and you should wait. It's only right.'

'Give us a kiss and then I'll remember next time.' He grabbed her round the waist and pulled her to him. 'By Jove, Sylvia, but you're grand. You always taste so sweet.'

'Willie.' Sylvia struggled to get free. 'At your time of life! Kissing in the middle of the morning. Really. Anyone would think you were in your teens.'

'I am. Where's that drink, I'm a working man and I need it.'

Educated at a co-educational Quaker boarding school, Rebecca Shaw went on to qualify as a teacher of deaf children. After her marriage, she spent the ensuing years enjoying bringing up her family. The departure of the last of her four children to university has given her the time and opportunity to write. Her latest novel in paperback in the Turnham Malpas series is *Intrigue in the Village*, and in hardback *Whispers in the Village*, also available from Orion.

By Rebecca Shaw

TALES FROM TURNHAM MALPAS

The New Rector
Talk of the Village
Village Matters
The Village Show
Village Secrets
Scandal in the Village
Village Gossip
Trouble in the Village
A Village Dilemma
Intrigue in the Village
Whispers in the Village

THE BARLEYBRIDGE SERIES

A Country Affair
Country Wives
Country Lovers
Country Passions

Talk of the Village
Tales from Turnham Malpas

REBECCA SHAW

ORION

An Orion paperback
First published in Great Britain
by Orion in 1995
This paperback edition published in 1996
by Orion Books Ltd,
Orion House, 5 Upper St Martin's Lane,
London WC2H 9EA

Tenth impression
Reissued 2005

A CIP catalogue record for this book is
available from the British Library.

ISBN: 0 75282 751 0

Printed and bound in Great Britain by
Clays Ltd, St Ives plc

www.orionbooks.co.uk

Inhabitants of Turnham Malpas

Gwen Baxter	A spinster of the parish.
Beryl Baxter	Her twin sister.
Sadie Beauchamp	Retired widow and mother of Harriet Charter-Plackett.
Sylvia Bennett	A villager from Penny Fawcett.
Willie Biggs	Verger at St Thomas à Becket.
Sir Ronald Bissett	Retired trades union leader.
Lady Sheila Bissett	His wife.
James Charter-Plackett	Owner of the village store.
Harriet Charter-Plackett	His wife.
Fergus, Finlay and Flick	Their children.
Alan Crimble	Barman at The Royal Oak.
Pat Duckett	Village school caretaker.
Dean and Michelle	Her children.
Bryn Fields	New licensee at The Royal Oak.
Georgie Fields	His wife.
Jimmy Glover	Poacher and ne'er-do-well
Revd Peter Harris MA (Oxon)	Rector of the parish.
Dr Caroline Harris	His wife.
Muriel Hipkin	Retired solicitor's secretary. Spinster of the parish.
Jeremy Mayer	Owner of Turnham House Health Club.
Venetia Mayer	Co-owner of the Health Club.
Michael Palmer	Village school headmaster.
Sir Ralph Templeton	Retired from the Diplomatic Service.
Vera Wright	Cleaner at the nursing home in Penny Fawcett.
Don Wright	Her husband.

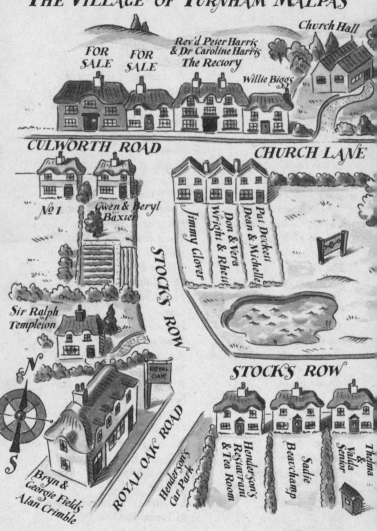

THE VILLAGE OF TURNHAM MALPAS

Church Hall

FOR SALE

FOR SALE

Rev'd Peter Harris & Dr Caroline Harris
The Rectory

Willie Biggs

CULWORTH ROAD

CHURCH LANE

Nº 1

Gwen & Beryl Baxter

Jimmy Glover

Don & Vera Wright & Rhett

Dean & Michelle

Pat Duckett

STOCKS ROW

Sir Ralph Templeton

ROYAL OAK

STOCKS ROW

Bryn & Georgie Fields
Alan Crimble

ROYAL OAK ROAD

Henderson's Car Park

Henderson's Restaurant & Tea Room

Sadie Beauchamp

Thelma Valda Senior

St Thomas à Becket

Muriel Hipkin

Anne Parkin

Liz & Neville Neal Guy & Hugh

GLEBE COTTAGES

GLEBE HOUSE

CHURCH LANE

Jimbo & Harriet Charrier · Plackett Fergus, Finlay & Flick Village Store

JACKS LANE

School House Michael Palmer

STOCKS ROW

Swimming Pool

Turnham Malpas School

SHEPHERDS HILL

Methodist Chapel

Sir Ronald & Lady Bissett Pond

SPARE LAND

BECK

TURNHAM

footbridge

FD '01

Chapter 1

Praise be! Ralph had come home at last. Muriel stood gazing up at his bedroom window, Pericles, beside her on his lead impatiently awaiting his morning run. The bedroom curtains were closed, so he was still in bed. She'd checked his house every morning for the last five days and now her vigil had been rewarded. Muriel glanced at her watch, a quarter to nine. She'd take Pericles for his usual walk and then when she'd dried his feet and shut him in the house, a visit to the Store would be next on her agenda. A nice home-made cheese cake, some fresh rolls, with some of Jimbo's special oak smoked ham on the bone would make a nice lunch for her and Ralph.

As Muriel gazed up at Ralph's bedroom window she felt an unexpected surge of excitement. It filled her heart and spread all over her. Suddenly she wanted Ralph's arms around her and thought it would be the best thing that had ever happened. So re-assuring, so comforting, so right, yes, that was it, so right for her and for him too, she hoped. Muriel tried to imagine what Ralph's face looked like, but the image of it had almost disappeared from her memory. Surely that couldn't happen in one month. Then the clean sharp smell of his after shave seemed to envelope her and with it his face and the whole feel of him came back to her. He was the first man, no,

1

the first person she had wanted to be close to in all her life. How could she have said no so emphatically. This business of not knowing her own mind would have to stop. Sometimes she really was a fool.

Pericles, bored with waiting, lay down on the pavement. Muriel felt the pull of the lead and looked down at him. 'Ralph's back Perry, isn't that lovely? Come along let's be off. Quickly now, no time for lying down.' Pericles stood up and shook himself, but the red wool coat he wore stopped it from being the refreshing activity he had hoped for. He trotted after Muriel pleased that her dilly-dallying was over.

As they walked past the Store, Jimbo came out to inspect his window display.

He raised his straw boater. 'Good morning Muriel. How's things?'

'Very well thank you, Jimbo. Isn't it a lovely day?'

'It is indeed. You seem very chipper this morning, looking forward to the New Year Party?'

'New Year . . . oh yes, that's right, I am. I'll be in later.' She left Jimbo still assessing his new display. Harriet came out to join him.

Harriet tucked her arm in his. 'Darling, I really think you've done the best display ever. I like the way you've tilted that basket with the dried flowers, and the way you've stacked the cheeses, kind of haphazard but planned if you get my meaning. Very effective.' She peered closely at the flower arrangement. 'I seem to recognise those dried poppy seed heads. Jimbo! They're from my display on the landing, it will be ruined now. Really. The corn dollies are a nice touch, bit out of season but appropriate.'

'Considering I was in a merchant bank a little more than three years ago plaiting nothing but paper, I've got quite good at this window lark haven't I?'

'Well, if this doesn't sell off the Christmas cheeses I

don't know what will. We'll do a tasting shall we?'

'Why not? Organise it if you please.'

'Certainly sir. Oh there's Linda. 'Morning Linda.'

Linda waved to the two of them. Jimbo with his striped apron, his white shirt and the bow tie matching the ribbon on his straw boater, bowed to her, Harriet in her 'taking out the Range Rover to pick up the fresh supplies from the farms outfit', curtsied and the three of them laughed.

Harriet said, 'They're queueing for their pensions already Linda.'

'Sorry I'm late.' Linda rushed in to begin the business of the day. Harriet went to start up the Range Rover and Jimbo went inside, well satisfied with having stayed up until twelve the night before to finish the window.

An hour later the door bell jangled and Jimbo looked up from serving a customer to find Ralph had entered the Store. Ralph was thinner, much thinner but tanned, his white hair even whiter if that was possible. But he was looking as aristocratic as ever. His holiday, or whatever it was that had made him disappear so surprisingly, had obviously done him good.

Jimbo went to shake hands with him.

'Delighted to have you back Ralph, we've missed you, specially over Christmas. How are you?'

'Very well, thank you Jimbo. You appear to be in tip top condition. Nothing seems to have changed in my absence.'

Jimbo clapped his hand to his forehead in mock despair. 'I slaved until midnight last night doing that window display and you say nothing has changed!'

'Blame it on jet lag, I've not come round yet.'

'Been somewhere exciting?'

'Visiting friends. I need to shop for my breakfast Jimbo, I've nothing fresh in at all.'

'Oh, I see . . . didn't Muriel get you anything in?'

'No, she doesn't know I'm back.' Ralph took a basket and began collecting what he needed from the shelves. Jimbo went to serve another customer.

When Ralph went to the cash till to pay for his breakfast Jimbo wished to ask why he had gone off so suddenly, but a tactful phrase simply wouldn't come to mind, so he had to reluctantly open the door for him and wish him good morning. In the hurly-burly of a busy pre-New Year shopping spree, Jimbo scarcely noticed that Muriel had been in to buy lunch. Working without Harriet, combined with having given his part-time girl an extra day off for working so hard before Christmas, he battled on by himself with little time for conversation. Muriel on her part was glad to escape without having to give an explanation of why she was buying two slices of cheese cake instead of her usual single slice.

When she got home she put the ham in the fridge and the cheese cake out on the worktop to defrost and then having been in the bathroom to titivate herself and spray on some of the perfume Caroline, dear Caroline, had given her on Christmas Day she sauntered as casually as she could down to Ralph's house. She wore her new, well, newest coat, wine red with a black fur collar and carried the black leather bag Ralph had brought her back from London. Muriel's fair hair, well, nearly white hair, peeped out from under her fake fur hat. She hoped her dark red lipstick didn't exaggerate her pale skin. One day I shall try some blusher she thought, but right now she was blushing without any artificial aid and trembling inside too. Oh good, he was up. The knock on Ralph's door had not been loud enough. She tried again. Oh dear, that was enough to wake the dead. The door was opened abruptly and there he stood, smiling tentatively down at her, his lovely fine-boned hands held out in greeting.

4

'Muriel my dear, come in.' As he took her hand Muriel burst into tears. She hadn't expected to, so she'd no handkerchief available. Ralph gave her his own and his thoughtfulness made her cry even more.

'Oh, Ralph, I have been a fool. Such a fool.'

'Never, Muriel, never a fool my dear.'

'Yes, yes. A complete fool.' She wiped her eyes dry and smiled shakily at him. 'Could you possibly come for lunch?'

'I've just finished breakfast, but for you I'll eat lunch too.'

'Oh not yet, I meant later about one o'clock.'

'I'll bring some wine shall I?'

Muriel was scandalised. 'In the middle of the day?'

'You drank it in the middle of the day when we were in Rome.'

'Of course I did. Yes then, bring some wine.'

'So be it.'

Muriel studied his face. She reached out to touch his arm. 'Ralph you've lost weight, have you been ill?'

'In my heart.'

'Your heart? Have you got heart trouble?'

'Don't you remember almost the last word you said to me?'

Filled with sadness she answered 'I said, "No". Forgive me for causing you so much pain. I did say I'd been a complete fool. I'm sorry I was so dreadfully unkind.' Muriel reached up, pecked his cheek and said, 'See you shortly.' She spun round and went out before she could reveal any more of how she felt. As she hurried along Church Lane past the Rectory Caroline came out and almost collided with her.

Caroline clutched hold of her. 'Steady Muriel.' They both laughed at each other. 'Where are you going in such a hurry?'

'Oh Caroline, I'm going to take your advice.'

5

'My advice? what about?'

'Ralph's home and I'm going to do what you said and orchestrate a proposal!'

'About time too. Peter will be delighted. He hasn't had many weddings to conduct lately, he was saying the other day he'd be losing his touch.'

'Oh dear, yes of course. Oh dear. I must be off I've got lunch to get ready. Oh dear. Oh my goodness.'

'Muriel do try to be happy, it's the first day of the rest of your life.'

'Of course, yes . . . what a lovely idea. Yes, of course it is. Bye bye.'

Caroline watched her dash off down Church Lane. Today was the first day of the rest of Caroline's life too, but she hadn't wanted to take away from Muriel's happiness by telling her. Today she, Caroline Harris would become a mother. A real honest to goodness mother of two. She and Peter were going at two o'clock to collect the twins from the hospital. Never again would she have to worry about Peter not having the children he wanted, because now he had his very own two children. Alexander and Elizabeth. Alex and Beth. Beth and Alex. Caroline stood watching Jimmy's geese as they grazed on the village green. In her mind's eye she could see the twins snuggled in their cots in the hospital, their tiny hands clenched tight, their eyelids fluttering a little as they slept. Thank God they'd decided to put weight on instead of losing it. Maybe they'd not fed eagerly because they were grieving for their mother. No that couldn't be it, could it? Still, they'd finally decided to feed well and gain weight so she needn't worry about them now. Just to get them home. Home! That sounded wonderful. She decided she was going to make a really successful job of bringing up the twins. Try to make them each feel they were the only one that counted. Full of anticipation she pushed open the door of the Store, in her pocket the list she'd made of the food she needed to fill the freezer before she became too busy to shop.

As Caroline dumped yet another basket of food by the till Jimbo asked, 'My word Caroline, I know Peter's a huge chap and has a big appetite but this is ridiculous. Do you know something I don't know? Is there going to be a siege or something?'

'Can you keep a secret?'

'Cross my heart and hope to die,' said Jimbo suiting the action to the words.

'I'm stocking the freezer because . . . well, we hardly dare believe it but the twins are well enough to come home, and we're collecting them this afternoon. I'm sure they'll be OK but you never know with them being so tiny, do you?'

'Caroline, I'm delighted for you.' He came round from behind the counter and hugged her.

Harriet coming out from the storeroom grinned. 'That's enough Jimbo please, hugging the customers. Whatever next? Is this a new sales gimmick? As the rector's wife, you ought to know better than to encourage him Caroline!'

Jimbo whispered, 'Hush Harriet, Caroline is collecting the twins this afternoon.'

'Oh how wonderful. I won't tell a soul or you'll be overwhelmed with visitors. Everyone is so excited and I'm so jealous of you having new babies in the house. I feel quite broody. We've made sure we've plenty of "new baby" cards in stock haven't we Jimbo?'

Caroline pulled their legs about their sharp eye for business. Having paid for the food she realised she should have brought her car round. 'I don't know what I'm doing this morning, I'm a complete idiot and so is Peter. He tried to start his car without the keys in this morning and wondered why it wasn't moving. Then he realised he'd left the Communion wine behind and had to come

7

back for it. If we're like this before the twins come home, what will we be like afterwards?'

Harriet assured her that things would all work out, and suggested she should bring everything across to the Rectory in the Range Rover which was still outside.

'Thanks very much. I appreciate that. Bye Jimbo.'

Mother's clock was striking a quarter to one when Muriel heard Ralph at the door. She checked her hair and face in the little mirror she kept for the purpose in her tiny kitchen and hastened across the living room to open the door. The small dining table in the window was already laid, all she needed to do was put the food on it.

Momentarily the two of them were silent as they looked at each other across the threshold.

'Shall I come in?'

'Oh yes, I'm so sorry, please, yes, please come in.'

'I'm early, I know, but I couldn't wait to come.'

'It doesn't matter, everything's ready. I shall never learn to be late. Sit down Ralph and I'll put the things on the table. Oh you've brought the wine.'

'Yes, I've had it in the fridge since you called, it should be just right.' Their hands touched as she took the bottle and Muriel felt as though she'd had an electric shock.

'Oh Ralph.' She stood on tip toe and pressed her lips to his. When she stepped back her face was flushed and she apologised. 'I'm so sorry, I beg your pardon. You sit down, I'll get on and make the coffee.' A wisp of hair came down across her forehead. Flustered and embarrassed she reached up to push it away only to find Ralph taking hold of her hand and putting it to his lips to kiss.

'It tastes of ham, smoked ham. Let me see, yes, that's right, vintage Jimbo Charter–Plackett.'

Muriel laughed. 'That's right.' She scurried away into the kitchen hoping for a moment's respite but Ralph

8

followed her in. Being such a small kitchen Muriel felt smothered by his presence there. She was acutely aware of him and couldn't avoid savouring the smell of his after shave or was it cologne or . . . She turned to pick up the coffee pot and bumped into him. In a moment his arms were round her and they were kissing as if their lives depended on it.

'Muriel, Muriel, I have missed you.' Ralph buried his face in her neck and she reached up to stroke his head.

'I've missed you too Ralph. If you still feel the same I desperately want to change that "No" to a "Yes".'

Ralph drew back and looked closely at her. He cupped his hands around her cheeks and said, 'Muriel Hipkin are you proposing to me?'

'Well, yes, I think I must be.'

'Hallelujah. What a day. Let's open the wine and drink a toast.'

He expertly removed the cork, poured them each a glass and raised his in a toast to her.

'To Muriel, my best beloved.'

'To Ralph, *my* best beloved.' Muriel sipped her wine and then said hesitantly, 'You haven't answered me yet.'

'The answer, my dear, is yes. I shan't let you forget you proposed though. Who would have imagined the day would come when you did that?'

'If my mother knew what I'd done she be ashamed of me.'

'Mothers don't always know best. To save you any further shame I'll ask you. Muriel Hipkin will you marry me immediately?'

'Yes. A thousand times yes.'

After lunch, during which they'd interrupted almost every mouthful to say something meaningful to each other, Ralph with a twinkle in his eye said, 'Do you remember when we were children I used to tease you about that initial "E" in your name and you would never tell me what it stood for. I used to try to guess, Ethel, Eloise, Edna, Enid, Elise, Evadne, Elsie . . . but you never told me. Seeing as I am shortly, very shortly, to become your husband will you tell me now?'

'Husband, oh my word. Oh dear, I shall be Lady Templeton. Oh, Ralph, what have I done?'

'Nothing yet, but you still haven't told me what the "E" stands for.'

'I have to have something of mystery about me, anyway it's so excruciating I can hardly bear to think about you knowing.'

'More wine my dear?' As he leant across to fill her glass he said, 'Still, I shall know on our wedding day because Peter will have to use your full name. I can wait.'

'Will he really? Oh dear, the whole village will know then.'

'Don't worry it will only be a nine days wonder.'

'Ralph!'

'By the way Muriel, in my male arrogance I assumed that when I proposed you would say yes . . .' Muriel reached across the table and stroked his hand. 'I am sorry about that, but you wouldn't have wanted me to say yes before I was sure would you?'

'No, my dear I wouldn't, so I made arrangements to buy Suzy Meadow's house as a surprise . . .'

'Oh Ralph, really? I thought you were going to buy Toria Clark's cottage.'

'So I was, but I decided it wouldn't be big enough for a married man. It's all signed sealed and delivered now, or it will be by the end of next week, so I intend moving shortly. Do you think you could live in Suzy's old house or would you prefer somewhere else?'

'Oh no, I've always liked her house.'

'We could always redecorate if you wish.'

'No, certainly not, I like it as it is. I shall really enjoy working in her garden.' Muriel couldn't help feeling sad at the prospect of leaving her beloved cottage. 'I shall miss my view of the churchyard. When I sell this house I hope the person who buys it loves it like I do.'

'We could live here if you want,' said Ralph.

'Certainly not, it wouldn't be suitable. And there isn't room for all your things and mine.'

'Well, I have got boxes and boxes in store which I have never looked at since I came home to England.'

'Well, there you are then, we need Suzy's house.'

After lunch Muriel cleared away. Ralph helped and they washed the dishes together talking about where he had been, and trying to decide where to go for their honeymoon.

'That does seem a foolish word to use, Ralph, for people as old as we are.'

'I'm hoping that even though we are older we shall still have a wonderful time together. It's the first time for both of us Muriel, so it can be as exciting or as dull as we choose to make it.'

Muriel was worrying and didn't know how to phrase the next thing she wanted to say. To give herself time she tested the little plant she kept on her window sill to see if it needed more water. She felt Ralph's hand on her arm. He turned her round and held her close and then stood away from her and smiled. 'You're very quiet, is there something you want to say?'

'Not just now . . .'

'Have you got some doubts?'

'Oh, no. No. It's not that.' Muriel rinsed the tea pot out again and dried it till it gleamed. It had been mother's favourite pot. She could almost see her mother's face reflected in the shining brown roundness of the pot. Her mother had never discussed anything to do with being a woman, not in all her life. Muriel realised she was as ill prepared for marriage at sixty-four as she had been at sixteen.

11

'I'm still here.' Ralph was leaning against the washer, arms folded, patiently studying her face.

'Ralph, you'll have to help me. I shall need help, you see, to get it right. I don't understand how to feel inside myself, because I've never had those kind of feelings. I don't know how it feels to want a m . . . I think passion is the word I mean. It's an old fashioned word but that's what I mean. I know you want us to be truly married, and so do I but . . .' Muriel blushed bright red and turned away from him to look out of the window. Her winter garden was just beginning to get a little colour, she could see the snowdrops peeping green through the soil. But soon she'd be leaving it for a whole new life and it would be someone else's winter garden. The enormity of what she'd done struck her and she felt intensely shy of the future. Why had she used the word passion? Now she'd have to face up to something she had avoided thinking about all her life.

'Muriel,' Ralph said gently, reminding himself as he spoke of the gentle delicacy of Muriel's nature and not wishing to trample all over it with some kind of hearty ho! ho! "it'll be all right on the night" kind of speech. 'I love you and you love me and because of that we'll make our married life absolutely lovely and satisfying in every way. We shan't rush things, we'll go steadily because that way we shall both reap rich rewards. I'll help you to feel passion, my dear, and I do love you all the more for your reticence. You can have confidence in me.'

'I can, can't I? You'll look after me, won't you Ralph?'

'Of course.'

'Please Ralph, let's go and see Peter about getting married. Can we get a special licence or something? If we wait a long time I shall get doubts and want to change my mind.'

'Very well, we'll go and tell Peter you can't wait to get married and which is his first free Saturday.'

12

'Ralph! You mustn't say I can't wait.'

'Well, I certainly can't.'

'Neither can I! I'll get my coat.'

They arrived at the rectory door still laughing.

It seemed a while before Peter answered their knock. 'Why Ralph, hello. Caroline said you were back.' He shook Ralph's hand. 'Lovely to see you, you're looking well. Have you had a good trip? We missed you over Christmas. Come in both of you. Hello Muriel, God bless you.'

'Hello Peter. Ralph has something to say.'

'Can we talk privately?'

'Certainly, come into my study. I'd offer you tea but Caroline's busy at the moment. Have you come to tell me something exciting? You both look very pleased with yourselves.'

Peter led the way into his study, and sat his two visitors in the easy chairs and then himself in his chair by the desk. Ralph cleared his throat, took Muriel's hand in his and asked Peter if he could fit in a wedding ceremony during the next few weeks.

'What? Oh I am delighted, absolutely delighted, I couldn't be more pleased. That's really great. Wonderful.' He stood up to shake Ralph's hand and then kissed Muriel on both cheeks. 'Just what we've all been waiting for. Is it a secret or can I tell Caroline?' Muriel nodded.

He opened the study door and shouted, 'Caroline, can you spare a minute?'

The moment Caroline saw the two of them in the study she knew they had come to arrange their marriage.

'Don't tell me, let me guess. You're getting married. I'm so pleased for you both, so very pleased. Peter, this calls for champagne.'

'Well, we have that bottle ready in the fridge for tonight. We don't *have* to wait till then do we?'

'In fact it might be best to have it now while all's quiet.'

Muriel looked curiously at the two of them. 'All's quiet? What's going to happen tonight?'

Caroline and Peter grinned at each other. 'You've only just caught us in, we've been to the hospital this afternoon . . .'

Muriel stood up quickly full of joy. 'You've been for the twins!'

'Yes.' Caroline hugged Muriel and she in turn hugged Caroline and then Peter.

'Oh where are they? Please let me see them.'

'Come on then, you too Ralph.' The four of them went upstairs into the nursery to gaze with love and admiration on Alex and Beth, each firmly tucked up in matching swinging cribs. Alex lay quietly sleeping, wisps of his bright blond hair just showing above the blanket, his tiny fists held close to his face. Muriel gently drew the blanket back and saw he still strongly re-sembled Peter, and felt uncomfortable at the thought of what the villagers would make of that. She rather hoped no one would notice. Loud sucking noises were coming from Beth's crib, and when Muriel peeped in she saw that little Beth had her thumb in her mouth.

Muriel clapped her hands with glee. 'Aren't they lovely Ralph? Just perfectly lovely. You must both feel so happy to have them safely home.'

'We are, but I'm terribly nervous. They'll be waking up any minute now for a feed and I shan't know where to begin, but we'll learn, we'll have to.' Caroline tucked the blanket a little more firmly around Alex and smoothed her hand around the top of Beth's head.

'How much do they weigh now, Caroline?'

'Alex is five pounds two ounces and Beth only just five pounds. But they are gaining a little every day now, thank the Lord. We'll go get that champagne before they wake up.'

They touched glasses and Peter said, 'May God bless

14

all four of us on this very special day in our lives. Ralph echoed his thoughts with 'God bless us all and give us all great happiness in the future.' Muriel clinked her glass with Caroline's and said 'Amen to that.'

Chapter 2

Jimbo, balancing on the top step of his ladder, was attempting to fasten a banner above the sign on his new restaurant. When he'd finally secured it, he leant back as far as he dare to read the words. 'CONGRATULATIONS ON YOUR WEDDING DAY.' That would give Muriel and Ralph a lovely surprise when they opened their respective bedroom curtains this morning. He climbed down from the top of his ladder and stood back to admire his endeavours. Turquoise and silver hydrogen-filled balloons, three at each end of the banner, were blowing briskly in the early morning breeze. A work of art Jimbo admitted to himself. In such good taste too. Oh well, lots to do, must get on. There was the cake to finish, and the bride to give away, to say nothing of the food to prepare for the village reception that evening. He folded up his ladder and turned to go inside, pausing for a moment's peace at the beginning of his hectic day, to look at the sleeping village.

Best day's work he'd ever done moving to Turnham Malpas. He'd been on a treadmill at that damned merchant bank. Living on his nerves and for what? A smart house, smart friends, smart garden, smart clothes? Trading it all in for a country store had seemed exceedingly rash at the time but what a superb business he, well Harriet and he, were making out of it. And the children were growing up in peace and quiet, that was the bonus. The sun was now well over the tops of the Clintock Hills; it shone on the Church of St Thomas à Becket and the old white-walled houses, making the village look at its best. This was a great day for them all. True, Sir Ralph wasn't Lord of the Manor any more, but he still carried that aristocratic air and all the old villagers acknowledged him as such, even after nearly fifty years without the Big House at the hub of their lives. As for Muriel, what a very exciting day it would be for her. Jimbo bustled inside. Lots to do, lots to do.

By five minutes to twelve the church was filled to overflowing, for the guests invited to the wedding and the breakfast afterwards had been joined by dozens of villagers. All eagerly awaited the bride's arrival. The choir was in place and the rector, Peter Harris, stood on the altar steps dressed in his white marriage cassock and his best surplice. The entire congregation was hushed in anticipation.

At a signal from the verger, Mrs Peel the organist burst into Mendelssohn's *Wedding March*. Sir Ralph rose and stood next to his best man, an old university friend whom no one knew, as Muriel Hipkin entered the church on Jimbo Charter-Plackett's arm. She wore a pale turquoise suit, matching shoes, and a tiny stylish turquoise hat with a fine veil softening its outline and covering her hair and forehead. In her trembling fingers was a small bouquet of white flowers. Muriel was nervous but triumphant. She'd been awake since first light, thinking about giving the whole of her future happiness into the hands of this man, Ralph. The momentous decision to marry Ralph, once she had made it, was so absolutely right.

As Muriel approached the altar steps she saw that Ralph had turned to greet her, his strong features

17

softened by love and by the sheer delight he felt at her arrival and at her charming appearance. He reached forward to take her hand and Muriel gave it to him without any reservations. Ralph leaned towards her and whispered, 'You look beautiful, my dear.'

When it came to the time for making their vows they turned to face each other and spoke steadily in firm, confident voices. The choirboys, dressed in their best ceremonial cassocks and ruffles, had to stifle giggles when they heard Peter say '. . . *this woman Muriel Euphemia Hipkin* . . .' Peter's address during the service brought some members of the congregation close to tears.

'I shall first read St Paul's thoughts on love, from Corinthians Book One, Chapter Thirteen.

'"Love is patient and kind; it is not jealous, nor conceited, nor proud; love is not ill-mannered nor selfish nor irritable; love does not keep a record of wrongs; love is not happy with evil, but is happy with the truth. Love never gives up; and its faith, hope and patience never fail. Love is eternal."

'It is only a short time ago that we welcomed Ralph on his return to the village after a long absence. His work in the Diplomatic Service has taken him worldwide, but the ties he had with the place in which he was born brought him winging his way back here when that work was done. He didn't know when he made the decision to return that Muriel, a childhood friend, had already come back. Some of you will recall that the bride and groom played together as children and that where Ralphie went, Moo was sure to follow. Recently we have watched them revive those early years. We all kept hoping that they would finally make it to the altar. There were some ups and downs, and at one stage it seemed we had all hoped in vain, but at last they have stood before God and declared their love. Muriel and Ralph, you have made your vows, secure in the knowledge that between you there is love which knows no bounds, love which *is* eternal. May God bless you both as you begin your married life together.'

When the wedding service was concluded the guests and villagers went out into the spring sunshine to watch the photographs being taken. They clutched their un-opened boxes of confetti, mindful of Willie Biggs' ire should they sprinkle it around within the church pre-cincts. The children from the village school formed a guard of honour down each side of the path. Dressed in their best and firmly instructed by their parents in the behaviour expected of them, they waved their Union Jacks and smiled until their faces ached. The bells of St Thomas à Becket rang out across the village filling the air with exultant sound. Everyone wanted to shake hands with the bride and groom and wish them the very best.

'Congratulations.'

'All the very best.'

'You look lovely Miss Hipkin . . . oooops Lady Templeton, beg yer pardon.'

'Lovely service.'

'Could 'ear every word you said, Muriel, and we all thought you'd be too shy.'

'Good luck to you both.'

'Get in the photo, Rector. At the back please, seeing as you're so tall, sir.'

'Them choir boys need keeping in check. Giggling all the time. Still 'er name was funny. Euphoria was it?'

'Wonder if they'll 'ave separate bedrooms, all them Dukes and Duchesses 'ave their own rooms.'

'Shut up, Pat. Now's not the time for that.'

Cameras of all shapes and vintage clicked and clicked again.

Once Ralph and Muriel were safely through the lych gate there was a concerted rush to shower them with confetti. Finally they were free to leave for their reception. Waiting in Church Lane was a beautiful open carriage and pair. The horses had their tails and manes plaited with turquoise and white ribbons and the driver wore a black coachman's coat and top hat. Ralph handed Muriel into the carriage with a flourish and seated himself beside her. Top hat in hand he acknowledged the cheers and good wishes with a wave as the carriage pulled away.

Harriet turned to Caroline and said, 'Don't they look splendid? What a send off.'

'They do. And they look so very happy.'

'I thought Peter's address struck just the right note.'

'He really laboured over it, it's so easy to wax dreadfully coy with a marriage service and he knew Ralph wouldn't like that at all. I'm just going to check that my parents are coping with the twins, so we'll see you at The George, Harriet.'

'Right. I'll find Jimbo and we'll be off too. He's in his element today. See you there.'

After the bridal party and guests had departed for the wedding breakfast at The George in Culworth, the rest of the villagers went home with the evening reception to look forward to. Lady Sheila Bissett longed to get home to kick off her shoes, she should never have bought them half a size too small just because they didn't have her size in stock. She'd be glad to get home anyway, because Ron was pestering her about her leopard skin coat. He'd never liked it but she did and that was what counted. Anyway, it was winter even if it was a wedding. And just wait till he saw her tonight, she'd show them all how to dress.

They'd had lunch and were fast asleep in front of the TV when Lady Bissett was awakened by frenzied barking. Oh no, not Flick Charter-Plackett's cats again. Pom and Pericles were behaving like crazed animals. Why Ron had promised to have Pericles while Muriel went on her honeymoon she never would know. They each encouraged the other where the cats were concerned. One whiff of a cat and they both went berserk. Sheila was sure that Chivers and Hartley came into their garden just for the fun of it. She looked out of the window. The two cats had just decided where they preferred to relieve themselves when Pom and Pericles pounced. Caught in mid stream as it were, the cats were at a disadvantage but fought their attackers with spirit. The spitting and snarling, the barking and growling could not be ignored.

Sir Ronald came out with Sheila hard on his heels. She was raucous in her annoyance.

'Ron. Ron. Get them both. Those bloody cats will tear their eyes out. Oh, Pom, come here darling.'

The protagonists ignored her cries. Pom and Pericles raced down the garden in hot pursuit, the cats spitting and clawing as they went. Sheila, abandoning any pretence of gentility, was shrieking at the top of her voice.

Sir Ronald charged down the garden carrying a large spade, looking as though he intended to flatten any cat within reach. By now Pericles had really caught the spirit of the exercise and was doing his best to murder Chivers. Confused by all the barking and still only half awake, Sir Ronald launched himself at Hartley, missed his footing and plummeted headlong into his ten-by-eight pre-moulded glassfibre pond with two shelves at differing depths for water plants, where his Harris tweed suit, purchased to make him look like a countryman, rapidly absorbed a good deal of water. Forgetting the dogs Sheila went to his rescue. As she gave him a hand to climb out the cats left the scene of battle and hurried out of the garden. Pom and Pericles, well satisfied with the mayhem they had caused, returned to the house, drank deeply from their water bowls and then lay down, each in his own bed, to contemplate their part in the chase. What Ron and Sheila had not realised was that Flick had been watching the whole proceedings from the side gate, her screams of protest unheard in the general mêlée.

Sir Ronald stood in the back porch removing his clothes while Sheila went inside for a large bath towel. The damage done to the garden and the pond by the skirmish was more than she could bear. The fish would sulk for at least a fortnight and the herbacious border, just when the plants were beginning to grow again, would most likely take all summer to recover. By the time she returned with the bath towel Sir Ronald had undressed down to his underpants. An angry voice boomed over the gate.

'Sir Ronald, a word if you please.' Jimbo Charter-Plackett, still wearing his morning coat, was striding into the garden. 'Got back early from the reception to find Flick running down Stocks Row in floods of tears saying you've tried to kill her cats with a spade.'

Unhinged by the ridiculous position he was in Sir Ronald stormed out of the porch and confronted Jimbo, his dignity considerably dented by the wet underpants clinging to his thick, overweight body and the pondweed coating his head and face.

His wife rushed after him with the towel but he waved her angrily aside.

'I'm sick of your bloody cats. They wander about all over the place. We're not the only ones who complain. Ruin my garden they do, they use it as a damned public convenience.'

Sheila tried desperately to rescue what little was left of Ron's dignity, 'Ron, Ron, please put this towel round you.'

'Shut up Sheila. Do you hear me Jimbo? It's open war from now on. I shall use cat powder and any other device I can think of to defend my garden.'

'Come, come now *Sir Ronald*, they're only young cats and it's caused Flick a great deal of distress. It's not fair to

22

threaten them with a spade. What have you been doing to yourself, by the way? You look perfectly ridiculous in those drawers, man. Get yourself covered up.'

'Covered up? It's your cats I shall be covering up, dead and buried they'll be if I have my way.'

Jimbo stepped forward and prodded his finger sharply on Ron's fat wet chest. 'Lay one finger on those cats and I shall have you prosecuted and I mean that. Flick's already had one cat drowned as you know, she can't cope with any more tragedies. Now go inside and get yourself attended to before you make any more of a spectacle of yourself.' Jimbo in a blazing temper turned on his heel and marched forcefully out of the gate, banging it shut and nearly breaking the catch. Sir Ronald took the towel, wrapped it round himself and strode, with what little dignity he had left, into his house.

Sheila knew when to keep quiet and now was the time. Normally she ruled the roost in the Bissett household, but there were days when even Sheila knew that silence was golden. She could hear Ron stamping about in the bathroom. He was so careless of all her frills and flounces: heaven alone knew what the lavender carpet and bath mat would look like when he'd finished. She'd chosen them so carefully to tone with the navy fitments. The cover on the toilet lid was lavender as well. She'd bought them all in Marks & Spencer and knew the moment she saw them that they would give the right effect. But it was the white basketwork shelving holding the glass jars of guest soaps and bath pearls and the lace tissue-holder which were the delight of her life. And the nets at the bathroom window, frilled all round the edges and draped tastefully over the frosted glass, were white as well with little sprays of flock flowers. The bathroom was one of her triumphs. Since she'd married Ron life had not had many delights for her financially, but these last few years, with his broadcasting fees and all the trips abroad he'd had with the Union and the expense account, things had improved considerably.

Sitting at her bow-fronted dressing table, Sheila heard the bathroom door slam shut. Ron came in stark naked.

'I've told you before, Ron, not to walk about like that.'

'Who's to see me?'

'Well me for instance, and it's not nice.'

'I'm not concerned whether it's nice or not I'm too occupied thinking about how to stop those damned cats from ruining our garden.'

'I thought Jimbo had rather a lot too much to say. Such a temper he has . . .'

'Barbed wire that's the answer. Cat powder only puts them off when they've got in, I've got to stop them getting in at all.'

'Barbed wire? We'll look like Colditz.'

'I don't care. Barbed wire it is. Or else we'll get a bigger dog who'll kill the blasted beggars.'

'Ron, you know I don't like language like that.'

'There isn't a word in the English language that fits those blasted cats.'

'In any case Pom wouldn't like another dog here. It would upset him dreadfully.'

'Might do him good, brighten his ideas up a bit. You make him too mamby pamby Sheila, I've told you about it before. He only comes alive when Perry comes to stay.'

'So you say. I think he's all right on his own. You should never have volunteered to have Perry. Three months' honeymoon in Australia, I ask you. That Muriel Hipkin's never been further than Bournemouth I should think, not till Sir Ralph came back. First Rome and now Australia . . . she's played her cards right, and no mistake. Managed to land him at last. What on earth he sees in her I shall never know. Ron, do you think they'll . . .

you know . . . ?'

'Eh? Oh that, I haven't any idea about that. I might as well put on the clothes I'm wearing tonight at the reception. Wish it could be my tweed suit. Bloody cats.'

'It wouldn't have been suitable anyway. People like us have to show the villagers the right way. You need your funeral suit love. With that nice spotted tie Bianca bought you for Christmas.'

'I'll look like a dog's dinner. You know I don't like that suit. I should never have let you persuade me to buy it.'

'Men in your position need to look smart. Whatever would they think if you went on telly with a ginger tweed suit on? Right country bumpkin that would make you look.'

'When I ordered that tweed outfit you said it would make me look like a country squire.'

'Well it does, but the telly people wouldn't see it like that would they?' Sheila concentrated on her nail varnish. One stroke down the middle of the nail and then one each side. This pale apricot would look splendid with her new dress. She couldn't wait to put it on. She'd never bought anything in Thoms & Curtis before, but one did have to set standards in the village. So easy to let things slide. The clothes that Caroline Harris wore, considering she was only a rector's wife, were unbelievably beautiful. Still, she had been a doctor all those years so she must have earned a lot of money in the past. And she did have style. Those twins, though, they must be hard work. Hardly any sleep at all some nights. They were lovely babies. Amazing how like Peter the little boy was. They say that about adopted children, how they start to resemble their new parents as they get older. But they must only be about eight weeks old at the most. Wonder what Harriet Charter-Plackett will wear tonight. Another of her Sloane Street creations no doubt. Still, wait till they see me in my outfit.

Sheila got up from the dressing table now her nails were dry and took the dress out of the wardrobe. She had little pot pourri bags hanging from each coat hanger to keep her clothes fresh. She bought them from a local girl who made anything and everything, edged with lace. Sheila was always popping in for something. One of her best customers she was. The dress was made of lime-green flowered brocade with a pleated peplum around the back which went flat as it came over the hips and across her stomach. It had a stand-up collar with large revers which crossed over just below where her cleavage began. Either side of the collar below her collar bones was a neat design of pearls sewn around the shape of one of the brocade flowers. She'd seen Ron look askance when she'd tried it on in the shop. She knew he didn't like her to display herself, but the dress was so right she couldn't resist.

She laid it on the quilted white satin bedspread and slipped off her négligé revealing a dumpy figure clothed in a Marks & Spencer slightly-too-tight underslip. When the dress was on, she turned this way and that inspecting herself in the mirrors on her wall-to-wall wardrobes. Yes, it was just right for the occasion, and just right for church in the summer, too. She'd make their heads turn. They were all beginning to accept that she was the lady of the village now. Her flower arranging and her organisation of the Village Flower Show had given her a real solid position in village life. They couldn't manage without her in Turnham Malpas now, no siree. Her black strappy high heels were uncomfortable but they'd soon wear in.

'You're ready too soon Sheila.' Ron yawned.

'I know. I thought I'd go and sit downstairs and give my shoes a chance to wear in a bit. There's a nice programme on the telly I can watch.'

'I wanted to see the sport.'

'Well, you watch it up here and I'll go downstairs. I'll

spoil my dress if I lie on the bed.'

Sheila let the dogs into the garden seeing as she and Ron would be out for a long time at the reception. That Pericles was a right card. Seemed to really enjoy being able to race about instead of being all stiff and starchy with that prim Miss Hipkin. She made their dinners for them and then installed herself in the sitting room. All the cushions on the beige Dralon three-piece had shiny curly fringes and huge embossed flowers in the centre. The arms were thick and solid and never failed to give Sheila a thrill when she looked at them. Perhaps they were a bit on the big side for an old cottage, but even so they added a real touch of class.

On the mantelpiece above the inglenook fireplace stood the wedding invitation card. *'Sir Ronald and Lady Bissett'* it read. Sheila ran her fingers along the embossed lettering and smiled with pride. They'd come a long way she and Ron. She switched on the telly and got out a box of Newberry fruits. She didn't rest her head against the cushion in case she ruffled her strawberry-blonde hair. She'd had the roots done only a week ago so it was looking its best. Hope this reception was worth all the trouble, she thought as her eyes began closing.

Chapter 3

By six o'clock that evening there was a steady stream of people heading for Henderson's Tearoom and Restaurant. Many of the guests lived so close they were able to walk to the reception. Most joined up with others and chatted and laughed their way through the village. Two of the guests walked alone. In the dark they were barely discernible and in their black coats and hats they appeared to the fanciful eye to be ghostly wraiths wending their way to some macabre feast. In fact they were Gwen and Beryl Baxter who'd lived in the village at number two all their lives. As children in the village school they'd always been considered odd, but in later years their oddities had become more pronounced. They rarely spoke to anyone and certainly no one could remember ever having been inside their house. If their windows were anything to go by, the habituées of The Royal Oak opposite guessed the house must be filthy. They were right. It was. Only Gwen went out and that was to the Store for food. Tonight the two of them were making one of their rare sorties out into the world.

They bumped into Peter and Caroline as they pushed their way through the restaurant door.

'Good evening to you both. How nice to see you.' Peter's hand, extended to shake theirs, was ignored.

'Isn't it lovely having a village party for Ralph and

Muriel?' Caroline tried. There was no reply.

'You go in first, ladies,' Peter suggested. He and Caroline followed them in.

Caroline looked up at him. 'Will mother be able to cope do you think? I'm so worried about Alex's runny nose.'

'My darling girl, your mother has had four children and she *is* a doctor and so is your father. Just be thankful they were free to come to stay, otherwise we wouldn't be here at all. Anyway, they've only got two minutes' walk to find us, haven't they?'

'Yes, you're right. I must make myself enjoy this evening. What I'd really like to do is go home and sleep all night without a break. That's the best present anyone could give me at the moment.'

'Evening Rector. Evening Dr Harris.'

'Left them two babies, Dr Harris? Hope they're in good 'ands!'

Peter and Caroline acknowledged the greetings. It was obvious the villagers were hell bent on enjoying themselves. Peter took his wife's arm and gently guided her through the crowd into the bright lights of the restaurant. Jimbo and Harriet had decorated the two rooms with pale turquoise and white flowers, and streamers complemented by silver garlands and bells. The food was already laid out on the tables, and an enormous three-tier wedding cake stood on a table by itself surrounded by a circlet of delicate white blooms.

Ralph and Muriel stood in the entrance greeting their guests. Muriel reached up to kiss Peter. 'Thank you, Peter, for conducting such a lovely service this morning. Ralph and I did enjoy it. You said all the right things.'

'I was only too delighted to take the service for you. My best wishes to you both. I know you'll be very happy.'

Caroline kissed Ralph and then Muriel. 'I do hope you

will, no, I'm sure you will, both be as happy as Peter and I. I couldn't wish anyone anything better than that.'

'Thank you Caroline, I'm so glad you were able to leave your two little ones and join us all.' Ralph leant forward and kissed Caroline on both cheeks.

'Give my love to Australia won't you Ralph? I was there for three months one summer when I was at university. I grew quite fond of the place.'

'Caroline, we shall be delighted to do just that. Come now, help yourselves to a Buck's Fizz and go and join in the fun.'

'Peter, don't they both look happy?'

'They certainly do. Now my girl, drink that Buck's Fizz and then another one and you'll be in just the right mood for a party.'

The party was in full swing, the band playing, the people dancing, the food rapidly disappearing when the door opened and in came Sir Ronald and Lady Bissett at full tilt and exceedingly flustered. Full of apologies they searched for Ralph and Muriel.

'We're so sorry we're late. We didn't realise how the time was going. Congratulations to you both. So nice for you at your time of life to have such a lovely sending off. Ron . . . ald could you pass me a drink please?'

Sheila and Ronald circulated, Sheila feeling she must make everyone feel at home. It was difficult for village people to know how to mix and make small talk. One had to do one's bit to make things go with a swing. She waved delightedly at Caroline, deep down experiencing that dreadful inadequate feeling when she saw Caroline's beautiful midnight blue floating creation. She might have known her dress would have been superb.

It was their misfortune to come face to face with Jimbo and Harriet, and Ron's drink spilled a little as he swerved to miss bumping into them. Harriet jumped back to avoid getting splashed.

Jimbo couldn't resist a jibe. 'Must say you're looking better than when I saw you last. Dressed in water and pondweed he was, Harriet. To the point of indecency.'

Sir Ronald spluttered his annoyance.

'It was your Flick's damned cats as you well know. Sick of 'em I am. Don't blame me if they don't get back home one day.'

'I've warned you about threats like that. Two cats in a garden the size of yours? What's the worry? Good for the soil I'd say.' Harriet, sensing Jimbo was brewing up for one of his big "put down" speeches, hastened to smooth ruffled feathers.

'Isn't everyone enjoying themselves tonight? I thought Muriel looked lovely at the wedding, like a ship in full sail coming into harbour.'

Sheila looked non-plussed by this flowery description of Muriel, 'Yes, I suppose so. Come Ron . . . ald I need another drink.' Sheila shepherded him, protestingly, on his way. Ron took a drink from a tray on the side and rapidly drank it down. Sheila recognised the signs.

'Don't you dare show me up by getting drunk. This is *the* social event of the year. I've spent a lot of money on this dress and I'm blessed if I'm going to have to go home before the party is well and truly over. We've missed quite a bit of it already with falling asleep.'

'It was you fell asleep, not me.'

'You could have woken me up, you knew the time all right.'

'I didn't, I was enjoying the football.'

'Just you remember we have a position to keep up. You're a national figure and they expect you to know what's what. Go and talk to Peter Harris or someone and keep well away from those two. And behave like a gentleman if you know how.' She said all this between clenched teeth and all the while smiling at anyone who came near. She'd kill him if he made a fool of himself.

31

Kill him she would. If only Bianca and Brendan had been here. They would have kept their father in check. He was so proud of them both. Bianca in that new job at the bank helping small business men start up, she'd done well for herself, and Brendan with his computer business. His degree from East Anglia had been a real stepping stone for him. Admittedly it was only a third but he could still put B.A. after his name. First one either side of the family who could do that.

'Hello Lady Bissett. How are you? What would you like to drink?'

Sheila turned to find Sadie Beauchamp, Harriet Charter-Plackett's mother, offering her a tray of drinks. If there was anyone in the room who could make her feel small it was Sadie Beauchamp.

'Thank you, I'll have a Buck's Fizz. It is a lovely party isn't it? I understand the children are to have an entertainer when they've finished eating.'

'That's right, Punch and Judy and then a magic show. Ralph and Muriel are so thoughtful. I love your dress, where did you get it? It's rare to come across something so unusual.'

'It's from Thoms & Curtis in Culworth. I saw it on display in the window and couldn't resist it.'

'I must remember that. I didn't know they sold such . . . interesting clothes.' Sadie made her way through the guests. Sheila watched her go. The slim-fitting understated floor-length black dress Sadie wore proclaimed money and taste and Sheila felt sick.

Harriet came to join Peter and Caroline.

'Good evening Caroline.' Caroline turned to answer her.

'Hello Harriet. Isn't this a lovely party? I like this idea of having an evening "do" for everybody in the village. Especially for Ralph with his past history of being Lord of the Manor so to speak.'

'Definitely Lord of the Manor no more.'

'What do you mean?'

'Didn't you realise? They've already started work on turning the Big House into a health club. The lorries have been going in and out of the gates for weeks.'

'A health club? I don't believe it!'

'True. True. Some people called Venetia and Jeremy Mayer have bought it and are spending thousands on it. And I mean thousands. Entirely new decor, swimming pool, jacuzzi, running track, gymnasium, aerobics classes.'

Peter asked Harriet how anyone could get permission to make such radical changes to such an old house.

'By dishing out backhanders to the Council, or so Neville Neal says and he should know shouldn't he? Considering the strings he pulled to get Glebe House built. Oh, of course that was before your time. Anyway now's your chance to get fit.'

Caroline groaned. 'Fit? I haven't time for anything but keeping my head above water at the moment. I don't know how two such small human beings can cause so much work, to say nothing of the lack of sleep. Every three hours they need feeding. There's no time for anything. Does Ralph know about the health club?'

'I don't know.'

When everyone had circulated and eaten and examined the wedding presents which were on display in a small side room, it was announced that the happy couple would shortly be cutting the cake. As many as could gathered round, and cameras clicked and photographers jostled as Ralph and Muriel stood holding the silver knife and smiled first this way and then that. When they'd done the cutting Ralph took hold of Muriel and kissed her for rather longer than necessary. The guests clapped heartily and Muriel blushed, which made them all clap and laugh even more. Ralph took her hand and kissed it

33

with all the aplomb of an eighteenth-century suitor.

'Ladies and gentlemen, thank you very much indeed for accepting our invitation to join us on this very special day. My wife and I . . .' cheers resounded through the room and Ralph laughed while Muriel blushed again, 'would like especially to thank Jimbo and Harriet. Jimbo for giving Muriel away and both of them for providing such a splendid reception for us and decorating the room in what can only be described as a tasteful and exuberant manner. And thank you one and all for the lovely presents you have given us. We have been quite overwhelmed by your good wishes. We both look forward to coming home again to you and enjoying many more years sharing in the life of the village. The children's show has finished, so would you all care to come outside and watch the firework display? Thank you.'

The guests just about allowed Ralph and Muriel to get outside first before they all stampeded onto the green. Jimbo's firework displays were renowned and they didn't want to miss one moment. Gwen and Beryl delayed leaving with the crowd, as they had designs on the food remaining on the table. The two of them wrapped sausage rolls and vol-au-vents, cakes and quiche in paper napkins and stuffed them into their handbags and pockets. Between them they had enough food for two or three days. Well satisfied with their haul they sauntered outside to see the last of the fireworks. There being no street lamps the fireworks showed up brilliantly from the first moment they escaped their containers. The children ooh'd and aah'd and the adults joined in. The grand finale consisted of a tableau made of catherine wheels in the shape of the bridal couple's initials. They all clapped Jimbo's genius. Soon afterwards someone brought Ralph's Mercedes up close to the crowd. It was decorated all over with balloons and "Just Married" signs. Muriel was handed courteously into the front passenger seat by Ralph, who then got into the driving seat and the Mercedes slid quietly away down Church Lane with the guests waving and cheering their goodbyes.

Sheila had managed to prevent Ron from getting drunk and apart from her twinges of envy about Sadie Beauchamp had thoroughly enjoyed herself. She wouldn't half be glad to get these blasted sandals off though, they were cutting into her toes. She kicked them off as soon as she got in. Ron got the dogs' leads and set off for a sharp walk to exercise Pom and Pericles before he went to bed. He'd been lumbered with walking the dogs because Sheila always considered it a man's job to take the dogs out late at night. Come to think of it she thought it a man's job first thing in the morning and during the day. Ah well, it was a small price to pay for peace.

As he passed The Royal Oak, Ron heard the sounds of loud laughter through the open door. Well why not? He tied Pom and Pericles to an ancient hitching post outside the saloon bar door and pushed his way into the crowd. As he neared the bar Ron remembered that the new landlord had taken over only this week. It seemed odd after all these years not having big Betty McDonald behind the bar pulling pints.

'A double whisky please, landlord,' he shouted. The landlord's round shining face was dominated by a huge 'Flying Officer Kite' moustache which more than made up for the lack of hair on his head. For such a youngish man he was certainly very bald. In the shiny smiling face was a pair of twinkling grey eyes. By any standards he was a big man. 'Good evening sir, and welcome to The Royal Oak. I'm Bryn Fields and this is my wife Georgie. Come here Georgie and introduce yourself.'

His wife was a petite and pretty blonde with a warm laugh. She reached over the bar to shake Ron's hand.

'Good evening, very pleased to meet you. And you are?'

'Sir Ronald Bissett.'

'Welcome to The Royal Oak. You know your first drink is on Sir Ralph with it being his wedding day?'

'Yes, I did know. Thank you very much. I hope this week is the start of a long and happy time for you here in Turnham Malpas. I see you've got a new barman too.'

Bryn called out 'Come here, Alan, and meet another customer. This is Alan Crimble, Sir Ronald, he's been with us for what is it . . . fifteen years now. We couldn't manage without him.'

Alan nodded a greeting to Ronald, who wasn't much impressed by Alan's weedy figure and ingratiating smile. 'Best cellarman in Britain is Alan.' Bryn clapped Alan on the back as he returned to serving drinks. 'Here you are then Sir Ronald, here's your whisky. Good health and a long life to Sir Ralph and his bride.'

'Here's to that.'

Ron downed his whisky and immediately asked for another. After all he had been nearly drowned today, he could be catching a severe chill. Pom and Pericles waited and waited. They were unaccustomed to being tied up for long and when boredom set in they began playfully snapping at each other. This rapidly became more than a game and before they knew it they were having a real fight. Neither could escape as both were firmly tied up. A passer-by unfastened their leads intending to pull them apart and then find their owner, but they took their chance and escaped. Their first thought was to continue the fight but having been released they changed their minds and raced for home. Pericles went to Muriel's house out of habit and Pom to Ron and Sheila's, where he sat yapping outside the front door.

Sheila, already in bed, woke up with a start when she heard him. She popped on her négligé and went to the window overlooking the front door. When she saw Pom sitting there with no sign of either Ron or Pericles she feared the worst. She went to bring in Pom, expecting that Pericles would be out there with him somewhere. He wasn't. She hung about nervously in the hall for a few minutes hoping Ron would return with Pericles. When he didn't Sheila went upstairs and got dressed with the intention of going over to Muriel's to see if Pericles had gone to his home by mistake. Sure enough she found Pericles shivering and crying outside Muriel's front door. As she wearily put the key in her own door on her return, she heard a burst of laughter from The Royal Oak.

'That'll be it,' she said out loud. 'He'll be in there drinking himself silly. Well, if he thinks I'm going to make a fool of myself dragging him out he's got another think coming.'

Sheila had been asleep about half an hour when she was woken by a loud thumping at the door. She snuggled down under her goose down duvet and deliberately ignored him for a while. Eventually she relented and went down to let Ron in.

Ron was standing unsteadily on the door step. 'Couldn't find the key, Tsheila. Tsorry.' He came over the threshold clinging to the door frame for support. He patted her arm, almost pulling her négligé from her shoulders as he slipped on the polished floor. 'You're a wonderful wife Tsheila. Best day's work I ever did marrying you. No one anywhere has a better wife than you. Blow Tsadie Beauchamp and that lot, I like something cuddly to get hold of. Give me a woman with curves I tsay. Come 'ere and give us a kissh.'

'Certainly not. What would the union people think of you now Ron?'

'They'd tsay good luck to yer Ron.'

He went into the downstairs loo, pale green fitments

37

with pale yellow accessories and a spray of artificial flowers tastefully arranged in a vase the shape of a penguin. She could hear him vigorously splashing himself with water. Ron came out rubbing his head and face with the pale yellow towel. More dirty washing.

'You're a big disappointment to me Ron. I try hard to turn you into a gentleman and you ruin it by coming home drunk as a lord.'

'I am a lord or very nearly. But you've tsome room to talk. That blasted fur coat, I told you not to wear it. I hate the blessed thing.'

'I don't know what it is that makes you think you know all there is to know about women's clothes.'

'I have got eyesh Tsheila, I can see what Tsadie Beauchamp wearsh, what Dr Harrish wears and it's not like what you choose.'

'Well, thanks very much. Been out having a good time without me and then come home criticising me and my clothes. Thanks very much Ron Bissett. I'm off to bed and think yourself lucky if I ever speak to you again.' Sheila stormed off to bed hurt almost beyond endurance by his cruel words, made worse by the fact that underneath all her bluster she knew he was right.

Chapter 4

The Monday morning after the wedding Peter followed his usual habit of praying from six thirty until seven and then going for his half hour run. He'd been awake since five helping Caroline to feed the twins so it already felt like the middle of the morning to him. He went down Jacks Lane, crossed Shepherd's Hill and then onto the spare land behind the Methodist Chapel and set off along Turnham Beck. He had the steady economical action of the experienced runner and having followed this route for nearly a year now, he didn't need to take particular notice of his direction. Just past the footbridge he became aware of someone coming at speed towards him. Lifting his head he saw what appeared to be a large oriental butterfly winging it's way down the path. It began running on the spot. Peter stopped to speak. 'Good morning.' The gaudy creature was dressed in an electric pink plush tracksuit with a matching sweatband holding back jet-black hair, which seemed to spring in a dense mass out of her scalp. Round her ankles were purple slouch socks and on her feet a pair of expensive snow-white running shoes. Her wrists and fingers were covered in bright jewellery, the kind Caroline would never dream of wearing.

'Hi! I'm Venetia Mayer from the new health club.'
'Oh right, I'm Peter Harris. Great day for a run isn't

it?'

'It certainly is. Be seeing you. Bye.' She carried on her way, leaving Peter shaking his head in amazement. He did a lot of thinking on his runs and this morning he was contemplating how he could best sort out Caroline's problems. Very soon she was going to be ill. The children being so small needed feeding frequently and were taking so much of her time both night and day that she was close to collapse. Much as he would have loved to stay in to help her he had his own commitments which she knew could not be ignored. What she really needed was another pair of hands all day long.

He stopped to rest for a moment, leaning on the gate into Sykes Wood. That was it, another pair of hands. But whose hands? There was no one in the village who sprang immediately to mind. No doubt the answer would come to him. Today, Lord, for preference, he prayed.

Mondays he tried to spend in Penny Fawcett, the first village travelling west from Turnham Malpas and one belonging to his parish. Its own church was long gone and the churchgoers from Penny Fawcett came to St Thomas' for their services. They still had their own village centre and there was always a mini market there on Mondays, so he knew he'd meet plenty of his parishioners. Peter parked his car and was about to go into the centre when a voice hailed him from across the road.

'Mr Harris, isn't it? Good morning. You won't remember me but I met you at the Hospital Garden Party last summer. My name's Sylvia Bennett.' She held out her hand to shake his. Peter racked his brain trying hard to recollect her, then, as he walked across the road he remembered.

'Oh. I know, you're a supervisor there. Yes, that's right, Caroline introduced us. How are you?'

'This is my cottage, come in and have a coffee before you go in the mini market. My coffee's a lot better than that stuff out of the paper cups they serve in there, their rubbish could rot your insides. I'll be glad for some company.'

They took their coffee from her bright shining kitchen out on to a little bench by the back door and sat catching the best of the winter sun while they talked. Peter warmed to her lovely kindly face and her big candid grey eyes, which never seemed to stop twinkling.

'Having a day off are you Mrs Bennett?'

'Well, yes, except it's a long day off I'm afraid. Been made redundant after fifteen years.'

'But you were a supervisor.'

'Makes no difference sir, nowadays. Re-organisation and out went Sylvia and got replaced by a young manager barely out of nappies who couldn't supervise a chimpanzee's tea party let alone a work force of twenty cleaners. Added to which I'm soon to lose my cottage. Landlord's coming back from abroad and has nowhere else to live, so out goes me. In fact it's not like me but I do feel a bit low today.'

Sylvia paused to put her cup down beside her on the path and then asked, 'How's Dr Harris? She was well liked at the hospital; we did miss her when she left. No edge you know sir, you'd as likely find her in the broom cupboard joking with the cleaners as find her perched on a desk in a consultant's office, explaining to him that he really shouldn't keep sick people waiting for hours while he played God with his private patients. Many's the one who's been hauled over the coals for it by Dr Harris. And what's more they did as they were told. And her so young compared to them.'

'At the moment she feels very far from young. You know, I expect, that she isn't able to have children, well, we've been very privileged to be able to adopt twins . . .'

'I had heard. I bet she's thrilled, she'll make a lovely mother.'

'Yes, she does, but she's exhausted. Living in the Rectory the phone is going continuously and she's trying so hard to do well by the twins, but they are tiny and they are much harder work than she'd anticipated. Well, no not that, we just didn't know what hard work such tiny babies are. There's lots of parish things she's involved with and she is a perfectionist as you know.'

Sylvia asked him if he'd like more coffee.

'No thanks, must be off. Lovely talking to you Sylvia, I'll tell Caroline I've met you. Thanks for the coffee. See you again sometime.' How could he introduce the idea of Sylvia helping out without giving Caroline the feeling that she wasn't coping. Lack of faith in her at the moment could cause serious damage to her already shaky confidence.

'Guess who I met today in Penny Fawcett?'

'Can't. I just want to get my dinner down before those two horrors of ours wake up. I'm sorry it's one of Jimbo's frozen dinners . . .'

'I don't think he'd appreciate the apologetic tone in your voice. He considers his frozen dinners are of gourmet standard.'

'Well, they are, but you know what I mean. Who did you meet?'

'Sylvia Bennett.'

'Oh, from the hospital. How is she?'

'Redundant.' Peter chose another roll and energetically buttered it while Caroline digested his news.

'Redundant? Has she got another job?'

'No, and another few weeks and the landlord wants her cottage back.'

'I see. I always liked Sylvia. We got on very well.'

42

'She likes you, she gave my darling girl very good references.'

'Did she? Jimbo's right, these dinners are good. Though I could eat a horse tonight. I got no time for lunch at all. Sylvia's a good cook you know.'

'Is she?' Peter continued enjoying his dinner, leaving a silence for Caroline to fill with her own thoughts.

'She doesn't know much about babies.'

'Doesn't she?'

As she finished the last morsel of her dinner Caroline said, 'She would be good for everything else though, wouldn't she?'

'Are you thinking what I'm thinking?'

'What's that?'

'She might be able to help us a bit here, just occasionally, you know from time to time.'

'Peter, you must be telepathic. Except I'd go one further than that.'

'You mean have her here every day?'

'Well, there are four big bedrooms here and . . .'

'So long as we always have one spare for visitors or the odd tramp in need of accommodation she could . . .'

Caroline triumphantly finished his sentence for him. 'Live in. Brilliant. We can afford it for a while, and she would save my life you know. She's very discreet, she wouldn't be a pest. Just till she found somewhere of her own you understand.'

'Of course.' Peter silently thanked the Lord for his intervention.

He came out of the church the following morning to find Jimbo limbering up outside as though he was about to take part in an Olympic marathon. He was wearing a pair of old rugger shorts from his university days and a sweat shirt with *Support the Whales* emblazoned across it.

'Good morning Jimbo.'

'Morning Peter. I'm taking up the challenge.'

'What challenge is that?'

'My beloved and valuable mother-in-law has said she will give me £10 each time I go for a run with you. She says I shan't manage it but I'm determined I shall. She ought to be called sadistic Sadie. She says I'm fat,' Jimbo patted his bulging midriff as evidence, 'so I'm definitely going to get fit.'

'Right, well, I shall be glad of your company. Here we go. I usually do a circular tour round Sykes Wood and back. Is that all right?' Jimbo quaked at the prospect but put on a brave face. He couldn't afford to allow his mother-in-law a laugh at his expense.

'Of course, nothing to it.' Peter set off at his regular brisk pace and almost immediately Jimbo realised he wouldn't make the grade. Just before he had begun showing serious signs of stress Venetia Mayer came into view wearing her pink track suit. She waved enthusiastically.

'Hi there.' She continued running on the spot while chatting, without any sign of shortness of breath.

'Good morning Venetia, have you met Jimbo from the village store?'

'Hi Jimbo. How perfectly delightful meeting two such fine specimens of manhood at this time in the morning. It seems to me that you are both prime candidates for membership of the health club when we open at the end of next month. Peter, I must say your physique is superb. Are you a sports fanatic?'

'Not really Venetia, simply a man who wants to keep fit.'

'Well, come to see me at Turnham House. I'll see you keep fit all right. We shall be holding "Executive Trim" classes, which I think will be ideal for you. What about you Jimbo? You need my services more than Peter. You don't strip quite as well as he does. Looks to be lots of flab

44

to be attacked with our special exercises. How about if I offer the pair of you an introductory course at half price. How's that for a bargain?'

Peter and Jimbo agreed it might be a good idea.

'Two Tarzans you would be before a month was out. Then all the women in the village would be after you both in a trice.' She laid a hand on Peter's arm, tweaked his muscles and winked at him. 'A few hours on a sun bed and you would look superb. There's nothing like a tan to increase a man's sex appeal!'

'Well, we must be on our way Venetia, thanks for the offer, we might take you up on it.' Jimbo hastened off, followed by Peter who couldn't stop laughing.

'I don't think she realises who I am, do you?'

'No, Peter, I don't. The woman really is the limit. Has she gone yet?' Jimbo turned round to check. 'Yes she has. It's no good I shall have to turn back. Do you think I can claim I've been for a run?'

'In all conscience, no, you can't.'

'You're right, I can't. You carry on Peter, and exercise your jungle man body. I can't keep it up.' Peter waved and carried on with his run. Jimbo turned back and slowly jogged his way home.

Sadie, having listened to their encounter with Venetia, was highly amused.

'How far did you run then Jimbo?'

'Not far enough. But I'm working on it.'

'So my ten pounds is safe then?'

'For the moment. I might take her up on the offer of membership. Keep the old flab at bay. Would you like to join, Harriet?'

'Yes, I would. Time I paid more attention to my body. In any case I can't let you and Peter loose up there with no one to keep an eye on you. If you're going in the jacuzzi, you'll go in it with me not Venetia. What's Jeremy like? Have you seen him?'

45

'No, and if he's as sexy as her we'll both have some fun.'

Sadie took hold of a fistful of Jimbo's sweat shirt. 'No straying James. You're married to my daughter and don't you forget it. I'm very handy with the garden shears.'

'Ouch! That's positively mediaeval. You wouldn't be so cruel would you darling?' He placed an arm round Harriet's shoulders and hugged her.

'Just try me.'

'Remember the garden shears James, that's all I ask.' Sadie laughed as she headed for the office to catch up on her mail orders.

Harriet's curiosity about Jeremy was satisfied later that morning when he came into the Store to enquire about the possibility of ordering food for the health club.

'I'm looking for quality food, fresh, well-presented and appetising. Ideally I need someone willing to provide all the food at competitive prices. There's no way we shall have time for shopping here and there and every-where once we open. I must admit I cut prices to the bone, there's no fooling me when it comes to overheads. And I shan't hesitate to change my supplier at a moment's notice if I feel I'm being taken advantage of.'

'We are not in the business of cheating anyone. Fair prices and consistent good quality is what we guarantee. In return we expect our bills to be paid on time. There's absolutely no credit.'

'Well, at least we understand each other.'

'Coffee?' Harriet stood with her hand poised on the lever of the customer's coffee machine.

'Yes, please.' She had to admit that Jeremy was a disappointment. Having heard about his wife Harriet had anticipated an Adonis. Instead he was thick set, if not downright chubby with a large bald patch in the middle of his grey hair. His heavy glasses enhanced him not one

46

jot. She couldn't see him doing an early morning run with his wife. More than likely he was tucking into bacon and eggs sunny side up while she was out jogging.

'How long have you been in the health club business, Jeremy?'

'New venture, actually. Venetia has the beauty and the experience and I have the brains and the money. This coffee's good.'

'Jimbo is out on business at the moment. If you could give me some idea of the kind of food you would be wanting and how you would like deliveries made and how often et cetera, when he gets back we could have a discussion about it.'

'Certainly. I've written down my thoughts on the subject so I'll leave them with you to browse over. Could I have another cup of coffee, please?'

'Of course. I've been wondering where you're going to get people from to fill up your health club. There's not many people around here who could afford to be members let alone stay there.'

'I have lots of business contacts and we intend promoting it as a place to send executives for a social as well as a physical weekend. Build company loyalty and morale and all that jazz. All paid for by the employers, of course.'

'I see. Well, here's hoping you have lots of success. I'm sure you will. As you say, with Venetia's beauty and your brains you're bound to be onto a winner.'

'Exactly. Must be off. There's our card. Give me a ring and we'll arrange a meeting. Remember though I'm in business. It's not a charity, so no fancy prices. Good day to you.' He left the store in a hurry, climbing into his BMW with more haste than grace.

'And so much for you Jeremy Mayer. No fancy prices indeed! If we didn't need the business I'd tell him what to do with his orders,' Harriet muttered to herself.

47

'Who's that just disappeared in a cloud of dust?' Caroline asked as she manoeuvred her pram in through the door.

'Good morning Caroline. That is the famous or is it *in*famous Jeremy Mayer from the health club. He's not anything like I'd expected.'

'I wonder if he knows his wife's been making passes at the rector? I shall be having a thing or two to say to her if she doesn't stop.'

'Don't take it too seriously Caroline, Peter's not so foolish as to be taken in by her. Can I lift Beth out?'

'Yes of course. I can't find my list, yet I know I put it out to bring with me.' Caroline tried all the pockets of her jacket and eventually found it tucked down the side of the pram mattress. 'I really think I've lost my marbles since I got these two. I don't know what I'm doing most of the time.'

'Would you be without them, that's the question.'

'Certainly not. But it does take some adjusting to when one's led an adult, shackle free existence for so long and then suddenly your life is not your own any more.'

'That will pass. Now little lady I'm going to put you back in your pram and pick up your brother for a cuddle. Mustn't show favouritism must we?'

Harriet picked up Alex and kissed the top of his head. 'What darlings you are.' Harriet cuddled Alex against her face. 'Mmmm little babies are lovely. I'm very jealous of you do you know that?' Harriet put Alex back in the pram and said, 'I'm thinking of joining the health club. Jimbo fancies it and I'm going to keep an eye on him. What do you think?'

'No time really Harriet. Peter might join but I won't. I'm not into exercise and all that right now.'

Whilst Harriet was putting Caroline's shopping together for her, Venetia dashed in. She'd changed her pink track suit for a pale green one, all colour co-ordinated with her headband and slouch socks. Emblazoned across her back were the words *Turnham House Health Club*.

'Harriet hi! I met your husband this morning. I'm trying to persuade him to join our health club. Do you think he will? Would you like to join as well? We're expecting a rush for membership so you'd better make your mind up quickly. He was out with this gorgeous man called Peter this morning. Now, he really is a superb physical specimen. Just the kind I like. Tall, well made, fair haired, with surprising muscles. I told him a few hours on a sunbed would just set the seal on him. My dear, he's devastatingly attractive. I could really make music with him. Can't think what he's doing living out here in the sticks. Do you know him at all? Of course you must, if he was out running with your Jimbo.'

Harriet tried to hush her up but it was no good. Caroline grew steadily more and more angry as Venetia blithely enthused over Peter's physique.

'Are you aware that you are speaking about my husband?' she asked finally. Venetia turned to study Caroline. 'You should be delighted to hear his praises sung so enthusiastically.'

'I'm not delighted, I'm very angry.'

At this Venetia only laughed and said, 'All's fair in love and war.'

Caroline left the Store without her shopping. She strode home in a furious temper and then burst into tears as soon as she got inside the rectory door. Alex and Beth, sensing her distress, also began crying. When Peter got home a few minutes later he found the house in uproar.

'Darling, whatever is the matter? Come here to me.' Peter took hold of Beth and put his other arm round Caroline as she sat herself on his knee holding Alex. She wept.

'I've been such a fool. I've made a complete idiot of myself. That dreadful Venetia Mayer came into the store and what had been a nice conversation with Harriet turned into a steaming row with Venetia.'

'What about?'

'You.'

'Me?'

'Yes, you. She thinks you are absolutely superb and wants to make music with you. Sunbed and all.'

'Did she not realise who I am?'

'No, not till I spoke up. I should just have laughed and made light of it, instead I got furiously angry.' Caroline began laughing through her tears. 'I really was a fool. I expect it's because I'm so tired, I take umbrage at almost anything. I shall have to apologise to her.'

'Don't do that, I'll go and see her, do the apologising and warn her off.'

'You'll do no such thing. *I'll* do the apologising. It was me who blew my top. She doesn't know you're the rector and I didn't enlighten her. I couldn't hide behind that as a reason for her to hold off.'

'I do love your sound commonsense Caroline. You do know I haven't encouraged her don't you?'

'Yes, I do. Absolutely. She's the threat, not you. I shall apologise the very next time I see her.'

Chapter 5

Caroline met Venetia a few days later when she was in Harriet's tearoom having morning coffee. She'd left the twins with Sylvia who'd promised to keep an eye on them while she did the ironing. Caroline was glad to escape for a little while and become a person again in her own right. Life was beginning to get a certain balance to it since Sylvia had come to live in. Her parochial duties having taken second place since the twins had arrived she was becoming aware of her neglect of Peter's flock. So this morning she would rectify the matter. And where better to meet people than in the tearoom?

It was half full when she went in. There was the usual sprinkling of tourists come to view the ancient tombs, the church murals and the stocks on the green and, dotted amongst them, were villagers out to meet anyone and everyone who might have some news to impart. She greeted the parishioners, smiled at a few of the strangers then took a seat at a table near the back. She ordered her filter coffee and a slice of Harriet's famous carrot cake and sat back to enjoy a grown-up interlude.

Venetia entered carrying a large poster. Her voice carried right to the back of the tearoom.

'I'm Venetia Mayer from Turnham House Health Club.' She spun herself round so the cashier could see the words printed on the back of her track suit. 'I'd like you

51

to display this poster in one of your windows. I'm going round to the store to ask Jimbo if I can put one on his Village Message Board but I thought one in here might be a good idea.'

The cashier looked warily at her. Caroline sensed a feeling of resentment in the look.

'Leave it here behind the counter and I'll ask Mr Charter-Plackett if I can put it up.'

'Oh, but I want to put it up now. You might forget.'

'I'm sorry, Mr Charter-Plackett employs me and I have to ask his permission before I put up notices. We can't have every Tom Dick and Harry littering the place with posters. He's very particular, is Mr Charter-Plackett. Doesn't want to spoil the ambonce he says.'

'Oh very well, but you won't forget, will you? I'll have an orange juice please.'

'The girl will come to your table and take your order. I deal with the money.'

'It's a wonder to me you get any customers in here at all with an attitude like yours. I wouldn't want to employ you at the health club.'

'No cause to worry yourself about that, I wouldn't want a job there anyways.'

'Well really! How rude. I shall have words about this with Jimbo. Such rudeness to a customer. Oh hello there, you're Peter's wife, aren't you?' She trotted down between the tables.

'That's right.' Caroline pulled out a chair. 'Come and sit with me.'

'These people are extremely rude. Are they always like this?'

'No, they're not. But I was very rude to you last time I saw you. I owe you an apology. It was entirely due to lack of sleep, I suppose. I'd been up with the twins a lot during the night and couldn't see straight at all. But that's no excuse. I'm so sorry.'

'That's fine. I didn't take any notice of you anyway. But you have to admit he is gorgeous. You are very lucky. I unashamedly admit I married money. Lots of it.'

The girl brought her orange juice and banged it down with little grace.

'See what I mean? They are thoroughly unpleasant people.'

Venetia sipped her orange juice and commented on its quality. 'We're buying all the food for Turnham House from Jimbo and Harriet. I imagine they provide some good stuff.'

'Oh yes, they are excellent. They've only been here for about three years, I understand. Jimbo used to work in the city but decided he hated it and it wasn't a good life for his children, so he and Harriet resurrected the village shop and they've made a great success of it.'

As Caroline finished singing the praises of the Turnham Malpas Store, Mrs Peel the organist left her table and came across with an envelope.

'Could you give this to the Rector for me, Dr Harris? Save me knocking on your door. He asked for a list of music I fancied buying for the Services. Said he'd pop into Culworth and order it.'

'Certainly Mrs Peel. I loved the pieces you played on Sunday. I thought that Scarlatti delightful.'

'Thank you, Dr Harris, I don't often get compliments, except from your husband, of course. Since he came I've felt that at last here's someone who could appreciate and inspire an organist.'

'I'm glad about that. The music is so important.'

'Old Mr Furbank never cared that much for the music. I could have played nursery rhymes and he wouldn't have been any the wiser. Good morning to you Dr Harris.' She gave a curt nod to Venetia and went out.

'Caroline! I had no idea that your Peter is the rector. What a laugh. Oh, well, maybe I brightened his day.

What on earth is such a super man doing being a rector? Oh my word.'

'Because he is a committed Christian, that's why.'

'Well, I may as well be honest. He won't be seeing me in church, I've no time for it. Hope to be too busy on Sunday mornings to go, even if I wanted to. See what I mean about the villagers though? She virtually ignored me. They don't want to know. Well, they'll have to put up with me because I intend staying and making a success of this place. Cheery bye. I'm off.'

Venetia waved a carefree hand and set off towards the door deliberately smiling and nodding at everyone as she went. The village people did not respond.

The regulars in The Royal Oak had plenty to say about the health club. Willie Biggs, the verger, confided to his drinking partner, Jimmy Glover, that it was an excuse for a sexual orgy like them Romans used to have.

'Wouldn't go as far as that Willie, but by Jove that woman in the tracksuit has plenty going for her. Nice bit of crackling and not half.'

'She ain't a woman, she's a walking sexpot skellington. See her eyes when she spots the rector. He's 'ad to change his route for his morning run to avoid her. They say she made eyes at him not knowing who he was. Dr Harris had a row with her in the Store because of it, and she's made sheep's eyes at Jimbo before now. Huzzy she is, Jimmy, a huzzy.'

'What I don't like is them making the Big House into a circus. Jaccersys and them naked Swedish steam things. Goes against nature. All them beautiful walls and them lovely paintings. I remember as a boy when we all went up from school to sing carols and then had mince pies and orange squash in the music room. Miss Evans getting bright red doing the conducting and then fidgeting with 'er 'ands and staring at her shoes when Sir Tristan made his thank you speech. Remember that Willie?'

'I do. I looked forward to that from one Christmas to another. And then Bonfire Night. Remember the cook used to do dozens of baked potatoes and yer ate 'em with yer gloves on 'cos they were that hot. Them bonfires were grand. That high they used to be, yer don't get bonfires like that nowadays. I could just fancy going this November to one o' them fires. Remember Sir Tristan used to come out and give each one of us a toffee apple to take home? Say what you like they were special people up at the Big House.'

'And where is it all now? Madame Butterfly won't be dishing out toffee apples, more likely condoms.'

'Shut up, Jimmy, what are yer thinking of?' Willie glanced round to make sure Jimmy hadn't been overheard.

'Well, I'm right. Everybody thinks the same; the good old days are dead and gone.'

''Ave you got that Sykes in 'ere? Yer know Bryn doesn't like dogs in.'

'Doesn't matter. I don't care. He never makes a sound, nobody knows 'e's 'ere.'

'I do 'cos I can smell him.'

'That's only 'cos he's drying out, he's been out in this old rain and he got soaking. In any case 'e's partial to a drop of Guinness as you well know, so we share a glass.'

'All right, all right. You're soft in the head where that dog's concerned.' Willie put down his pint of Tetley's and waved to Pat Duckett, beckoning her across to join them. 'Sit 'ere Pat and tell us the latest from the school. Still wearing you out, is it?'

Pat carefully placed her plump behind on the settle and launched into the story of Venetia's visit to Mr Palmer.

'Headmaster, I ask yer and there she is prancing about in the playground demonstrating some exercises he could do to correct his stoop. "Come up and see me sometime", she says, sounded like Greta Garbo in that film. Or was it Marlene Dietrich? Anyways them children were all gathered round with their mouths open listening to all this. I had the kitchen window open on account as I was washing up in there and it was steamy. I could hear every word what she was saying. I heard Mr Palmer say, "I'm afraid the subscription would be beyond my teacher's salary, Mrs Mayer." "Oh," says she, "call me Venetia do." Waggles her bum and dances off.'

'Been making eyes at the rector an' all,' said Jimmy determined to inflame Pat's wrath.

'Never. That's it then, she is a tart. Whatever would Mrs Rector think if she knew?'

'She does.'

'Never. The poor dear. She might be a Doctor and well brought up but she is pleasant to everybody. No hoity toity with her. Tell you what, I wish Sir Ralph was up at the Big House and it was like my mum remembered it before the war. The Village Flower Show in the grounds, all them side shows and the flags flying . . . that's how it ought to be, not all tarted up like she's making it. Our Dean went up there on his bike the other day, says it's like a building site. That Jerry Mayer bossing 'em all and diggers and machines all about. It'll never be the same again. Never.'

'It's what's called progress,' Willie moaned. 'But it will mean jobs. They've been advertising.'

Pat banged her lager down. 'If she offered me a king's ransom I wouldn't work up there. All them bare folk plunging about, it's not decent. My Duggie would turn in his grave if I worked up there, God rest his soul.' She raised her eyes piously to heaven and sketched a cross with the hand that wasn't holding her glass.

'Your Doug didn't have much time for God when he was down here Pat. Reckon he went up there do yer?'

'That's enough from you Jimmy Glover. Yer'll be civil when yer talk about my Doug. He was always kind to me.'

'I could tell that by the black eyes he kept giving yer.'

'That's as maybe, but he didn't mean it.'

They were sitting right by the door so they had a full view of the stranger when she walked in. She had a kindly fresh country face, with twinkling eyes. Well, they had the potential to be twinkling, but she was nervous just now. She wore a royal blue coat and smart high heeled court shoes which helped to increase her height. She went to the bar and asked for a white wine.

'Who's that?' Jimmy asked.

Pat nudged him and said, 'Isn't it Sylvia Crossman that was? Worked over at Culworth Hospital for years as a cleaning supervisor. Wonder what she's doing here?'

Sylvia looked around the bar for a table but they were all occupied. Pat caught her eye and, hitching further along the settle, invited the newcomer to sit down.

'You're Sylvia Crossman that was, aren't you?'

'Yes, I'm Sylvia Bennett now.'

Jimmy introduced the three of them to her and then followed it up by saying they hadn't seen her in the bar before.

'No, well, I only moved into the Rectory this week. Dr Harris needs help, what with that big house to run, and the twins, and helping the rector and answering the phone all day long. I rented a little cottage over at Penny Fawcett for years but the landlord wants it for himself now and I couldn't afford a bigger rent, everywhere I looked the rents were far too high, so Dr Harris suggested I lived at the Rectory for a while till I find something. I've got a lovely room and I have my own bathroom too. They're both so pleasant to work for. Do you know them very well?'

Willie didn't answer so Jimmy answered for him,

'Willie 'ere, who seems to have been struck dumb, is the verger at the church.'

'Oh well then, you won't need me to tell you how nice they are. Those babies are a delight. I love looking after them. Dr Harris feeds one and I feed the other and we sit chatting, or watching the TV. It makes a real change from supervising at the hospital, I can tell you. I've never been in here before.'

'We all know one another and we get on fine. Some of the newcomers are a bit pushy . . .'

'Who had you in mind Pat?' Jimmy asked, knowing full well to whom she would be referring.

'Well, that Sir Ronald and Lady Bissett. Ron and Sheila really, but they stand on ceremony a bit. Think they're somebody special 'cos he's on telly now and again. Most folks is all right. Funniest folks is Gwen and Beryl Baxter. They've lived here all their lives, if yer can call it living.'

Pat, sensing a chance to pass on some local gossip, hitched herself closer and began regaling Sylvia Bennett with the story of Gwen and Beryl. Willie hadn't spoken because he couldn't. He felt as though he'd been pole-axed. He stole glances at Sylvia when she wasn't looking, and found himself more delighted with her than he could possibly have imagined. Every move she made fascinated him. He'd been around a bit, but it was the first time he'd ever met a woman who had affected him in this way. One glance from her lovely grey eyes and his insides melted. He felt ridiculous. His heart was racing, his blood pressure seemed to have gone clean through the roof and he was sweating as though it was high summer and he was hay making. At his age . . . fifty eight and his heart beating twenty to the dozen. It must be this new beer the landlord was selling. That was it, it was the drink. He stood up pushed back his chair and, cutting across Pat's monologue, said abruptly, 'I'm off home.

Goodnight.'

'What's up with Willie?' Jimmy inquired as Willie pushed his way past a crowd coming in. 'He's in a hurry.'

Willie went home to his little cottage between the church and the rectory, bewildered by his reaction to Sylvia Bennett. He took one look around his sitting room and his heart sank to his boots. He saw everything with new eyes as if he'd never been in his own cottage before. He'd never noticed how awful it was. Something would have to be done. If ever he plucked up courage to invite Sylvia in he'd be mortified. In fact he couldn't invite her in. It was all too dreadful. He'd do what he'd been promising himself for years, dip into his savings and get it done up. He needed a new bathroom for a start. Couldn't ask Sylvia Bennett to go up the garden to that old privy when she got caught short.

Chapter 6

The news about Willie's improvements not only to his cottage but to his general appearance too, caused a great deal of interest in Turnham Malpas. The first meeting of the newly inaugurated Flower Festival Committee provided a good moment for an exchange of views, as Willie, co-opted onto the committee to advise on the feasibility of their plans, was unable to attend due to a severe cold. Peter had arranged the chairs in a circle to give the impression that no one person was in charge though nominally it was himself. Harriet Charter-Plackett, Mrs Peel the organist, Lady Bissett and Sylvia Bennett with Peter and Willie constituted the committee. Their speculation as to the cause of Willie's sudden burst of activity drawing no conclusions, they had to reluctantly begin the business of the meeting.

Lady Bissett removed her imitation Burberry and got down to brass tacks immediately. 'I'm full of ideas for this Flower Festival. We did one in Culworth Church, and it was compliments all round. Good organisation is the key.' Sheila Bissett had a vision of all white arrangements punctuated here and there by soft green foliage.

'Why all white, Sheila?' Harriet asked.

'Because it is restrained and tasteful.'

'Downright boring if you ask me,' Harriet retorted. 'There's no variety in that. I'm not much of a flower arranger but even I know there's not much to catch the eye if every arrangement is white.'

'Believe me I do know,' Sheila bridled. 'I've been a member of the Culworth Flower Arranging Society for the last five years. They did a very effective one in the Cathedral only two years ago. The variety comes in all the differing shapes of the petals and the foliage.'

Harriet pressed her point, 'The Cathedral is very light though, full of huge windows, while our church is small, dark and mediaeval. We have those beautiful murals and the painted tombs. Surely it would be better to echo the colours in those?'

'I agree,' Sylvia said. 'I think the colours of the murals and the tombs would look good. Rich reds and purples and pinks and blues. Quite excellent.'

'Who's the one with the experience here? Me. I'm the only one who is even a member of a society. Please allow me to know what is best.' They could see Sheila was beginning to lose her temper.

Adept at stepping in when storms were brewing, Peter cleared his throat and said, 'Were we celebrating Easter, marriage, baptism or confirmation then I'm quite sure Lady Bissett, that your idea of an all white display would be highly appropriate and very effective, but we are celebrating summer and the beauty of our church. Mrs Peel and I have been planning some very buoyant and cheerful music for our recital and I think that coloured arrangements would be more suitable at this time. We'll let the committee vote, shall we? Those in favour of coloured arrangements please signify.'

Every hand bar Lady Bissett's went up.

'That settles it then: arrangements reflecting the colours of the church. Now Lady Bissett, do you think that your society would do us the privilege of arranging the flowers? We would foot the bill for the flowers of course. Their expertise and your flair would I am sure provide a

61

wonderful display. The money we raise will go towards urgent church repairs. I wish we were well enough off to give it for charity, but I'm afraid that's not possible. I think cups . . .'

'Just a moment Mr Chairman, I haven't said yes.'

'I'm so sorry, I thought you'd accepted the decision of the Committee.'

'I have not. The way I feel at the moment I could very well say that I won't have anything to do with the Festival at all.'

'Come now Sheila, you can't have everything all your own way,' Mrs Peel objected.

'If it's about flowers I can. I've worked my fingers to the bone over the church flowers and now when it comes to the best bit, my wishes are completely disregarded. It's not fair. I think all white arrangements would set off the colours in the church beautifully.'

Peter, trying to be as diplomatic as possible, argued that the committee had voted and they had to take the decision of the majority.

Sheila drew herself up and said with tight lips, 'I know why they voted like they did. It's not because they didn't want white flowers, it's because they don't want me.'

'That's hardly fair, Sheila. We all know we couldn't manage without you,' Harriet protested.

'Well Rector, the decision is yours. Either we have all white flowers and I do it or you have coloured ones and someone else does it. I would have thought that you of all people would have backed me up.'

'We are doing this to help the church, not to satisfy our own egos, and I feel that . . .'

'Are you saying I'm wanting my own way for the glory of it?'

'No, not that at all. It's just that . . .'

'Oh yes, you are. Well, that's that then. I shall have nothing to do with your festival at all. You can organise

62

it all by yourselves and then we'll see what a mess you make of it. You'll soon be crawling to me to do it for you, but I shan't. I wash my hands of it completely.' Sheila stood up, pulled on her raincoat and stormed out of the vestry.

'Sheila won't you recon . . .' But Peter's words went unnoticed.

The remainder of the committee sat silently for a moment gathering their thoughts.

'We've done it now, Peter,' Harriet murmured.

'It looks very much like it. But it's no good, I don't honestly think all white would be a good idea.'

'Neither do I. I have a friend,' Sylvia said quietly, 'who is a member of a flower arrangement society and I'm sure she would be delighted at the opportunity to organise a festival in such a lovely church as we have here. She would accept it as a real challenge and she's very talented. Would you like me to put it to her?'

'That sounds a very good idea, don't you think so Mrs Peel?' Harriet said, seeking support.

'Indeed I do. We've all had enough of being bossed about by Sheila Bissett.'

'I don't think we should be too critical. She has put in a lot of work while I've been here.' Peter shuffled his papers together and suggested that Sylvia should contact her friend and perhaps could let him know the outcome as soon as possible. With that the meeting closed.

Sheila spent the next morning in readiness for Peter coming to apologise and agree to her suggestions. She'd plumped the cushions, vacuumed the carpet, re-arranged the flowers, and given her houseplants a spray of leaf shine. She'd dusted the coffee table, left a few of her flower magazines on it and put some new drops of essence in the pot pourri on the bar. Should she offer him a drink or would it be better just to offer coffee? Coffee would be best. Sheila got her best coffee set out in readiness.

When it got to one o'clock and he still hadn't come she knew she'd lost. 'Ron, who else could they get to do it? They'll be cancelling the whole thing next, just you wait and see.' But in the church newsletter the following Sunday the date and details of the festival were announced. Sheila seethed with annoyance. 'I shan't be going to church any more. That's the thanks you get for being a stalwart. Christian indeed! Some Christian that Peter Harris is. That's definitely settled it. I'll get my own back and I know how.'

She didn't tell anyone how she intended doing this, but the very next morning she was in Harriet's tearoom nice and early. She settled herself at the table in the window, waiting for a suitable listener.

She didn't wait long. Before the morning was out a considerable number of the villagers were convinced that Peter was the father of the twins whom he and Caroline were adopting. Sheila had started it off by questioning the babies' parentage. 'Isn't it odd how much like the rector little Alexander is? It's a funny coincidence isn't it, seeing as how Suzy's husband had dark hair? Before it had been passed on more than a few times it had become a fact.

Harriet overheard two of her customers talking about it in the Post Office queue.

'And Lady Bissett says that she knows for a fact that the twins are the rector's own.'

'No! Well, I don't believe that. Surely to goodness, it can't be true.'

'Well, she says it is. Says how little Alex is so like the rector they can't deny it. And he is yer know.'

'Well, he is the same colouring I expect. Well I never, whatever next.'

'Rector having a bit on the side, takes some swallowing that does.'

'It's Dr Harris I feel sorry for. If it's true I think she's been very brave taking them on.'

'So do I.'

'Question is, who do we really want, a lovely young rector who's strayed a bit or that Lady Bissett as she likes to be called. I know who I prefer.'

'Well yer right there, that Lady Bissett isn't half a pain in the arse. He's lovely and he's worked so 'ard since he came, what with the Cubs and the Brownies and the Women's Meeting and the pensioners' Luncheon Club. I don't know how we managed with that old faggot Mr Furbank. It was time the good Lord gathered 'im to His bosom and no mistake. My turn is it Linda? Two second class stamps. Thanks.'

Harriet at her first opportunity went in search of Jimbo. He was sitting worrying over his accounts.

'It's no good you know. The restaurant is not pulling its weight. I shall have to think seriously about . . . Why whatever's the matter?'

'Jimbo I don't know what to do. Two of the customers have been saying that Sheila Bissett has said that Alex and Beth are Peter's.'

'We know they're Peter's; they're adopting them.'

'No, they mean actually *Peter's*. You know, that he's the real father and that's why they've adopted them.'

'You mean Suzy Meadows and Peter . . . No, no, no. I don't believe it. That can't be right. Peter would never let Caroline down like that. I mean God, he's the rector. No, of course he wouldn't. Absolutely not. I'll have a word with Peter, man to man when we go for our run in the morning. Devil of a job bringing up the subject though. But this gossip will have to be stopped. I can't believe it's true. Spreading lies like that. The woman's malicious.'

'I know why she's done it, it's because we wouldn't do

as she said about the Flower Festival. She expected Peter would go running round next morning and apologise and beg her to run it, but he didn't because Sylvia Bennett asked a friend of hers to do it and she's jumped at the chance.'

'I feel desperately sorry for Caroline. Do you suppose it really is true and she doesn't know it?'

'I haven't the faintest idea. We are good friends, but she wouldn't tell me something like that would she? It's much too private.'

When Jimbo met Peter the next morning he wasn't quite sure how to broach the subject. Then Peter himself mentioned Sheila Bissett, saying she'd resigned and how difficult it made things.

Almost as an aside Jimbo asked, 'Have you heard the rumour she's spreading as her revenge?'

'No. What is she saying?'

Jimbo stopped by a farm gate and leant on it. 'Let's have a rest before we turn back.'

Peter wiped the sweat off his face with the sleeve of his running shirt and said, 'Well?'

Jimbo, breathing heavily as much from the quandary in which he found himself as from the running he'd done, looked Peter straight in the face and came out with Sheila's malicious gossip.

'No good beating about the bush. I feel very awkward telling you this, but you've got to know. Sheila Bissett is spreading the story that your Beth and Alex are really yours and Suzy's . . . you know . . . that you well, you are their real father. That's why you're adopting them. There, that's it in a nutshell.'

Peter went pale, turned his head away from Jimbo's direct glance and said quietly, 'What's that old saying? "Be sure your sins will find you out."' He leant on the gate looking across the fields towards Sykes Wood. 'We didn't have an affair. It happened the week Patrick died. She was desperate for comfort and I have to admit I was stunned by her, quite stunned. Then I found out she was expecting twins and I thought it was the end of everything, my marriage, my vocation everything. Caroline was magnificent, said it wasn't to be allowed to make any difference to us. We were partners for life and she wouldn't permit something like that to separate us. What Suzy longed for and planned for, was that Caroline would want to adopt the twins, and that's exactly what she did want.'

Jimbo silently absorbed what Peter had said. God! What a situation. What was there to say? He waited a while for Peter to compose himself and then said in a matter of fact tone, 'Then you've nothing to fear: the two of you can stand together on this. I know in my heart that the whole village will be behind you. They don't like Sheila Bissett, but they do love you and Caroline.'

'I promised Suzy faithfully that we would never disclose the truth, just as she promised us that she would never tell, either. How has the woman found out?'

'She's put two and two together and made five. That's what.'

'I must get straight home.' Peter turned away from the gate and set off at such a cracking pace that Jimbo couldn't keep up. When he got back to the Rectory, Peter went straight up to the bathroom for his shower. He arrived in the kitchen for his breakfast already dressed in his cassock for the regular Friday morning school assembly in the church.

'Sylvia, do you think you could leave Dr Harris and me for a moment, I need to speak to her about something.'

'Of course Mr Harris, I'll just get on making the beds. Your eggs are ready.'

'Thank you.'

67

Caroline, who was loading the washing machine, reminded him to ask Michael Palmer about the children doing some singing in the church on the day of the festival.

'Caroline come here.'

'I really am busy, Peter. I shall have to start bathing the twins soon and I've the drier to empty and a thousand other things to do. Can't it wait?'

'No, it can't. Please come here and sit down.'

'Be quick then.' She sat on the edge of the chair ready for immediate flight.

'My darling girl, the one thing I don't want to do is to hurt you any more than I have done already. God knows I've done enough damage one way and another, but there's something I must tell you. You know we promised that we would never explain about the twins? Suzy promised and we did for everybody's sake. Well, I'm afraid that someone has put two and two together and arrived at the conclusion that they are mine.'

'Oh please God, no. Oh no.' Tears began brimming in Caroline's eyes and she got out her handkerchief to wipe them away. 'Are you sure?'

'We should have known we couldn't get away with it. We should have been honest from the start.'

'C . . . c . . . c . . . could we deny it?'

'That wouldn't be right would it, not in the long run?'

'No, it wouldn't. Oh, just when everything was going so well. Just when I was beginning to feel like a normal woman instead of a peculiarity.'

'Was that how you felt?'

'Yes.' Caroline wiped away the new tears beginning to run down her cheeks. 'The barren woman syndrome, you know. I was beginning to forget. What the hell are we going to do?'

'I've not had time to think. Jimbo's just told me.'

'How does Jimbo know?'

Peter finished buttering his toast before he told her, 'Because Harriet overheard someone talking in the Store.'

'Then they all know.'

'Yes, I'm afraid so.'

'Who started it?'

'Sheila Bissett.'

'I might have known. I've never liked that woman, always pretending to be something she isn't. Now she's really done for us. What are we going to do?'

'Go and have it out with her.'

At that moment the door bell rang and Caroline composed herself and went to answer it. Jimmy Glover was standing on the step holding a plastic carrier bag.

'Morning, Dr Harris. Thought you might like a couple of rabbits for the pot. Fresh this morning they are and I've dressed 'em all ready like. There's nothing to do 'cept rinse 'em and pop 'em in the pot. Rector'll like a bit of rabbit I expect.'

'That's very kind of you, Jimmy. Can I give you something for them?'

'Not at all, Dr Harris, they're a gift from me as a thank you for all you and the rector do for the village. We all appreciate you both and them babies. Good morning.' Jimmy raised his foul old cap and stepped briskly off across the road back to his cottage.

She closed the door and tears came into her eyes again. He hadn't said anything specific, but she knew what he meant.

'Peter that was Jimmy Glover with two rabbits for us. He knows and he's trying to tell us he doesn't mind. Isn't he lovely?'

'Yes, he is. I wouldn't have thought it of old Jimmy. Rascal that he is. That will test the cook tonight. I bet you've never cooked rabbit before have you?'

'No, but I'll get Sylvia to give me some ideas. It

69

doesn't help what's happened though does it? What shall we do? I'm so upset.'

'I'm going to see Sheila Bissett straight after I've taken the school assembly. I've got to face her with it and get the matter cleared up. We can't have it festering away for ever.'

'You've got more courage than I have.'

'Well, in my book it has to be done.' Peter drained his cup and then said, 'Must be off. Don't worry about it too much my darling, I'll get it sorted out. We'll have a difficult few days but there'll soon be something else for people to talk about.'

When the school assembly was finished Peter lingered in the church for a while. The prospect of facing Sheila Bissett was causing him anguish. One of the reservations he had had about taking on the twins had been this very thing. Maybe in the long run being completely truthful, after Suzy had left, would have been the better course of action. He'd dreaded the hurt Caroline was now feeling, to say nothing of how he felt. One mistake, just one fall from Grace and he was still paying for it. Rightly so, but Caroline shouldn't have to pay too. The children were flesh of his flesh and he was bound by ties he never knew existed before they were born. He'd even found that he would kill for them rather than have them hurt in any way. For a man who claimed to be a pacifist that was a strange thing to discover about oneself. Waiting for the adoption papers to be processed was torment. Caroline felt so certain that it would all go through without a hitch, but he lived in dread until it had all been signed and sealed. For Caroline's sake he had to find the right words. He knocked on Sheila's door and waited for a reply. Sheila opened it and looked defiantly at him.

'Good morning, Rector. You've managed to call then at last.'

Peter looked down at her and gave her a tentative smile. 'Good morning. May I come in for a moment Lady Bissett?'

'You may.'

He followed her into the sitting room. She indicated the sofa with a nod of her head. Peter clasped his hands and took a deep breath.

'It has come to my notice, Lady Bissett, that a rumour is going round the village to the effect that Alexander and Elizabeth are my children by Suzy Meadows.'

'Is there?' Momentarily, Sheila looked uncomfortable and then defiant.

'I can't deny it, because it is the truth. I won't go into the circumstances which brought it about, but I will say this; my wife, the one person in the world who should have felt entitled to take her revenge on me, in fact did not do anything of the kind. When she found out that Suzy couldn't keep her twins, Caroline asked to adopt them, as much for my sake as for her own. As you know she can't ever be a mother herself, but out of some great store of compassion, she decided that adopting the twins would make everything right for everyone. Suzy wanted that too. If Caroline can find such love and understanding when she has the most right to feel deeply hurt, is it not possible that you could find it also?'

Sheila didn't answer.

'I have no right to ask for sympathy for myself, but perhaps I have a right to ask for it for Caroline.'

Still Sheila didn't answer. With her hands resting on her lap she sat staring at Peter, waiting for him to continue.

'There really isn't anything else to say. I hope that you can find it in your heart to show some of the compassion which Caroline has shown me, and that you will endeavour for her sake not to make life more difficult for her than it is. Please don't encourage the gossip, that wouldn't be right, but put the situation in the best light that you can?'

'I like your wife, and in the circumstances I wouldn't want to make matters worse for her. But it's only for her sake not yours. You can't be forgiven for what you have done, not a man in your position. Just as you can't be forgiven for letting me resign.'

'With regard to your resignation, we run the Flower Festival through the committee and the others didn't want all white displays. We did decide democratically, Lady Bissett. I'm only sorry that we have not the opportunity to benefit from your flair and expertise. I have been giving the matter some thought and I wondered if you might like to put some all white displays in the church hall? Everyone will be going in there for refreshments and will have plenty of opportunity for seeing the displays. The hall is rather bare as it is now isn't it?'

'Would I have a free hand?'

'Absolutely.'

'Then I shall be in charge of the church hall flowers on the day.'

Peter stood, and so did Sheila. He took her hand and, looking straight into her eyes, thanked her for her understanding and told her that there were few people in this world who could have overlooked the committee's decision with such generosity of spirit. Sheila found herself blushing with delight. She squeezed his hand and assured him of her intention to make a real success of her task. 'You won't regret asking me, Peter. And I'll remember about Caroline.'

'Thank you, Sheila. Thank you.'

Caroline, knowing she must be brave and go out to meet people, set off for a walk with the twins on the pretext that they wouldn't settle so she thought perhaps an outing in the pram might get them both to sleep. Pat Duckett was leaving her cottage on her way to get ready for school dinners. She called across to Caroline, 'Morning Dr Harris. Isn't it lovely? Just right for getting the twins a breath of air. Aren't they coming on?' She poked her head in the hood and tickled Beth and then Alex under their chins. 'You two be good for your mum. My they are looking great. You must be so proud of 'em.'

'Yes, I am, Pat.'

'Bye then, I must be off. I tell you what, I wish you'd bring them in for the children to see. I'll ask Mr Palmer if it's all right shall I?'

'I don't think he'd want me coming into school.'

'He would if I asked him. Walk round with me and I'll ask him now. Come on. No time like the present.'

The children were delighted. They asked her questions about how the babies could be twins when they were a boy and a girl. Caroline explained as best she could. They all wanted to cuddle them, and eventually when the twins started getting fractious, Caroline said she must be going. Michael Palmer came to the gate with her.

'You and Peter have their loyalty, you know. Never doubt that.'

'Thank you, Michael, very much.' She smiled at him, trying hard not to let him see how much she was affected by their kindness.

When she called in the Store to do a bit of shopping she found Harriet deep in conversation with Venetia.

'Why, hello, Caroline,' Venetia enthused. 'How lovely to see you. When we have our opening night will you and Peter be able to attend? I wondered if he would take the first swim in the pool that night as a way of celebrating our little enterprise? He's such a good advertisement for a healthy body.'

'Oh come on, Venetia, let it rest. There's plenty of other men who could do that for you with a lot more verve and sex appeal than Peter.'

'I tell you what, after the rumours I've heard this morning, I realise now why you're so touchy about him. I think it's very courageous of you to take on those twins. Not many women would do it.'

'I'd better leave, Harriet, before I say something I shall regret. I'll come back later when you have more time.' And Caroline opened the door wide and pushed the pram out, blinded by tears she was determined not to let Venetia see.

Harriet exploded. 'How dare you make a remark like that? How dare you?'

'I was complimenting her on her courage.'

'Complimenting her? Oh, so that's what you call it. We are all very upset about this nasty gossip that Sheila Bissett has been spreading and we're standing behind them both on this. There was no need for you to say what you did. I'm so mad I think we'd better postpone our discussion to another day. If indeed I ever feel like discussing it with you ever again.'

'You're letting sentiment get in the way of business Harriet. Jimbo wouldn't let that happen. Have it your own way. Perhaps Jimbo has more of a business brain than you. I ought to have known.'

She tripped out of the Store leaving Harriet fuming at the woman's lack of sensitivity. She went through to the back office in search of someone to whom she could let off steam.

'Jimbo, where are you? Isn't he back yet Mother?'

Sadie looked around and said, 'No, he isn't. She's right you know. You did let your feelings get the better of you. No one can afford to turn business away nowadays.'

'You agree with what she said then?'

'No, but it is a free country.'

'Not in our Store it isn't.'

*

74

Peter found Caroline in the kitchen with Alex and Beth fast asleep in their pram.

'Sorry it's taken me so long to get back I . . .'

'Shush . . . keep your voice down. I've just got them to sleep. What did she say?'

'Sylvia in?'

'No, she's having some time off. How did you get on?'

'Reading between the lines, Sheila had been expecting me to go round the morning after the Flower Festival to apologise and agree to her all white job. When I didn't go, she decided to get her own back. I have unashamedly used every trick in the book to persuade her of the error of her ways. I told her she was quite right, that Alex and Beth are mine, but that we had decided to say nothing both for the children's sake, for Suzy's and for yours. It seemed the best of all the options. So we've come to a compromise. She's apologised to you through me, I've apologised for the Flower Festival Committee being a bit high-handed and disregarding her wishes, and in return she's doing flower displays in the church hall where we shall be serving refreshments all day. I've no doubt they will be so magnificent we shall be able to charge for visiting the hall as well. So honour is satisfied all round.'

'Thank God for that. I feel shattered about it all. You were quite right, we couldn't really expect to keep it a secret. Let's hope it's a nine days wonder. I've received nothing but kindness from everyone, except from Venetia Mayer. The woman is totally lacking in tact. She could cause a lot of trouble for you, Peter. Apparently she wants you to be the first to dive into the pool at the Health Club on opening night. Something about you being an "excellent advertisement for a healthy body".'

'Oh help, what will the woman think of next? I'm glad Jimbo's running with me at the moment. At least there's safety in numbers!'

'I think maybe we shall weather the storm. Do you?'

'Yes, I do. You don't regret adopting Alex and Beth, do you Caroline?'

'Never for one moment. Except sometimes in the night when I've had hardly any sleep then I *do* wonder if I'm right in the head. But not seriously.'

'I love you, my darling.'

'And I love you too.'

Chapter 7

When Peter heard the heavy hammering on the rectory door he knew it was Willie. Willie always knocked as though there was a major emergency on hand. He opened the door to find his verger standing on the step holding a large box full of plants.

'You're looking very smart today Willie. I hardly recognised you.'

'Thank you sir. Thought I'd spend a bit of money and get done up.'

'You've certainly got done up and no mistake. If I didn't know better I'd think you were courting. I assume those plants are for me. Are you staying to put them in?'

'Well I could, sir, if you like. I'm not dressed for it, but I don't mind.'

'I'm going to get Sylvia to make me a coffee. My wife's taken the twins for their injections this morning so Sylvia's in charge. Come into the kitchen and we'll get her to make one for you as well.'

'Right, thank you Rector, I will.'

The two of them went into the kitchen to find Sylvia almost hidden behind a pile of ironing.

'You know Willie our verger, don't you Sylvia?'

'Yes I do, Mr Harris. How are you, Willie?'

'Fine thanks Mrs Bennett.'

'Sylvia's the name.'

'Right well, Sylvia then.'

Peter offered to make coffee. But Sylvia declined his offer.

'I shall be glad of a break thank you. I'll do it.'

They all three sat down in front of the Aga with their coffee. Peter asked Willie how his house alterations were going on.

'Very well indeed Rector thank you. Nearly completed they are.' The telephone rang and Peter went to answer it.

Willie cleared his throat and asked Sylvia how the Flower Festival was going on.

'Very well indeed. You know Lady Bissett is doing the flowers in the church hall, do you? She tried to take over the whole thing but we wouldn't let her.'

'Sounds just like her. I was in Culworth yesterday. I see they've got a nice musical on, done by the Operatic Society, *The Mikado* it's called. Have you seen it?'

'No, I never have.'

'I just wondered. I fancied going.'

'Oh, I see.'

Willie drank some more of his coffee trying to think how to phrase the big question without risking a rebuff.

'Do you get plenty of time off while you're here?' he began casually.

'Usually every evening. And most weekends, unless there's something special on.'

'I see. So if you wanted to go out you could.'

'Yes, I can and I do.'

'So if I came up with two tickets for it you'd be free to go?'

'Oh yes.'

'Shall I do that then?'

'Willie Biggs, are you asking me out?'

Willie pondered the implications of this question and then decided that in for a penny in for a pound.

'Well, yes I am.'

Peter came back in. 'Old Mrs Woods in the alms-houses in Penny Fawcett is dying and she's asking for me. I've got to go out there straight away. Tell Caroline I shan't be back for a while, will you Sylvia?'

'Certainly Rector.'

'I'll settle up with you for the plants when I get back, Willie. Next time I see you we'll have a word about clearing out the boiler house store room.'

Bracing himself for Sylvia's answer, Willie looked up vaguely at Peter and said, 'Right sir.' Peter smiled to himself and hastened off to old Mrs Woods.

'Very well, Willie, if that's an invitation I'm accepting.'

'Accepting? Oh right then. I'll see about the tickets and let you know.'

He banged down his cup by the sink said, 'Thanks for the coffee' and hurried out without a backward glance. Sylvia, washing up the cups, was bent over the sink laughing. He didn't expect a yes I bet. Well, why not? What have I got to lose? Nothing at all. And he's nice enough. Thinks I haven't noticed he's smartened himself up. Usually means a woman in tow when a bachelor smartens up. Done his house up too. Must be serious.

After Willie had put the plants in the rectory garden he went home to admire his cottage. He'd given it a good clean and tidy up after the building work and he was almighty satisfied with it. Having done all the work he'd have to pluck up courage to ask her back after *The Mikado* and no mistake. Since he'd had the bathroom made and the kitchen fitted out with those units from MFI that were going for a song, he'd realised how much the new things showed up the rest of the cottage. As a result he'd acquired a new carpet, new curtains and new chairs for his little sitting room. He'd also bought some house plants and special pots to put them in. Altogether home was beginning to look like one of those places he'd seen in the magazines at the dentist's when he'd been forced to go with that raging toothache; cosy but a bit special. The old stuff had gone on a bonfire in the churchyard along with a lot of other rubbish he'd kept ever since his mother had died. Sylvia wouldn't be going in the bedroom, so if he kept the door closed while she was there he could set about clearing that out in his own good time. She didn't know it, but he'd bought the tickets on the off chance when he was in Culworth yesterday. He'd call round tomorrow and tell her he'd got them. He just hoped he hadn't shown how agitated he was, he'd only to come near her and he felt like a boy of sixteen with his first love. Well, she was his first love and . . . The door bell rang. Willie went to answer it, hoping it wouldn't be Sylvia saying she'd changed her mind.

It wasn't. It was Gwen Baxter.

'Hello Gwen, what can I do for you? First time since I can't remember when that you've knocked on my door.'

Gwen always spoke as though she was on the bridge of a ship during a violent storm. Willie stepped back to avoid not only the smell emanting from her but to lessen the impact of her gruff voice. 'Wouldn't be knocking now if I wasn't needing help. There's something wrong with the tank on the roof and we need help. Beryl's standing watching the bucket. It's filling up with water nearly as fast as she can empty it.'

'What do you want me to do?'

'Attend to it of course.'

'I'm not a plumber, Gwen.'

'I know that. But you could look at it for us.'

'Well, I'll look, but I'm not promising anything.'

She marched across to her cottage with her long strides, Willie dashing along in her wake. The stench

80

which greeted him as he walked through the back door made him feel sick. She took him into the little hallway. The shoulder-high piles of newspapers baffled him. They'd go up like tinder if ever there was a fire. He squeezed between the towering columns and followed Gwen upstairs. Every step had things stacked at each side till it was only possible to put one foot at a time on the step. Basking in the righteousness of his own recent clear out and the improvement it had made, he suggested to Gwen that she had a bonfire too.

'A bonfire? Whatever for? We need all these things.'

Beryl appeared at the head of the stairs carrying a heavy bucket. She waited till they got to the top and then raced downstairs as fast as she could to empty it.

'I shall have to get in the loft, you know,' Willie told Gwen.

'There's a trap door in the ceiling in our bedroom.' She opened the door to their room.

'Have you got a ladder?'

'Yes. Wait there I'll get it.'

Willie looked round. It was not the kind of bedroom he would have liked to sleep in. His own was a prince in comparison. Every item in here needed either throwing away or a thoroughly good wash. Preferably throwing away. He began to itch, first on his ankles and then further up his legs. Oh Lord, surely they hadn't got fleas? The sooner he was out of here the better. He saw Beryl galloping up the stairs with an empty bucket. Gwen appeared with the ladder and he managed to push open the trapdoor and heave himself up into the loft. It was a burst pipe. A major joint, botched by some amateur plumber in years gone by, had opened up and water was pouring from the slit through the floor onto the landing below. He shouted down.

'It's no good Gwen, there's a big slit in the pipe up here. I'll have to turn off the water and you'll need to get a proper plumber.'

'Can't you do it?'

'No I can't, I haven't got the right equipment.'

Willie dropped down onto the ladder and pulled the trap door shut.

'Where's the stop tap?'

'Under the sink.'

He pushed his way between the newspapers and went into the kitchen. Willie bent down and after a great deal of effort turned the tap completely off. 'It'll be a while before the water stops running. You really will have to get a plumber to come, Gwen. Use the phone in the Store.'

'So far you've told me to have a bonfire, get rid of our belongings and now phone the plumber. Anything else you'd like to instruct me about?'

'No. I'm only offering advice.' Beryl rushed through with another bucket and emptied it with more vigour than sense into the sink. Willie stepped out of the way just in time.

'Well, don't offer any more and what's more don't go out and tell people about our house. What we do under our own roof is our affair. I don't want you tittle tattling about us in The Royal Oak. I've seen you going in there.'

'No harm in that.'

'Drink is the devil's work and I ought to know.'

'You mean yer father.'

Gwen swung round and glared into his eyes from only a few inches away. He had all to do not to get his handkerchief out to hold over his nose.

'What do you mean by that?'

'Well, we all know what he was like, Gwen. Went home rolling drunk six nights out of seven didn't he? Be honest.'

'What he did six nights out of seven was his affair.'

'How your mother put up with it I don't know. She

82

was such a clean woman, always washing and scrubbing you all.'

'You find something odd do you in her being so clean?'

'Now, don't take on so.'

Beryl dashed past again with another bucket.

'Well, do you?'

'No, I don't, it just seemed such a pity that she tried so hard and he undid it all. It must have been a relief when he died. Pity she went first. Anyway I must be off.'

'Off to see your lady friend are you?'

'Lady friend?'

'Yes, Sylvia Bennett. Going out for a bit of that there 'ere. Disgusting it is. Disgusting.'

'Later today the rector has a funeral to conduct and I am going to make sure the church is looking its best and to contact the funeral director in the absence of the rector to make sure everything is in order. And I'll thank you not to make nasty remarks about my private affairs.'

'Affair is it now. That's why you've had your house done up. Making it nice for taking her back there. I've been watching you. I know what your evil designs are.'

'Next time you want any help don't send for me.'

Willie went out through the narrow opening of the back door, enraged at Gwen's dirty mind. He had a good wash in his new bathroom and as he changed his clothes discovered bites all the way up his legs. All during the funeral he had to exercise the utmost control to stop himself from scratching. He explained to Peter when the funeral party had gone.

'Sorry, sir, if I've been behaving a bit odd during the service, but I'm afraid I must have got fleas.'

'Fleas? Where from Willie?'

'Gwen and Beryl Baxter's. They've got a leak and I went in to investigate it. They need a plumber but I bet they won't bother with one.'

'Have you had to turn off the water?'

'Had to else that house of theirs would be flooded. Mind you, not a bad thing. It's foul, like their minds, begging your pardon Rector.'

'I'd better go across and see if I can help. They can't manage without running water.'

'I wouldn't if I were you. They'll only be abusive, sir. Not fit for your ears.'

'Willie, I have not lived in an ivory tower all my life, I have been around a bit.'

'Very well sir, as you please.'

Peter tried knocking on the front door and, getting no reply, went round to the back. He knocked loudly and then did as he did at most of the village houses, he opened the door and said, 'It's Peter here from the Rectory, can I come in?'

He pushed open the door as far as it would go and stepped in.

'Hello, Miss Baxter, are you there?' He stepped further into the kitchen. 'Hello?'

There was a sudden rush of feet and Beryl entered the kitchen with a carving knife held threateningly in her hand.

'It's only me, Miss Baxter – Peter from the Rectory. It's all right.'

'Yes?'

'I've come to see if I can help about the leak you have. Have you rung the plumber?'

'That's for Gwen to decide.'

'Is she here?'

'Yes.'

He heard more footsteps and then Gwen burst in through the kitchen door.

'What do you think you are doing entering our house without asking?'

'I'm sorry but I usually knock and then walk in when I

84

go visiting. In future I'll knock and wait for you to answer. I've come about you having to get Willie to turn the water off.'

'Well, he's done it.'

'How are you going to manage without running water?'

'Quite well thank you.'

'We could let you have some water from the Rectory if that would help until the plumber gets here.'

'We don't want any favours.'

'If you like I'll phone the plumber on your behalf and in the meantime Willie and I will bring you some water across.'

'We do not require help from someone who professes to be a goody goody and then fornicates with his neighbour. I don't think Jesus had that in mind when he said love thy neighbour.'

Peter had no answer to that.

'Don't think that because we don't socialise we don't know what goes on. We have a complete view of the comings and goings of this place from our windows. Nothing goes on that we don't know about. I saw you go round to see that slut and saw how long it took you to leave. Then when we saw her getting bigger, we knew. Oh, yes we knew. Then your wife tries to cover your tracks by wanting to adopt them. What a joke. Standing by her man. Ha. No man living deserves loyalty like that. Not one of you. You're all scum. Scum, do you hear?'

'I think it would be better if I take my leave. No person is totally perfect and I above all am aware of the fragility of both man and woman, but we can ask for forgiveness. Perhaps you need forgiveness for thinking the way you do. May God bless you both.' Peter forced open the door and left.

'Get out, get out and don't ever come back. Fornicator.'

When he got home he went straight upstairs, undressed, showered, put fresh clothes on and went into his study and got out what Caroline called the 'parish whisky'. He poured some into a glass and sat at his desk trying to erase from his mind the evil he had just encountered. Caroline came in carrying Beth who was in her permanently happy mood. Nothing ruffled her calm.

'They actually live in this village day in day out and their lives are so foul, Caroline, I can't believe it. How on earth can it have happened, that they turn out like that?'

'Here, nurse your daughter for a while, she'll restore your faith in human nature. I would have thought that by now you could no longer be surprised by the infinite variety of the human condition.' Peter took Beth in his arms propped her carefully against his shoulder and rubbed his cheek on hers to remind himself that there was still something beautiful left in the world.

'This is something much, much worse. You can feel the evil in the air. To say nothing of the smell. Don't ever call on them Caroline please. Nor let the children near them either. There's something very wrong there, believe me. Beryl came into the kitchen brandishing a carving knife.'

'You mean holding a carving knife?'

'No *brandishing* it. They must be unhinged. Completely unhinged. Apparently they watch all the comings and goings from their window and claim nothing goes on that they don't know about.'

'Heavens above, I shall hardly dare go out.'

'Exactly.'

Had Peter been able to see them at that moment he would have seen them struggling to get the top off their old well. Running water had been put in when their parents bought the house on their marriage, and the old well had been covered up. More than sixty years of rain and earth and neglect had wedged the lid tight. Beryl found a spade and dug away some of the earth and grass. Gwen got a steel rod from the shed and used that to prise it loose. Eventually they got the lid off and both peered in. Beryl picked up a stone and threw it down. They listened for the sound of it hitting the water.

'I didn't hear it, did you?'

'No. Throw another one in.'

She did and they both heard it hit the water. In the shed they found a long piece of rope. Beryl emptied the metal rubbish bucket from under the sink and they tied the rope to the handle and dangled it down the well.

After several attempts it came up filled with water.

Gwen grimaced.

'I knew we didn't need a plumber. Interfering sods those men are. Go fill the kitchen sink with it and we'll let it down again.'

Beryl put the plug in the sink and emptied the water from the bucket into it. Things were swimming around. Funny little things with lots of legs and some that wiggled along with no legs at all. And it was green.

'Gwen, I don't think it's fit to drink.'

'We'll boil it.'

'There's funny things in it swimming about.'

'We'll sieve it first.'

'What if it makes us ill?'

'We'll get used to it. Take this bucket full. That'll do us for today, better than tap water with all the chemicals they put in it nowadays.'

'Well we shan't need the plumber shall we?'

'No. We don't use much water anyway.'

Chapter 8

No one realised that Gwen and Beryl had been taken ill through drinking the well water. The first day they drank it without concern, but then after that they developed serious intestinal infections which laid them low.

It was only when Willie noticed their curtains had not been drawn back for two days that anyone decided to do something about it. Willie, Jimmy and Pat went across together. They tried the front door but couldn't get in so they went through the side gate and pushed open the back door as far as they could. Pat got her handkerchief out and covered her mouth and nose. Even Jimmy, used to a very haphazard regime in his own home, was appalled at what he saw. They called out downstairs and looked in the sitting room but there was no sign of the two sisters. Willie suggested they made their way upstairs together. They tried to push open the main bedroom door and found it almost impossible because of the newspapers piled up from floor to ceiling. They tried the next bedroom and found the two of them prostrate in bed. They had used various containers to be sick in as well as having been sick in the bed, and they lay there, two gaunt, exhausted and unconscious women in dire need of help.

'Right Jimmy, out to the Store, dial 999 and get an ambulance. Tell them what you like but they've got to get here quick.'

'What about asking Dr Harris to come while we wait? Maybe she could give 'em something to 'elp,' Pat suggested.

'Certainly not, we can't ask her to come into this mess. It's enough to make me ill just looking at it. In any case she might get something and give it to them babies. No, that won't do. Have you gone yet Jimmy?'

'I'm just off.'

Pat reached out and tentatively shook Gwen's hand as it lay over the edge of the bed.

'Is this Gwen, Willie, I can't tell the difference? Gwen are you all right? Gwen? Gwen?'

'She's breathing I can see. Go round the other side and try the other one.'

Pat did. She could see that Beryl or Gwen, whichever one it was, was breathing, but she got no response.

'I reckon we've caught 'em only just in time Willie.'

'So do I.'

It must have been all of twenty minutes after Jimmy got back before the ambulance came. Even they, who must have seen some dreadful sights in the past, were appalled at what they saw. They wrapped the sisters up, put them on stretchers and with Willie and Jimmy's help manouevred them down the narrow staircase.

When they'd gone Willie locked up and went to tell Peter what had happened.

'I reckon they're touch and go, sir. Don't know what's caused it, but by Jove they aren't half poorly.'

'I'll ring the hospital and then go in to see them tomorrow. Though if my last encouter is anything to go by it will be far from pleasant.'

'They's too ill to be nasty sir, far too ill.'

'Right Willie. My word, they are two very peculiar women, aren't they?'

'Peculiar is putting it mildly. They weren't that bad as

kids. They've gone funnier and funnier since they got into women. You should see the house.' Sylvia came down the stairs and Willie smiled and nodded to her.

'Hello, Sylvia.'

'Hello, Willie.'

Peter tactfully retired to his study.

'There's a good film on in Culworth this week. Funny title, *Fried Green Tomatoes in a Whistle Stop Cafe*, or something. I'm told it's good. Wondered if you'd like to go see it.'

'I would indeed. And when we've been perhaps you'd like to come back here for a coffee.'

'Right you're on. I'll look up the times.'

'I'm buying myself a little car, if it's arrived by then, we could go in that.'

'Didn't know you could drive.'

'Well, I had a car for years for getting into work and then it packed up. But I've decided to get another one. Only an old banger mind.'

'Never mind so long as it goes. I'll be in touch.'

Peter couldn't get to the hospital for two days but he reassured himself by phone that they were recovering. When he did manage to visit them they were unrecognisable, not only because they had lost weight but because they were so scrupulously clean.

'Sister Murphy, how are you?'

'Why, hello, Mr Harris, long time no see. These two parishioners of yours are going to be all right, though heaven knows why. They were in a terrible state when they came in. Dreadfully dehydrated, absolutely filthy and in need of a lot of loving care. Could you come into the office and give me a few details.'

Peter told all he knew and then went to speak to them. He hardly knew which was which.

'Hello, Gwen? Is it Gwen? It's Peter here from the

Rectory. How are you today?'

Her eyes opened slowly and focused on his face.

'Go away.'

'I've come to see you because you've been very ill.'

'I don't need you.'

'Very well, my dear. You're in good hands. All you have to do is get yourself better, then you can go home.'

He went to the next bed took hold of Beryl's hand and spoke her name.

'Beryl, are you awake?' She opened her eyes, looked him full in the face and whispered, 'I told her we shouldn't drink it. I told her.'

'What did you drink Beryl?'

'It was the well.'

He could learn no more from her. She'd fallen asleep again.

The sisters were due home at the end of the next week. Apart from Peter no one had visited them. He organised a plumber to attend to the burst pipe but other than that he did nothing to the house, outfaced by the enormity of the task and afraid of intruding.

The social services were there when he called at the hospital a couple of days before they were to go home.

'We really cannot understand how two people have been allowed to live like they do. Does no one in your village have a conscience about them at all?'

'I know things look very bad and that the house is in a terrible state, but these two women will allow no one in. They shun all friendship, all overtures and totally refuse to accept that they need help. The reason why they drank the water from the well was because they didn't wish to have a plumber in their house. You tell me how to help them in those circumstances?'

'It is difficult I know. But you must persist. In the

91

1990s its wicked for old women to be living like they do. The whole village should take responsibility for them. No wonder we find old people have been lying dead in their houses for days before anyone realises. Someone should check them regularly.'

'Well, how about if you talk to them. You've seen the house, you know how unhygienic it is, in fact downright filthy. You offer them help to clean up and decorate or whatever it is you have the ability to instigate and see what kind of a response you get. You can't force people to have help if they don't want it. And they don't. As far as they are concerned their home is all right. It's just how they want it.'

'I'll have a word, I'll persuade them to let us help.'

'I've paid for a plumber myself and he's been in and mended the leak so the water is turned on again and they won't need to use the well. So at least they won't be back in here.'

'Well, that's something. I have a fund which I can use to help them, so I'll see about it straight away.'

Peter nearly said, 'And the best of luck' but didn't, being mindful that he might need their help at some future date for other parishioners.

Despite Gwen and Beryl stoutly refusing all offers of help the social services came to the village, borrowed the key from Peter and cleaned the twin's bedroom and the downstairs rooms and took away all the out of date packets and tins which had accumulated over the years. So when the twins went home from the hospital at least the worst of what had taken place while they were ill had been cleared up.

Gwen and Beryl were horrified when they found out and sent the social worker away with stern reminders that she was not to call to see them under any circumstances and that now they were well again she could cross them off her list.

The day before they were due home Sheila couldn't resist going round and taking a peep through their windows. A golden opportunity she called it. Ron, unwilling to allow her to go alone, found himself sneaking through the side gate. They had a peep through the windows.

'Ron, just look at this kitchen. It's absolutely antiquated. They haven't even a washing machine. No wonder they always look dirty.' Sheila reached up on tip toe and by holding on to the rotting window sill could see into the pantry.

'There's scarcely any food in the pantry, but the shelves have all been wiped. How can they live in there? Someone should do something about it.'

'You offer to go round and clean then.'

'Who'd want to clean up in there I ask you?' She turned round to hear his answer but he'd gone.

'Where are you Ron?'

'I'm down the garden looking at this well.'

Sheila struggled through the undergrowth. She knew she shouldn't have put her high heeled sandals on, but she pressed on. Ron was on his knees throwing stones into the well.

'It's mighty deep is this well. Fancy drinking water straight from this.'

Sheila peered down and sniffed the damp mossy odour. 'It's like those caves we went to see, near Bath was it? Why do they have their house like it is. Anyway no one can help them. The social services have helped a bit but they've not done enough. What do we pay all these taxes for?'

'Let's be off.'

'Shouldn't we put the lid on the well, Ron?'

'Yes, OK.' He pushed the heavy rotting old lid over the top as best he could. 'Surprises me they could move it in the first place. They must be stronger than they look,

93

those two.' He stood up, dusted the earth from his trouser knees, and they walked towards the side gate. As they approached, Gwen and Beryl appeared from the front path.

Gwen became immediately enraged. 'How dare you, what do you think you're doing? Thought we weren't home until tomorrow did you? Well, we discharged ourselves early. Couldn't cope with their interfering ways. What do you think you're doing creeping about our garden like this? Get out, go on get out.' Gwen was angry, but Beryl was frightened. 'Go away, please go away,' she called.

Ron tried some of the assertiveness training he'd learnt on a course for union leaders. Assuming his most authoritative voice he marched towards them saying, 'Now Miss Baxter we've been in to make sure the lid was on the well securely. Couldn't take the risk of one of you falling down it could we? All's well, now I've attended to it, you've no need to fear. Glad you're well enough to come home. Take care of . . .'

Ron got no further. Gwen picked up an almost bristleless broom and raised it above her head, obviously intent on hitting him with it. The head of the broom caught Ron on the side of his head with an enormous thwack. The words he'd just used about her being stronger than he'd thought came back to him as she struck him again and again. Sheila intervened in an attempt to help Ron, but Beryl came behind her and gripped her arms. Suddenly Gwen stopped. She went quite pale and very short of breath.

Beryl let go of Sheila and went to Gwen's aid. The two of them unlocked the back door and Gwen and then Beryl squeezed inside and shut the door.

'Ron, Ron, let's get home before anyone finds out.'

'Quick, through the gate. I feel such a fool.'

Inside their own home, Ron turned on Sheila.

'Can you tell me why I listen to you? It's you who got me into this predicament. I've that interview to do tomorrow for the ITV programme. All kinds of a fool I'm going to look with a bruise and a swelling the size of an egg on the side of my head.' He tenderly examined his head with the tips of his thick fingers. 'You're nothing but a confounded nuisance Sheila and after all these years it's time I stopped listening to you. In future *I* say what we do.'

'Well really, when I think of how I wait on you hand and foot, you don't do a hand's turn in the house and now you say I'm a confounded nuisance.'

'Well, you are. Don't ever suggest that we have anything to do with those two damned women ever again.' He stamped off upstairs to Sheila's navy and lavender bathroom, angry about the impression he would give on the TV programme. Maybe if he sat on the left hand side of the discussion group the lump would not be too obvious to the audience. The media certainly made one conscious of one's image. Talking of images, he wished Sheila looked more like Harriet Charter-Plackett or Caroline Harris. No not them, more like Sadie Beauchamp. Now she always looked stylish. Sheila never quite got her clothes right. And that dyed hair, he'd have to have a word about that.

His afternoon tea was ready when he got downstairs. Neat little brown bread sandwiches and a plate of scones with jam. No cream because of his cholesterol. The china teapot, the tea strainer and a neat little pink serviette for his knee. He'd much rather have had a big cup of strong tea, at the table in the kitchen and some well fried bacon between two slices of fresh white bread.

'There's a possibility I might get a chance to sit on the Question Time panel Sheila.'

'Honestly? Why didn't you tell me straight away? Oh

Ron that really is something. Question Time, well I never. Could I sit in the audience?'

'It's not quite the thing to do that. In any case I wouldn't want you there.'

'Would I make you nervous?'

'No, embarrassed.'

'Embarrassed? That's nice.'

'I mean it. You spend ridiculous money on clothes and somehow you never quite make it. That leopard skin coat will have to go for a start.'

'My leopard skin?'

'Don't keep repeating what I say.'

'I don't keep repeating what you say.'

'You do, you've just done it again. Anyway, that coat'll have to go. And when you go into Culworth to the hairdresser's you can get your hair made back to what it ought to be.'

'It cost a lot to get it like this.'

'It's not worth it, believe me. If I'm going to move in Question Time circles you've got to move with me. Hair done like when you were serving in The Case is Altered is not right now. We've moved up from then.'

'I do try.'

'No, you don't, you've stayed stuck like a gramophone needle. I bet Sadie Beauchamp spends no more money on clothes and hair than you do but she looks like a lady.'

'If I don't look like her and she looks like a lady, what do I look like then?'

'What you always looked like, a barmaid.'

'A barmaid?' Sheila's feelings were hurt in a way she couldn't remember ever before. This then was the thanks she got for trying. She stood up, scattering her sandwiches over the coffee table, 'This will cost you and not half Ron, not half. You wait and see.'

'Yes I will. You're Lady Bissett now, not Sheila with

her brassy hair, twinkling away to get the punters to buy more drink. When I get back tomorrow night from Birmingham we'll lay some plans.'

Chapter 9

As Harriet dashed across to the Church to help water the arrangements the flower society had worked on the day before, she noticed Ralph's Mercedes parked in front of his and Muriel's house. Oh good they're back. And in time for the Festival too. How nice to see them again.

She got there and found Sylvia had arrived first.

'Good morning, Sylvia. You're early.'

'Well, I decided to get absolutely in front of myself this morning, because Dr Harris and the rector and I want to spend time here today and of course the rector is giving the recital too, so we're sharing the work load so that we can all enjoy the festival in turns.'

'It's a lovely day. Let's hope it brings the crowds and we make lots of money.'

'Let's hope so.' They went from arrangement to arrangement feeling the oasis and deciding how much water, if any, the holders needed. The church looked quite the best it had ever done. Willie Biggs had worked marvels with spotlights and floodlights emphasising the flowers in all the right places.

'There's more to Willie than meets the eye isn't there Sylvia? Who'd have thought he would have had the sensitivity to know how to show the flowers and the murals and tombs to such good effect?'

'Yes, there is more to him than one thinks. He

certainly has an ear for music.'

'Oh how's that?'

'Well, to tell the truth we went to see *The Mikado* together in Culworth last week and he can sing some of the songs really well. If he wasn't the verger, he should be in the choir.'

'I didn't know you and he were . . .'

'Well, we are just good friends that's all.'

'Just like they used to say in the papers! Have you any water left in that jug? This arrangement under the pulpit needs a drop more.'

'Yes, here you are. I don't need to ask you not to say anything do I?'

'I shall be as silent as the grave, Sylvia.'

'Thank you, Mrs Charter-Plackett. He'd be so embarrassed if he thought everyone knew.'

'You won't keep it a secret for long as he well knows. Nothing can go on in this village without everyone knowing. Although come to think of it there have been a few well kept secrets in the past.'

Sheila chose the morning of the Flower Festival to launch her new image. Ron had been with her to Culworth to help choose her outfit. After a lot of wrangling on Sheila's part, he had persuaded her to buy a very expensive suit which he declared would come in useful for all sorts of occasions. It was a soft olive green and Ron had chosen a delicate cream blouse to wear with it. The collar of the blouse flowed over the neck of the collarless jacket. The most astounding difference was her hair. It had been made a soft mousey colour with slight blonde highlights and cut quite short but flatteringly around her face. Instead of her usual strappy stilettos she had chosen a pair of medium heeled dark chestnut shoes with a small matching handbag. Ron had surreptitiously been making mental notes of the way Sadie Beauchamp made up her face and had supervised Sheila's make up, having slyly hidden her rouge and the bright blue eye shadow she normally affected.

She purposely arrived in the church hall a little late pretending to be checking whether or not her flower arrangements needed more water. Several early visitors to the Festival didn't recognise her. 'Why Lady Bissett, we didn't see you there.' They would have bitten their tongues out before they could be friendly. They hadn't quite forgiven her yet for pointing out that young Alexander was so like the Rector. After all some things were best left unsaid. Out of the corner of her eye Sheila saw Sadie Beauchamp arrive for her morning coffee. This she knew was the great test. Sheila went to buy her third coffee that morning quite coincidentally at the same time as Sadie.

'Why hello, it's Sheila. I hope you don't mind me making a comment but, I must say, you look absolutely charming. And your hair too!'

'Thank you.'

'Where did you buy your suit?'

'Fisk's.'

'They have some lovely things in there. You've made a good choice.'

Ron watched the exchange from across the Hall and felt well satisfied with his campaign.

The church hall had a continuous queue of customers for refreshments. Harriet had to go back to the Store three times for more milk and bread and cakes, and also for another ham to carve for the rolls and sandwiches. The flowers in the church hall were not all white as Sheila had insisted upon. They were mainly white but here and there she had placed pale yellow flowers to give warmth and they were pronounced a great success. To her delight several customers said they'd put an extra fifty pence in the cash box as a fee for viewing her flowers.

There was such a steady stream of visitors to see the flowers in the church that Willie was in attendance all day keeping a watchful eye on anyone who might be a threat to the arrangements. Sylvia's friend, who'd been in charge of the church arrangements, blushed with delight when Peter complimented her on the effective way her society had picked up the colours of the stained glass windows and the murals.

'Wonderful, truly wonderful and we do appreciate you standing in at such short notice,' Peter said, whereupon Sylvia's friend blushed again to the roots of her hair and had to retire to the church hall for a cup of tea while she recovered. The organ recital, given by Mrs Peel and Peter, filled the church and most satisfactory of all, it was full again when the school choir did their performance prior to the church closing at seven.

Ralph and Muriel, having travelled through the night from the airport, didn't put in an appearance until the school choir was performing. Willie Biggs, adjusting some lights so they shone on the children while they sang, was the first to notice their arrival.

He whispered, 'Welcome home Sir Ralph, Lady Templeton.'

Muriel whispered back that he had no need to stand on ceremony, they were still Ralph and Muriel as before.

Harriet, standing at the back, gazing full of love and motherly pride on Fergus, Finlay and Flick singing on the front row of the choir, felt a slight nudge at her elbow. When she saw Muriel she broke into a delighted smile and whispered, 'See you afterwards.'

When the church was finally closed for the night Harriet suggested that Ralph and Muriel, Peter and Caroline should come over to her house about eight thirty when she'd had a chance to get the children to bed and they could all catch up on Ralph and Muriel's news.

Caroline arranged with Sylvia to babysit for a while. 'I shall be glad to, my feet are nearly killing me. Would it be all right if I asked Willie in for a bite to eat? It'll be his first chance of a meal all day. I thought afterwards we'd watch TV.'

'Of course, that will be fine. I've got the twins to sleep so they shouldn't be any trouble. Go and ask him to come in. Peter and I are nearly ready to go. Don't forget to switch the baby alarm on in case the twins cry, will you?'

'I'll do that. I won't be a moment asking him.'

Caroline grinned at Peter. 'As fast as we get one romance sorted out there's another one to be tactful about.'

'I don't think anything will come of it, do you really?'

'Come here, your shirt is out at the back. Why not? One should grab happiness while one can. There's too little of it in this world.' Peter turned round and linked his hands around Caroline's waist.

'Except here in this house. I thought I was completely happy before, but I had no idea what happiness was till now.'

'Thank you for saying that. I know I gave you a hard time when I found out about Suzy; I honestly believed the end of my world had come. That was until I recognised how much I needed you.'

'I love you my darling. Give me a kiss.'

'Peter, we mustn't start kissing. Sylvia will be back with Willie, and we've got to go.'

'Have we? Well, yes, I expect we have. Just one then. Did you notice Sheila Bissett today? I hardly recognised her.'

'Bought her outfit in Fisk's in Culworth.'

'How do you know?'

'I asked her when I complimented her on how charming she looked. Ron grew about two feet taller.'

'Shall I check Beth and Alex?'

'Yes please. You played beautifully today, Peter.'

'Thank you, my darling girl.'

Willie was installed in the kitchen with Sylvia cooking an omelette on the Aga when they got downstairs.

'We shall only be about an hour, Sylvia.'

'Be as long as you like Dr Harris. Willie and I are going to watch TV so we shan't notice the time. We'll listen for Beth and Alex.'

'Good night Willie.'

'Good night sir.'

Sadie was already there when they arrived at Harriet and Jimbo's.

'Good evening you two, escaped for a while from your family cares?'

'Good evening Sadie. No, we've escaped from playing gooseberry.'

'Playing gooseberry?'

Caroline winked at Sadie and put her finger to her lips.

'Not able to disclose.'

'Oh I see. It's Sylvia is it?'

Harriet pushed a drink into her mother's hand. 'Hush, mother, you're getting into a real village gossip. Don't pry.'

'My dear Harriet, what else is there to talk about but the goings on in the village? I swear I could write a column every week for the local rag on the comings and goings in this village. "Village Voice", I'd call it and I wouldn't be short of items for it either. A couple of evenings in The Royal Oak and I'd have enough material for three columns in no . . .'

'You never go in The Royal Oak.'

'I could always start. Do you suppose the Culworth Gazette would pay me for it?'

'Don't say you need the money,' Harriet retorted.

Peter laughed. 'Compose your first column Sadie,

103

right here and now.'

'OK here we go. Item one. Venetia and Jeremy Mayer are opening their new health club in two weeks' time. The local rector is performing the opening ceremony by being the first to dive in the pool. He has been chosen because of his superb athletic figure, Venetia Mayer told your reporter. Local people are expected to gather in their hundreds to witness their trendy rector performing this duty.'

'Oh no he's not,' Peter declared amidst a lot of laughter.

'Item Two. What is this we hear? Villagers are no longer friendly caring people as in the past. Two local residents lay ill for three days before anyone realised. Their lives were saved by the prompt action of the verger. Village life is not what it was in days of yore.

Item Three. What has prompted the said verger to spruce up his house, put a bathroom in and a new kitchen and buy new clothes? Is there romance in the air we ask?

Item Four. A local aristocrat has abandoned her unbelievably tasteless clothes and become quite civilised. The hairdresser in Culworth has thrown away her last bottles of peroxide. Her best customer has gone mousey.'

'Mother, that is cruel.'

Caroline agreed. 'Very cruel Sadie. She has made a real effort.'

'Yes, you're right, it was cruel. She is trying, I have to admit.'

Peter suggested that Sheila was quite nice once she'd dropped her pretence of being landed gentry.

The door bell rang and Jimbo went to answer it, to find Muriel and Ralph at the door bearing gifts.

'Come in, delighted to see you both. Have you had a good trip?'

'Absolutely wonderful Jimbo. But we're so glad to be

104

back. We couldn't wait another night. Ralph drove us straight here from the airport.'

'Hello, everyone.'

Muriel stood in the doorway looking tanned and radiant. Sadie went towards them crying, 'Why, Muriel you look ten years younger, what have you been doing?'

Harriet blushed, 'Mother really, what a thing to say to someone just back from their honeymoon.' Muriel took the innuendo in her stride. Her arms were full of presents.

'We've brought presents for everyone. This boomerang is for Fergus, this is a fearsome Aborigine carving for Finlay, and these carved wooden beads are for Flick. Harriet this is for you. It's a wrap for you to put on when you come out of your pool. Jimbo, we've bought you a beach shirt from Bondi Beach. Here are some toys for the twins, Caroline. I nearly got them some clothes but I wasn't sure of the size, babies grow so quickly. The huge parcel Ralph is carrying is a sheepskin rug for you Peter and for you Caroline. I do hope you like it. Sadie this is a silk scarf for you. I hope I've made a good choice, you're always so clever with your clothes. I do hope you all like them.'

'Muriel spent most of the honeymoon choosing those presents. To say nothing of all the things she's bought for the house and for me.'

'Ralph, I did no such thing.' They all smiled at Muriel's indignation.

'Let's all have drinks while we open our parcels.'

When they'd opened their presents and caught up with some of the news from Australia and Turnham Malpas, Harriet suggested they went into the kitchen and collected whatever they liked from the left overs of the Flower Festival catering. And if Jimbo opened some wine they could sit down and talk some more.

Caroline, about to put a roll filled with ham and cream

cheese into her mouth said, 'This ham looks delicious Jimbo. In fact everything you sell is delicious. You don't sell rabbit do you? We had some a while back. It was gorgeous. We used a recipe of Sylvia's grandmother's, all herbs and spices and things. Why don't you sell them in the Store, Jimbo? I'm sure Jimmy Glover could keep you well supplied and it would be a nice little addition to his income for him.'

Jimbo glanced questioningly at her and said, 'Jimmy gave you them did he?'

'Yes, that's right.' She unconcernedly continued eating until Jimbo said, 'I'm surprised at you Caroline.'

'Surprised at me, what have I done?' Harriet tapped his knee and shook her head but he ignored her. 'I wouldn't have thought you would have condoned eating an animal that had been trapped and no doubt been in excruciating pain most of the night.'

Caroline put down her fork and looked at Jimbo in surprise. 'What do you mean? He *shoots* the rabbits . . . doesn't he?'

'No, he traps them.'

'You're wrong, Jimbo. I've seen him with a gun.'

'That's as maybe, but he traps his rabbits. Ask any of the villagers, they all know he does it.'

'He wouldn't give me rabbits he'd *trapped* now would he? You're quite wrong Jimbo, isn't he Peter?'

Ralph answered her question, 'He does trap rabbits, Caroline, and has done all his life and his father and his grandfather and no doubt his great-grandfather before him.'

'I don't believe you. Traps them? I thought that all stopped years ago.'

Ralph shook his head. 'It may have declined but Jimmy still does it. Prides himself on using the same type of snare his father used. I'm sorry Caroline.'

'Not as sorry as I am. It's barbaric, absolutely barbaric.

106

And I ate them. I feel terrible.'

Peter stood up and went across to her, taking her plate to prevent the contents sliding onto the floor. 'Darling, please don't upset yourself. You didn't cook them knowing how they'd . . . died, did you?'

'That's the kind of remark people make about torture and mass executions. What could we do about it they say, we didn't know and they think it makes it all right. They think that takes away the guilt. It doesn't. He has to be stopped. Peter, I very nearly gave the twins a taste, but decided the gravy was too rich. I can't bear to think of how I would feel if I had done that. Oh God.' Caroline shuddered.

'There you are then, at least they haven't eaten them.'

'But they could have done. What time is it, I'm going round to see Jimmy right now.'

Jimbo, who'd spent the last couple of minutes feeling decidedly uncomfortable and trying to avoid Harriet's angry looks, decided he must pour oil on the trouble he had stirred up.

'No good going tonight Caroline, I expect he'll be in The Royal Oak by now. Sleep on it, you'll feel better in the morning.'

'Sleep on it? Ignore it, it'll go away. The rabbits won't feel the hurt so much if Caroline sleeps on it, is that it? I've eaten one of those rabbits. Actually eaten one and it makes me feel sick. The children have rabbits on their eiderdowns and they look so sweet, they're doing head over heels all round the edges, and I do love them.' She looked up at Peter, her eyes filling with tears.

Peter started to feel real concern about Caroline, he couldn't remember when he'd seen her so distressed, apart from . . .

'I think we'd better be getting home, we've left Sylvia quite long enough and it is her day off really.'

Caroline jumped to her feet, 'I know, you go home

and I'll go into the pub and look for Jimmy.'

Muriel, wishing the floor would open up and swallow her, murmured quietly, 'Don't you think The Royal Oak is a bit public for a discussion of this nature?'

'Muriel! I thought you of all people would be on my side.'

'Oh I am, I am, but I think you need to sleep on it first. Don't be too hasty.'

'Ralph what do you think? And you, Harriet, where do you stand?'

Harriet answered first, 'Frankly, I'm on your side but I'd want to act quietly rather than making a big public fuss.'

'And you Ralph?'

'Well Caroline, I suppose you could say I am at heart a country man having spent my childhood here and I have to admit to going poaching with Jimmy's father when I was a boy. When I think of the sum total of all the agony in the world, a few rabbits in Sykes Wood are a very minor incident aren't they?'

'I'm afraid I can't agree with your argument.' As Sadie had contributed nothing to the discussion Caroline asked her how she felt.

'Frankly one more or less concerns me not at all, there are far more pressing problems in this world than the demise of a few rabbits,' Sadie yawned. 'In any case I'm off home now.'

Caroline pulled a disapproving face and said, 'Right, Peter, we'd better go, as you say. Thank you for the supper Harriet, I do hope I haven't upset things too much but . . . Anyway I must go.' Caroline marched for the door leaving Peter to follow. He thanked Jimbo and Harriet for their hospitality, wished Ralph and Muriel a goodnight and went out after his darling girl.

As they passed the church she said, 'It's no good, Peter. I'm going to see if he's in the pub. You go on home.'

'Please Caroline, please don't.'

'When we married we both agreed that there would be no trespassing on each other's moral ground. You are always free to behave according to your dictates and now I'm behaving according to mine.'

'Please darling, I think you're rather overwrought, you've had a long day and . . .'

Caroline turned to face him. 'I sincerely hope you are not humouring the little woman, Peter.'

'Oh no, of course not, no, no, but I do think . . .'

'See you later.'

Caroline pushed open the door of the saloon. Being Saturday the bar was full. From every corner there were great gales of laughter and smiling faces. Such a contrast to the desolation she was feeling. It seemed as though three-quarters of Turnham Malpas were here tonight. And why not? It was a lovely summer's evening and they were all out to enjoy themselves. The glass doors into the little courtyard at the back were open and she could see people sitting out at the tables Bryn and Georgie had put there. In the far corner near the other entrance to the bar, ensconced on the settle, were Pat Duckett and Vera Wright. Jimmy sat opposite with a pint in his hand. Alan asked Caroline what she wanted to drink, but she refused. He shrugged his shoulders and stood watching her threading her way between the tables. Nice bit of stuff that rector's wife he thought. Well off too, by the looks of it. He'd remember that.

Pat moved up to make more space. 'Good evening Dr Harris. Would you like a drink? You'll have to be quick, it's nearly closing time.'

'No thanks.'

'Getting away from them twins for a bit are yer? How are they getting on?'

'Very well thank you. I've come to see Jimmy

109

actually.'

'What can I do for yer Dr Harris? How did them two rabbits turn out I gave yer?'

'That's what I want to talk to you about, Jimmy. It has been suggested to me tonight that you snared the rabbits you gave me. Is that correct?'

'It is.'

'Has it ever occurred to you that it is a very cruel way of catching an animal?'

'No more cruel than most kinds of deaths.'

'But they'd've been there all night probably, terrified out of their minds struggling to escape.'

'Well, they is only rabbits yer know, not people.'

'They are still God's creatures aren't they? I'm very upset by it. I can't bear to think that I ate animals killed in that way. What's worse, I did contemplate giving the twins some of the gravy but decided it was too rich for them. If I had done, I can't imagine how I would be feeling right now.'

'But that's what life's like in the country. It's a townee way of looking at things to think the country is all little lambs frolicking about and fluffy Easter chickens. It isn't. The country's tooth and claw, really yer know, and I'm part of it.'

'If I asked you to stop would you do that for me?'

Pat weighed in on Caroline's side. 'Jimmy I've told you before about them rabbits, you know I've stopped 'aving 'em from yer. Our Dean's dead against 'em since he saw yer coming 'ome that morning with that one with it's leg dangling.'

Vera, incensed by what she saw as disloyalty to one's own, snapped, 'You've been glad enough in the past to 'ave Jimmy's rabbits. Saving money was 'ow you saw it, but now suddenly you've got principles.'

Caroline intervened, 'Well, Pat, I admire you for changing your mind and sticking to it, now all we've got to do is to get Jimmy to stop.' Something brushed against Caroline's leg and she jumped. 'What's that?' She looked under the table and saw Sykes, Jimmy's dog, under there. Beside him was an empty tankard.

'It's only Sykes, mi dog. I gave you those rabbits because I'm glad you're both 'ere, and I'm glad you've got them twins, and because I was mad that time when Sheila Bissett was spreading them rumours, which most of us knew already but weren't telling. This is the thanks I get.'

Alan called out, 'Time gentlemen please. Come along now.'

Caroline silently absorbed what he'd said. 'I appreciate your kindness Jimmy, nobody appreciates it more than me, but will you stop Jimmy?'

'No, Dr Harris, I won't. I've been catching rabbits all mi life and I'm not going to stop now. I 'ear what you say and I'll think about it. Can't be fairer than that.'

'I really wanted a promise to stop altogether.'

'That you won't get.'

Vera chipped in with 'Quite right Jimmy, it's a free country.'

'Not for them rabbits it isn't if Jimmy goes on snaring 'em.' By now Pat was getting very indignant. She liked Caroline and had no intention of her coming off the worst in the argument.

Vera chipped in, 'It is a free country Pat. There's few enough things we can do nowadays like what we want so what the heck, you keep right on going Jimmy.'

'Don't come looking to me when you want to borrow a couple of pounds for the insurance man, Vera Wright. You've had the last borrow of my money believe me.'

'Righteo then, at least we know where we stand.'

'Yes, we do. And what's more Jimmy, you can give some thought to what Dr Harris has said. Just think of them poor babies eating that gravy. It makes me want to chuck up.'

Jimmy drank the last of his pint, wiped his moustache dry with the back of his forefinger, stood up and said loudly, 'I shall continue to catch rabbits in whatever way I think fit.'

Caroline pleaded, 'I wouldn't mind if you shot them Jimmy, at least they wouldn't suffer would they?'

'They might if I didn't kill 'em straight off. Then they'd go away and hide and still die in agony.'

'Well, why kill them at all?'

'It's my right. Good night. Sykes.' Sykes crept out alongside Jimmy, as though he knew full well dogs were not allowed in the bar.

Alan watched, and smiled to himself. He wasn't prepared for the uproar which erupted once Jimmy had left.

'Quite right Dr Harris, quite right.'

'It should be stopped, it's wicked.'

'He gets the social, why does he need to torture poor rabbits, he always catches more than he can eat.'

'He has got rights yer know.'

'What rights?'

'Something to do with the rights of villagers on common land, I think, from way back.'

'Sykes Wood belongs to Home Farm. He's trespassing.'

'Still, he isn't stealing is he? Tain't as if Home Farm know how many rabbits they've got.'

'If you decide to get a petition up I'll sign it Dr Harris.'

'Oh well I hadn't thought about doing that.'

'Well, it does need stopping.'

Finally Alan had to become quite stroppy with his customers. 'I need to lock up ladies and gentlemen. Please. I don't want the Sergeant coming round or Bryn will kill me, to say nothing of what Georgie will do.'

Caroline went out, wished everyone goodnight and

headed for home.

Peter was feeding Beth and Alex was crying.

'Where's Sylvia? Why isn't she helping?'

'She and Willie have gone for a walk. It *is* her day off you know. Alex's bottle is ready, just check it first.'

When Caroline had got Alex settled with his bottle, Peter asked her if she'd found Jimmy.

'Yes, I did. He won't stop and said as much to everyone in the bar. We've had a big argument and he's defiant. They've all had a row. Pat and Vera are on opposite sides, and I'm exhausted and angry.'

'You sound to have caused a real furore. Enjoy feeding Alex and we'll get them both to bed and get off ourselves.'

'Apparently most of the villagers had guessed already about these two babies of ours, but were keeping mum.'

'Oh, my word. Had they.'

Chapter 10

When Ralph woke during the night after only a few hours' sleep he knew he would be awake until breakfast time. Jet lag seemed to affect him more as he got older. He turned over in bed hoping he wouldn't disturb Muriel.

'Ralph,' Muriel whispered. 'Are you awake?'

'I'm so sorry my dear, did I wake you?'

'No, you didn't. I've been awake for ages. I didn't realise that flying could upset one's personal clock so much. I didn't notice it when we went out to Australia. I suppose that was because I was so excited. How long will it be before I'm back to normal?'

'A few days that's all.'

'Ralph isn't it lovely to be back home again?'

'Yes my dear, it is.'

'You don't sound as enthusiastic as I am.'

'Oh I am, I'm all mixed up I suppose. You see, it's coming home for you, but I haven't quite found my feet yet.'

'It feels as if you've always lived here.'

'Does it?'

'Yes.' Muriel turned over, snuggled up to Ralph and put her arm around him. 'Doing this, putting my arm around you, feels the most wonderful thing in the world. You see I've always had a bed of my own, a room of my own, and now sharing it with someone I love is so comforting. No matter how afraid or upset I am now, I've always got someone who will listen. It's surprising, isn't it, what one can tell someone in the dead of night when the curtains are closed and the whole world is asleep.'

'And what kind of things would you like to say to me at this moment? Have you some dark secret you have refrained from disclosing, Lady Templeton?'

'Doesn't that sound grand? Definitely not. I am very worried about Caroline.'

Ralph released himself from Muriel's grasp and got out of bed.

'Would you enjoy a cup of tea and a slice of toast?'

'Yes Ralph, but I'll get it.'

'No, no, I will. You rest there and allow your beloved husband to wait upon you.' He searched under the bed for his slippers, put on his dressing gown and went downstairs. Muriel lay back in bed admiring the pretty wallpaper and matching curtains. She was pleased she had resisted Ralph's insistence on redecorating. She loved the Laura Ashley papers and in any case the house had seen enough sorrow; it needed leaving alone for a while. Poor Suzy giving up her babies like that. Still it was the best decision in the end. They had two wonderful parents now.

After a while Ralph returned to the bedroom. He'd found the best tray, Muriel's favourite tray cloth and the morning tea set her cousin had bought them for a wedding present. The toast was keeping warm under a silver cover with the family crest on, from Ralph's old home. Muriel couldn't help but reflect on how affronted an earlier generation might have been to find their son and heir tucked up in bed with their head gardener's daughter. Things had changed.

Ralph poured the tea and presented Muriel with her

toast and a paper napkin. 'My mother would have fainted at the prospect of paper napkins. White starched linen was *de rigueur*, so starched it nearly cut one's mouth if one was so foolish as to use one. What a ridiculous set of standards they had.'

Muriel popped the last piece of her toast in her mouth, and drank the remains of her tea. Ralph got up. 'Here let me take your things.' He put their cups and plates on the tray and got out of bed to place it outside the bedroom door.

He took off his dressing gown, climbed back into bed and took hold of her hand. She squeezed his hand with both of hers and smiled.

'What do you think about Jimmy and the rabbits, Ralph?'

'Frankly, I think Caroline is making much too much fuss. If we went into it I'm sure we'd be horrified at the way chickens are killed, and the way cows and pigs and sheep are killed. A few rabbits hardly matter in the scheme of things do they?'

'That's not quite the point though, is it Ralph? Just because others are suffering it doesn't mean to say it's all right for those rabbits does it? It's like people say, "Oh, well, everyone else is taking pens and paper and equipment home from the office so it's all right if I do it." It's still stealing isn't it?'

'Yes, you have a point. But I'm not going to join her in her "Freedom for Rabbits" campaign. I'm too much of a countryman at heart.'

'Well, I'm afraid I'm on her side. It has to stop.'

'Muriel, please, you will not get embroiled.'

'Why not?'

'Because I don't want you to.'

While Muriel mulled over a side of Ralph's character she hadn't met before, he turned towards her and began caressing her neck in the way he knew she enjoyed. He tried to turn her to face him but she resisted.

'Ralph, it's the middle of the night.'

'Not to me it isn't, but in any case is the time relevant in some way?'

'No, but we haven't sorted out about the rabbits. I hate being at cross purposes with you, Ralph.'

'I didn't know we were.'

'*You* said you didn't want me to get embroiled, I didn't say I wouldn't.'

'Well, leave it for now and we'll sort it out in the morning.'

Ralph was still caressing her neck and Muriel could feel her bones beginning to melt; a sensation she had grown to appreciate these last few months. 'Very well dear. Ralph I do love you. Listen! What's that noise? It's Perry drinking the tea out of the bottom of our cups! He is a naughty dog, but it's so nice to have him back. I have missed him.'

'There's a little girl in you who has never quite grown up and every now and again she emerges. It's that youthful quality of yours which I love.'

'Is that all I am, just a little girl?'

'Come here and prove otherwise.'

The two of them were very late waking the following morning and to Muriel's chagrin they missed morning service. 'Oh Ralph, I did want to hear how much they'd got with the Festival yesterday. Peter will think us very neglectful not getting to church.'

Ralph picked up the clock and saw it was already eleven. 'When I see him I'll tell him why you slept in.'

'Ralph!'

'Stay another half an hour, and then we'll have brunch and this afternoon we'll take Pericles for a long walk, have an early tea and go to evening service.'

'What a good idea. It's so nice to have someone to

117

make up my mind for me. Put your arm round me and we'll have a little doze.'

She changed her mind about going for a walk, deciding she needed to answer some letters which were awaiting urgent attention. Ralph had only been gone a few minutes when Muriel heard an urgent knocking at the door. She opened it to find Jimbo there.

'Muriel, please, have you seen Flick?'

'Flick? No, why?'

'We can't find her. She was with the Brownies this morning in church and we went home with the boys, thinking she would follow in a little while when Brown Owl had dismissed them. She hasn't though. We've looked everywhere. I've even been up to the Health Club and Venetia and I have searched up there, but there's no sign of her. I've left Jeremy looking round the grounds and the people from Home Farm are searching their barns. We're absolutely at our wits' end. Harriet's being so sensible but underneath she's terrified.'

'Oh Jimbo, I'm so sorry. I'll get my cardigan and keys and I'll come to help you look.'

'Is Ralph in?'

'No, he's gone out for a couple of hours. I'll set off and walk with Pericles along the beck. She might have gone wandering off with her cats.'

'Thank you. We're getting really desperate now. It's been an hour and a half you see.' Having tried each house in the immediate vicinity of the green Jimbo went home to Harriet.

'Harriet, I've had no luck. Have you heard . . . no obviously you haven't.'

'Jimbo, it's time to ring the police.'

'I know, I know. Look phone round some more of her schoolfriends will you. She might have gone off with one of the Brownies, fancying having lunch with them or something. You know what children are like. "Oh I've

118

asked Mummy and she says it's all right." Go on, darling, ring. Ah, Sadie, you're back.'

'She's not at my house hiding or anything. Have you been angry with her about something Jimbo?'

'Not at all. As far as I know she is perfectly happy. God I'm going mad. Harriet's ringing up some more of her friends. If she has no luck then I shall contact the police. It's no good relying on the local Sergeant, we need more brains than his.'

Harriet came back into the room. 'Mother, what's the name of that girl whose mother held the barbecue and nearly set the father alight?'

'Now she tells me. What kind of friends do we have?' Jimbo grunted. 'Idiots?'

'She's called Jenny something,' Sadie remembered, 'I know, Jenny Barlow.'

'That's it.' But Harriet returned, having drawn a blank. She said she couldn't think of anyone else to ring. 'I know, I'll ring Brown Owl and see if she noticed where Flick went. I should have done that in the first place.' And she went off to the telephone once more.

'Jimbo, I didn't like to ask this in front of Harriet, but did you try at the Baxters' house?'

'Yes, Sadie, but there was no reply.'

'Well, I think we should try again.'

'So do I, but they're not going to let me in, are they? And if I ask, they'll say no they haven't seen her, even if they have. That's why I want the police. They can insist on looking, whereas I can't.'

Fergus and Finlay were standing listening.

'I know I've asked you two this before, but do you have any clue at all about where Flick might be?'

'None at all Daddy. We finished before the Brownies did, 'cos they'd got a lot of notices. She didn't say anything to us.'

'Have you been needling her?'

'No, we've been very good today. Aren't we going to find her Daddy?'

'Yes, of course we are. Don't be silly. We will, won't we Grandma?' Jimbo appealed to Sadie as much for reassurance for himself as for the boys.

'Yes, we will. Let Grandma make you a nice drink. I think I might be able to find a KitKat for each of you, if I have two sensible boys.'

'We'll save one for Flick for when she gets back.'

'Of course.'

As far as Jimbo was concerned, that last remark of the boys made up his mind for him.

'Right Harriet, no news from Brown Owl?'

'No. Jimbo what are we going to do? I can't think straight.'

'Neither can I. It's the police next, there's no doubt in my mind.'

The Sergeant, roused from his afternoon sleep brought on by a surfeit of Mrs Sergeant's jam roly poly pudding, knew that this meant the end of his Sunday and possibly his Monday as well. They'd gone for years in this village without so much as the theft of a bicycle bell and now this. Murder, suicide, sudden death. It was all happening in Turnham Malpas. Now worst of all, a missing child.

'I have to tell you this Sergeant, the only house where I have had no response is the Misses Baxter's. All the other people have answered their doors, looked in their sheds and gardens, and done their best to help. Three quarters of the village is out looking for her, but there's no news yet. I don't know what to think any more. I do know that something serious needs doing though.'

'Right Mr Charter-Plackett. It seems to me that we can't dismiss this on the basis that she will turn up shortly. It's been two hours now, you say, and all she had to do was walk from the church to your house. That would take one minute at the outside. I want you to go find Willie Biggs and get him to search the churchyard with you and the church and the church hall as well. I'll get onto the station in Culworth. Keep looking in all the most unlikely places. She may have got locked in somewhere.'

'That's it! She could be locked in the vestry or something, couldn't she? I'll see Willie straight away.'

The two of them searched the church, unlocking the vestries and the boilerhouse, looking behind the old tombs and in every nook and cranny. They then began methodically combing the churchyard. Willie kept the grass between the graves absolutely immaculate so the chances of her being found there were nil, but they still persisted. Jimbo wished the churchyard was overgrown and that he would find her hidden in the long grass with a broken ankle or something. Anything but this total blank.

When he got back to the house, the police from Culworth had arrived. Harriet was showing them a photograph of Flick. The Sergeant took the Detective Inspector on one side and after a short consultation the Inspector went off with his Detective Constable to the Baxters' cottage. Meanwhile the village Sergeant accompanied Jimbo to the school to knock on Michael Palmer's door and ask to search the premises.

Detective Inspector Proctor had no preconceived ideas about the Misses Baxter. So far as he was concerned this was just another house in a dead alive hole which he wouldn't live in if his salary was doubled. DC Cooper knocked loudly on the front door and they both waited. The Inspector thought he saw the curtain move slightly but couldn't be sure. He always said it was his wife who was intuitive but today he acknowledged his own instincts were sending signals that all was not as it should be in this house. 'Knock again Cooper,' he growled impatiently. 'I haven't all day. God what a dump.'

There was still no reply. 'Right. Down the back and see what you can find. I'll have a dekko through the window, that's if I can make anything out through the filth.'

The Constable went off round to the side gate while Inspector Proctor shaded his eyes with his hand and peered through the dirty glass. He recoiled, startled to find himself staring straight into a pair of brown venemous eyeballs as close to the glass as his own. He jumped back and then knocked on the window and pointed to the front door shouting, 'Open up please!'

He waited for the sound of footsteps coming to the door but there were none. Cooper came round the corner and said, 'No reply, guv. Not a sausage. We could find all sorts 'ere. The garden's like a jungle; wouldn't surprise me if Tarzan didn't come swinging through it shortly.'

'Good, we might be needing him. They are in, I've just seen one of 'em looking at me through the window. Not a pretty sight. They're a queer lot. We're definitely not going without seeing them. Go round the back again and make a pretence of searching the garden. That might flush 'em out.'

'Right guv.'

'Cooper we're not filming *The Bill*; drop the guv bit. It's either sir, or Inspector.'

Cooper thrashed about with the broom that Gwen had used on Sir Ronald. He waved it this way and that, pushing the grass aside as he went. He glanced once or twice at the kitchen window to see if they were watching him, but he didn't catch them looking. Inspector Proctor came through the side gate. He banged on the back door and shouted, 'It's the police. Open the door or I shall have to break it down. Come along now, please, we only want to ask you some questions.' A small crowd of villagers had gathered by the front garden of the house. Amongst the crowd was Sheila Bissett.

'They are mad you know. I bet it's them have got her. You wait and see. I just hope she's still all right.'

'Come on, Lady Bissett. What harm could they have done her? We know they's crackers but they won't murder no one would they?'

'Wouldn't they? Don't you be too sure.' The crowd watched the police officers standing outside the back door. The Detective Constable and the Inspector had a whispered conversation and then they said, 'One, two, three!' and barged at the door with their shoulders. Their combined weight and force broke the latch and the door burst open. Inspector Proctor was unmoved by the condition of the kitchen. There wasn't much that could surprise him about people.

'Hello there, it's the police. Can we have a word?'

Gwen appeared. 'Just you keep well away from me. We don't want you here.'

'Believe me madam, we wouldn't be here at all if it wasn't for the fact that we have a little girl missing. Yours is the only house we haven't been able to check, and check it we must.'

'Where is your warrant?'

'We haven't time to waste getting a warrant. Everyone else has co-operated willingly. We need to make sure she hasn't been shut in somewhere by mistake.'

'What are you accusing us of?'

'Nothing, madam. It is simply a case of looking to make sure she hasn't been taken ill somewhere and can't get help or has locked herself in an outhouse and can't make herself heard.'

'You can search the shed if you want. You'll find nothing in there. It's always locked.'

'Give me the key and my Constable will look.'

Gwen put her hand in the pocket of her apron and handed him the key. While Cooper searched the shed, the Inspector questioned Gwen, 'Did you go to church this morning?'

'Certainly not.'

'Where's your sister?'

'Having a nap.'

'Could you get her to come down to see me?'

'No. She's not at all well.'

'Then in that case I shall go upstairs to see her if you will accompany me.'

'You won't.'

'If you won't go with me then I shall have to go alone.' He made to brush past her into the hall. Gwen stood aside, then changed her mind and went up the stairs in front of him.

Beryl lay huddled in the big double bed they shared, apparently asleep.

'Wake your sister for me.'

Beryl stirred at the sound of his voice.

'Good afternoon Miss Baxter. I'm making inquiries about a little girl who's gone missing. Felicity Charter-Plackett. I understand she's always called Flick. Have you seen her today?'

Beryl's eyes slid from his face to Gwen's and then back again. 'No.'

'Would you recognise her if you did?'

'Yes.'

'Have you been out today?'

'No.'

'Has your sister been out today?'

'No.'

He looked at Gwen and said, 'There's a Sunday newspaper in the kitchen. Mr Charter-Plackett doesn't deliver newspapers, so how have you got it into the house?'

'Well, that's all I've done. I didn't think you meant popping out for two minutes for a paper.'

'What else do you think I hadn't meant?' He heard Cooper return to the house. Cooper shouted up the stairs. 'It's full of old clothes, guv . . . sir. I haven't moved everything, we'd have to clear the whole shed out to do that.'

'Do it, Cooper.'

'Yes, guv.'

Gwen glared at him. 'You'll have it all to put back again.'

'We will.'

The Inspector went back downstairs again but not before he'd opened the big bedroom door and looked in. He estimated that the piles of newspapers hadn't been disturbed, though he could be wrong. He opened the sitting room door next, looked in and then returned to the kitchen. Moving a pile of papers from a kitchen chair he sat down to wait for Cooper to empty the shed. He looked round the kitchen hoping to unnerve Gwen and make her say something. She stood watching him. He picked up the Sunday newspaper and began reading.

'Nothing better to do with your time than sit there? What about repairing that door?'

'We'll send someone round.'

Jimbo came to the back door to report that they had had no success in the school.

'We're being invaded. Get out, go on, get out.'

Cooper came back from the shed sweating and dirty. 'Nothing in there guv.'

'Thanks, Cooper. Put it all back.'

'Back?'

'Yes, back.'

Jimbo, by now almost incoherent with anxiety, asked Gwen if she knew where Flick was.

'Please Miss Baxter we need to know.'

'I don't know.'

'Are you absolutely sure you haven't seen her going past the house? I know you like to watch people going by. Perhaps you happened to see her after church. Or you saw someone stop to speak to her. Think Miss Baxter, think.'

'No, I didn't.'

'We'll search the garden now, Miss Baxter.' The Inspector stood and turned to go out. Jimbo followed him and they went to the far end of the garden and began looking section by section. They unearthed an ancient mangle, a roll of rotting carpet, and various old boxes and an old mower, but of Flick they found nothing. It was Jimbo who came upon the lid of the disused well.

'Oh my God. I didn't know they had a well. Inspector, come here.'

'That's recently been disturbed.' Jimbo went deathly white. The Inspector looked at him. 'Go and find the village Sergeant for me, will you, Mr Charter-Plackett, and ask him for his torch. He'll have one with a powerful beam.' Jimbo hurried off, glad to be of use.

'Now we've got him out of the way, we can get the lid off and look down.'

Between them they managed to lift it off. The Inspector threw a stone down. 'It's very deep. Go and get the torch from the car, Cooper.'

Willie arrived to offer his help. 'You don't think she's down there do you, Inspector?'

'We have to look at every possibility. My instincts tell me there's something odd here. I can feel it in my bones as they say. Good lad, Cooper.'

He shone the torch down the well. The surface of the water gleamed greenly back at him. He moved the beam of light slowly up and down the walls of the well. There were no signs of anything having rubbed against the brickwork as it was pushed down. He decided to have another go inside the house. They heaved the lid back on again.

Jimbo arrived with the Sergeant's torch.

'Oh thanks sir, my constable remembered we had one in the car. I'm glad to say there's no sign of your little girl down there.'

Gwen and Beryl were both in the kitchen when he returned to it.

'You're feeling better are you Miss Baxter?'

'Yes.'

'Right, Cooper. Upstairs. And search properly, every drawer, every cupboard, don't miss a thing. Both bedrooms.'

This upset Gwen and Beryl. They both rushed to block the door.

'You've already searched. You can't search again. We won't let you.'

'I'm afraid I can. Move to one side please.' He noticed Beryl's eyes stray momentarily towards a chest of drawers, which was standing in front of what was obviously the understairs cupboard. When he looked at the floor he saw marks which showed that the chest had been dragged across to its present position. How had he missed that?

'Cooper, move this chest.'

Cooper pushed and strained but couldn't budge it, so Willie went to give him a hand. At this the two women became more and more agitated. Suddenly Gwen snapped. She went straight for Cooper and lunged at him and beat him with her fists.

'This is our house. Stop it, stop it! You've no right!'

Inspector Proctor took hold of her and forcibly restrained her from attacking his constable. She kicked and struggled to get free, shouting at Willie and Cooper to stop. The two men pulled open the door of the cupboard and Cooper shone the torch inside.

'Here we are sir. She's here.'

He knelt down, reached inside and came out backwards on his knees, holding Flick in his arms. She had been bound and gagged and lay limply. Constable Cooper bent his head and listened for her breathing.

'She's OK. She's breathing.' He laid her down on the kitchen floor. Jimbo undid the gag, unbound her arms and ankles and then held her to him and forced back the sobs which, despite his strenuous efforts to retain self control, would keep coming into his throat.

'I'll go tell her mother, Mr Charter-Plackett,' offered Willie and he ran from the house shouting. 'She's all right, we've found her.'

The crowd outside cheered. They caught snatches of Inspector Proctor saying, 'I arrest you both . . . and anything you might say . . . I must ask you to accompany me to the station.'

The procession to the police car was followed by dozens of pairs of eyes. Pat Duckett shouted, 'Yer nasty pair of old baggages. Yer deserve all yer get. What did yer want to harm a poor little girl for?'

The Sergeant, who had arrived too late to help, importantly cleared the way. 'Move along please, move along.'

'Harriet are you awake?'

'Yes, I've not been to sleep yet.'

'Neither have I, and what's more I don't think I shall. God what a day. Never again.'

'I'm going to check if she's all right.' Harriet went across the landing to Flick's bedroom and stood looking down at her. Flick was curled on her side, her hand tucked under the pillow in its usual position. Harriet gently stroked the hair from her cheeks and pulled the duvet a little closer around her shoulders. She went back to bed and lay staring at the ceiling.

128

'She's fine, sleeping like a baby. Never *ever* do I want to go through a day like today again.'

Jimbo lay on his back staring at the ceiling. 'I've been thinking: it's my fault this happened.'

'Your fault? How could that be?'

'I've put everything into making a success of this business . . . mostly for my own satisfaction but also as one in the eye of those City people who said I'd be back there inside six months. It's made me ignore my own children.'

'You haven't.'

'Yes I have. I don't mean I ever stopped caring about them. How could I? They're our own flesh and blood, for God's sake. But today, when I thought we'd lost Flick I realised that under pressure from me we've let that bond between ourselves and the children grow weak. That's why she feels free to just wander off as she likes. Because we don't put restraints on her. We're always busy and, to be honest, we've been quite glad if she's not bothering us.'

'But we take such care of them. The boys don't go off and they're older.'

'They don't seem to feel the need. You see, there's two of them so they always have someone to share games with. It makes Flick quite an outsider, you know.'

'So what's the remedy?'

'From now on, I don't care what it costs, but whenever Flick and the boys aren't at school I want you home there for them. I know it means employing people in the shop and the kitchens when you're not there. But no matter what it costs, that's what we're doing. We came within a hair's breadth of her being dead. I can't imagine what hell that must be but I know it would be double hell if we had ourselves to blame. I just can't take a chance of that happening.'

'But I enjoy working in the shop.'

'I didn't say you would do nothing, Harriet, I said you weren't going to be involved whenever the children are at home. And that's final. I'll work twice as hard to make it possible. You are their mother and I want you to be there.'

'Jimbo, since when have you told me what to do?'

'As of now, but then I've never been so frightened as I was this afternoon. You know, waiting to see if a big deal had come off when I was at the bank, the old adrenalin would be riding high, my palms would be sweating, my nerves at top pitch, and that awful patch of fear at the pit of my stomach would be there gnawing away. But it was nothing compared to today. I am not going through that again.'

'She ought to be able to go about alone in a place like this.'

'She ought, but obviously she can't.'

'You're quite right of course, and I shall do as you say. And tomorrow when the police come to question her, make certain they don't frighten her, won't you? We don't want to make matters worse than they already are.' They were quiet for a while, then Harriet said, 'All that trouble with Caroline and the rabbits last night doesn't seem very important today does it?'

'But, Inspector, I didn't go in. I saw Chivers running down Church Lane when Brown Owl dismissed us. He's always wandering off, and I'm frightened he'll get lost, he's only small, he's not even had a birthday yet. I ran after him and he went to Misses Baxter's side gate and climbed over. I went to the gate and called "Chivers, Chivers".'

'Did you open the gate Flick?'

'No..o..o.o. I stood looking over, calling. Daddy said I mustn't go in people's gardens after my cats. So I didn't. But then she came out.'

'Who came out?'

'Gwen.'

'What did she say?'

'Nothing.'

'I can't understand why she was so very very cross with you if you didn't go in.'

Flick looked uncomfortable and glanced anxiously at her mother. Harriet patted her arm and said, 'Just tell the Inspector the truth, Flick.'

Flick swallowed hard and whispered, 'Daddy's told me not to go in people's gardens after my cats, but I did twice. They like Miss Baxters' garden because it's all messy and piled with rubbish and they like to play in there, it's such an *interesting* garden for cats you see. So they've told me twice not to go in there and shouted at me and she said, that is Gwen said, she would punish me if she caught me again. This time I didn't go in but she just opened the gate and before I could run away, she grabbed me and dragged me inside. I told her Mummy would be cross. But she wouldn't listen. She used some naughty words I've heard the boys use, and Daddy once when he dropped a box of baked beans on his foot. She held me tight and Beryl said, "Let her go. You must let her go." But Gwen didn't listen.'

'Where did she hold you? Pretend you're Gwen and get hold of me like she got hold of you.'

Flick grabbed Inspector Proctor's neck and his arm. 'Like that but really tight. I couldn't get away.'

'What happened next?'

'She told Beryl to get some old cloths and then she tied me up and stuffed me in the cupboard. It was so hot and I couldn't breathe and then Daddy was holding me. I don't know how long I was in the cupboard.'

'Did Beryl help to tie you up?'

'No. She was crying and saying "No, no, no." She said she was so upset she'd have to go to bed.'

131

'So Beryl didn't do much then?'

'No. Beryl must be nicer than Gwen, mustn't she?'

'Well, I'm not too sure about that, she didn't stop Gwen or go to get help did she?'

'No, she didn't. Can I go and play now?'

'Is there anything else you need to tell me. Your Mummy is here and we don't have secrets from Mummy do we? So tell her and me right now if you can remember things I've forgotten to ask.'

'I've told you everything. I'd like to go now please.'

'Are you quite certain you've told us everything that happened? Did they take you anywhere else besides the kitchen?'

'No, nowhere else. Nothing else happened at all. Will they go to prison for being nasty to me?'

'We'll wait and see.'

'May I go now, please?'

'Yes, but before you go I want to say something. Your cats know you love them Flick, because you look after them so well. They're not daft, they know when they have a good home. So don't, whatever you do, go looking for them again. It might be a while before they get back home, but they will. Thank you for answering all those questions. You've been a great help. Off you go.'

Flick got down off the chair and went to find the boys. She thought she'd go back to school tomorrow, they'd all want to know what had happened, and she'd be able to tell them about the doll Venetia had sent her that morning. It was absolutely gorgeous and had the most wonderful lace dress on and beautiful long blonde hair. She didn't know which was lovelier, the doll or the box it had come in. She'd call it Venetia, that was a perfectly splendid name for a perfectly splendid doll.

When she left, the Inspector stood up to take his leave. 'Thank you, Mrs Charter-Plackett. There's bound to be some after effects, like bad nerves and nightmares. Your daughter will need lots of love and reassurance. We shan't be able to keep those women locked up for ever, much as we might like to, so take care. If Felicity lets slip any more information, no matter how slight, will you phone me at this number? If I'm not there leave a message to ring you. I'll be in touch.' The Inspector shook hands with Harriet and went out to his car.

Chapter 11

Despite Caroline's anxiety about Flick she still felt as strongly about Jimmy and the rabbits and was determined to swing public opinion onto her side. She made a point of mentioning the subject to everyone she met. Some villagers met her idea with downright hostility. But aided and abetted by Pat, who made it her business to introduce the subject to as many of the school parents as she was able, many of the villagers came round to her way of thinking. Michael Palmer, having listened several times to the story of what had happened in The Royal Oak on the Saturday night, agreed with Caroline.

'Knew yer'd see it her way, Mr Palmer,' Pat commented gleefully as she tidied the hall after school dinners. 'She's a lovely lady is Dr Harris, she's really cut up about them rabbits, feels right bad about 'em. I don't understand how some people don't see her point of view. I tell yer who would be on her side . . . Mrs Meadows. Now she was always very keen on kindness to animals. She had that campaign d'yer remember? Not long after she got 'ere, about stopping foxhunting. Yer remember she got the Council to stop the hunt going across the Big House land. 'Spect that Health Club lot won't care too hoots about poor foxes. Do you ever 'ear from Mrs Meadows, Mr Palmer? I always thought you two got on really well.'

Michael Palmer hesitated for a moment and then gave an emphatic 'No'. Pat smiled to herself. She hadn't lived thirty-nine years without learning something about human nature. She guessed from his answer that it wasn't strictly the truth.

In his pocket Michael had the latest letter from Suzy's mother, this time at the bottom was a short note from Suzy herself sending him her good wishes. It was the first time she'd written anything at all and the first time he realised that she knew he'd been writing in response to her mother's request. In future he'd have to be careful what he said about the twins. It was one thing divulging news to a devoted grandmother, quite another telling a mother news of the babies she'd given away. He fingered the envelope, carefully tucked away in the pocket of his tweed jacket. One day perhaps she'd write a real letter to him. In his mind's eye he could see her long fair hair, her lovely rounded cheeks and the sweet, so sweet smile which lit up her face. He imagined his hands cupping her cheeks and himself placing a kiss on her dear mouth . . .

'Shall you be having football this afternoon, Mr Palmer, with it being wet? 'Cos if you are I'll put newspapers down in the cloakroom, that floor's murder to keep clean.'

'Shall I be having what?'

'Football, yer know with the boys.'

'Oh right, yes, I shall.'

'I hope you'll bring it into your nature and science lessons about cruelty to rabbits and explain to them children about using snares . . . Our Michelle can speak up about it, our Dean's explained it all to her.'

'We'll see, we'll see.' Michael gazed out of the window and saw Caroline coming across the playground. Oh no, not more rabbits he thought.

'Good afternoon Dr Harris, what can I do for you?'

'Hello Michael. I want to know if I can persuade you to

talk to the children about cruelty to animals. Especially in connection with the way in which we kill them, in particular the killing of rabbits. If you don't feel able to, will you let me have a word?'

'Mrs Duckett has already informed me several times as to my duty to the children concerning this matter. If you would like me to do it then I shall. I feel quite as strongly as you do.'

'Oh thank you Michael, I do appreciate that. I've been so upset about it all. If we can teach the *children* that it's wrong then that's the most important thing, even if we can't convert diehards like Sir Ralph.'

'Country people do see things differently Dr Harris.'

'I know, I know.' One of the children came to Michael with a problem about his football kit. 'I won't keep you. Thanks anyway. Bye.'

'Good afternoon.'

Caroline, on her way back to the rectory, met Muriel out with Pericles for his afternoon walk. 'Hello Muriel. Isn't it a lovely day?'

'It certainly is. Now, are you feeling any better? I thought you were quite drained on Saturday night, and greatly in need of a rest.'

'Muriel! Is that how you saw my protest? As some kind of hysterical outburst?'

'Oh no, I didn't mean it like that. I think you're quite right about Jimmy, but I did think at the same time you were needing a change.'

'Well, perhaps I am, and perhaps not. But I'm still angry about Jimmy, it doesn't alter that does it?'

'No, it doesn't. I'm afraid Ralph and I are on opposite sides. It's a bit uncomfortable.'

'Oh Muriel, don't let it upset things for you, that's the last thing I want.'

'I can't do as Ralph says *all* the time can I?'

'No, that's right you can't, but don't let it come

between you. I can fight my own battles, you know, when it comes to it.'

'I know that Caroline, but you must be careful. These last few days there's been an awful lot of upsets over this rabbit question. I understand there was a row in the Store in the pension queue on Monday. Jimbo had to step in and sort it out. He refuses to be drawn on the matter, of course, because he has customers on both sides, though we both know how he feels. Linda slapped the change down for some person who'd declared themselves on Jimmy's side and they complained to Jimbo and he had to tick her off in front of everyone and she had yesterday off, said she was sick, but Jimbo's not too sure about that. First day's sickness she's taken in two and a half years. Lady Bissett's given someone a real telling off at the flower arrangement class because they criticised you. One of the members confided in me that she'd used language more suited to a saloon bar than the church hall. Some of the ladies quite ruined their arrangements they were so upset.'

'Oh, Muriel, I'd no idea things were so serious. It won't affect Jimmy will it though? It won't make him change his mind?'

'I doubt it, he's very thick skinned. Must go, Pericles is getting impatient.'

Peter stormed into the rectory half an hour after Caroline got home. She was unprepared for the onslaught she got from him.

'Cup of tea Peter?' she called from the kitchen. 'You've timed it nicely, darling.'

He came into the kitchen and sat down at the table. 'Thank you.'

'Biscuit?' She turned round to hand him the tin and saw how angry he was. His eyes were almost black with temper and his jaws were clamped so tight his cheeks were white.

'Peter, what's happened?'

'What's happened? I'll tell you what's happened. I've spent, what is it, eighteen months? carefully nurturing this village back to life. Back to being a caring community, back to church, back to having some social life together. I've started Brownies and Cubs, a women's group, a luncheon club for the elderly, I've revitalised the choir and the music, I've improved the finances and heaven knows what else. And now *you* are destroying all my work. I can't believe it of you, Caroline, I really can't.'

'What have I done?'

'You know full well what you've done. It's these damned rabbits.'

'Peter!'

He dragged the lid off the biscuit tin, chose a biscuit and banged the lid back on again. But he was so enraged he had to put it down uneaten, his hand shaking with anger as he laid the biscuit on the table. 'I've said nothing these last three days, but I can keep my own counsel no longer.' He began ticking off facts on his fingers. 'One, Bagheera and Brown Owl aren't speaking, so the Jumble Sale they are supposed to be holding jointly a week on Saturday to raise money to help parents who can't afford uniforms, is in jeopardy. Two, two of my senior choirmen have resigned because the choir master has instructed the boys about the cruelty of snaring rabbits and they think it is none of his business to indoctrinate them, which it isn't. Three, Mrs Peel has had a row with Willie and he refuses to unlock the church early and to make sure the electric is switched on so she can practise first thing on Wednesday and Saturday mornings. And four, old Mrs Woods' son and daughter, who were coming to see me about their choice of some elaborate kind of headstone for her grave, have argued so fiercely about the rights and wrongs of killing rabbits, the daughter has declared she is about to become vegetarian, and neither of them can keep the appointment about the headstone because, though they live in the same house, they are no longer speaking. You knew my calling from the first day we met in your surgery. I cannot lay that calling aside as you well know. As my wife, Caroline, you should behave more circumspectly. Your actions are causing serious damage to the parish, and I must ask you to reconsider before it all becomes irretrievable and, for me, unforgivable.'

Caroline was defiant. 'Because I am the wife of a priest I am not permitted to have opinions then? I must allow things I disapprove of to happen and stay silent? None of this is my fault anyway.'

'Whose fault is it then? I've just met Pat Duckett and she was praising you to the skies for having got Michael Palmer to instruct the children in the school on the rights and wrongs of the situation. Is there no end to your activity on behalf of these rabbits?'

'The fault is Jimmy's not mine.'

'Jimmy has been killing rabbits in this way for years. Until you decided to begin this crusade nobody minded.'

'Then it was time their consciences were woken up.'

'Woken up? They've certainly been that. Caroline, I don't know when I have been so angry. The repercussions have been far beyond anything I expected. Far beyond. Irreparable damage is being done.'

'Go and see Jimmy then and persuade him to stop. I can't.'

'Oh no, you go and see Jimmy. This hornet's nest is all your doing.' Peter stood up, and taking his cup of tea with him stormed off to his study. Sylvia put her head around the kitchen door and asked if there was any tea going or should she beat a hasty retreat?

'Come in Sylvia, the storm clouds have departed. Are

the children OK?'

'Yes, they're asleep in the garden in their pram and yes the cat net is on.'

After a moment Caroline said, 'Peter has never spoken to me like that in all the time I've known him. I have never seen him in such a temper. It's very . . .' Caroline got out her handkerchief and blew her nose.

Sylvia poured herself a cup of tea. 'Well, to be honest, Dr Harris, it has caused a lot of trouble believe me.'

'It would all blow over if I could just get him to stop it.'

'You won't, only an instruction from the Almighty could stop Jimmy. I'm sorry, Dr Harris, but you're going to have to let it go.'

'My conscience won't let me.'

'Willie says Jimmy is such a law unto himelf anyway, that all this trouble will bother him not one jot. Seeing that the rector is so upset, maybe you'd better just let matters rest.'

'But that's it, that way nothing gets done, no reforms are made, no bills through parliament, no injustices righted. When I think of eating those rabbits I feel so sickened.'

Sylvia took a deep breath and spoke her mind. 'If it had been Beth missing on Sunday instead of Flick, believe me, Dr Harris, you wouldn't be worrying your head about rabbits this week.'

Caroline looked at her in horror. As she leapt to her feet, her chair crashed over onto the floor, but she ignored it and rushed out into the garden. Sylvia stood the chair up and went to the window. She saw Caroline lift Beth from the pram and hold her tightly to her chest. Sylvia watched as she began to sob, deep, searing sobs which tore at Sylvia's heart. She tapped on the study door. 'Excuse me, Rector, but I think Dr Harris needs a hand.'

Peter looked up from his desk. 'Needs a hand?'

'Yes, she's in the garden crying, sir.'

Peter strode out and gathered Caroline and Beth into his arms. He stood stroking her hair and kissing her, hushing her as though she was a little girl.

'My darling, my darling, I'm so sorry for what I said. Please forgive me, please. I can't bear you being so upset. Please, please stop. I should never have spoken to you like that. I know how devastated you felt about the rabbits and I'm deeply sorry for the way I spoke. If you want to crusade for the rabbits you can, I shan't mind.'

Caroline raised her head from his chest and looked up at him. 'Oh Peter, what if it had been Beth missing on Sunday?' Peter felt as though he'd been kicked in the solar plexus: the breath went from his body. He forced air back into his lungs with a great heave of his chest. He couldn't trust himself to speak, so he took out his handkerchief and wiped her face dry with his trembling hand. When he'd composed himself he said, 'Caroline, I'm sorry it was Flick, and, I sound selfish, but I thank God it wasn't Beth. She's here safe and sound with us, loved and cherished, fast asleep in her mother's arms. What more could a baby ask?'

He bent down to kiss his little Beth, who was blissfully asleep and unaware of the crisis unfolding around her. Peter stood holding the two of them closely in his arms comforting Caroline, hugging her and telling her she was safe with him. When he felt her relax and no longer shaking with sobs, he stood back from her and said, 'There we are, now let's put her back in the pram with Alex, and we'll leave them to sleep the afternoon away.'

They walked back together into the kitchen. Sylvia had gone.

'Come and sit on my knee, and we'll finish that cup of tea you were having.' He refilled her cup and the two of them took turns drinking from it. The hot tea gave Caroline back her voice. 'I'm so tired Peter, so tired.'

141

'I've been thinking about that. Can I be in charge for a while and make some positive suggestions?'

'Anything you like.'

'I'm going to do some ringing up and some organising and hopefully you're going up to your mother's for a few days.'

'Oh, I couldn't manage driving all that way with the children. I couldn't face it.'

'I know that. You're going on the train by yourself, and Sylvia and I will look after the children between us, and if we get desperate Willie can come in as support troops. Or Harriet or someone. We shan't be short of volunteers believe me. Three or four days walking along your beloved cliffs, with the wind blowing your cobwebs away, will do you all the good in the world.'

'It sounds wonderful. But I've been such a failure. How can an intelligent woman, with a loving husband, with all the help I have available and the babies I desperately longed for, be so hopeless?'

'My darling girl, you're not hopeless, you're a brilliant mother, and that's the problem. You're suffering from exhaustion, brought on by hard work and lack of sleep, that's what.'

'I would be so grateful for a respite. Mother will be pleased. Please forgive me for this rabbit business, I shouldn't have been so persistent. Never having lived in a village before I didn't realise that everyone would be taking sides. I still mean it about the rabbits though, it must be stopped.'

'Of course.' He held her close, then said, 'I don't know how I shall manage without you.'

'Don't worry, you'll be so busy I shall be back before you know it! Thanks for being so wonderfully under-standing. Give me a kiss, a real proper humdinger of a kiss.' When he released her she said, 'M..m.. m.. m. m. Let's have another.'

Chapter 12

Pat Duckett sat waiting on her favourite settle right by the door where she could see people coming in. Her port and lemon stood on a little brewery mat in front of her. If she sipped it slowly it might last half the evening and then Jimmy or Willie might buy her another one. No good hoping Vera might, for Vera was as strapped for cash as herself. She was tired, she'd had a hard day. It had been raining and the school floors had got muddy footprints all over. It had taken her ages to get them cleaned up. Sometimes she wished she could give the job up, but what would she do for money then? Bringing up two children on your own wasn't much fun and the bigger they got the more they ate and the more it cost for their bally clothes. The door opened and in came Vera and Jimmy.

'Hello, get yourselves a drink and come and sit down.'

'Hello Pat.'

'Evening Pat.'

When Jimmy and Vera had settled down with their drinks Pat said, 'Have you heard that Dr Harris has gone up 'ome for a few days?'

Vera looked surprised. 'No, I hadn't. Has she taken the twins with her?'

'No, the rector's looking after 'em with Sylvia.'

'Sounds as if he's put his foot down then about her

rabbit crusade.'

'Well, it did cause a lot of bother and, come to think of it, I don't know why I'm drinking with you, Jimmy. Anyways, I understand they had a blazing row, and then she cried and next day she's off to Northumberland.'

'Last time she went there was when . . .'

'That's right, when she found out about . . .' Pat glanced round to make sure she wasn't being overheard. 'about Suzy Meadows and them twins. Heaven's above you don't think it's happened again?'

Jimmy scoffed at their speculation. 'For crying out loud you two, I'm not that keen on Dr Harris at the moment as you well know, but he can't be straying again. Surely to goodness 'e's learned 'is lesson.'

'You have to admit Jimmy, he's very handsome. There's many a one would fancy 'im and no mistake.'

Jimmy laughed. 'You're wrong. She's gone away for a rest, believe me.'

'Who says?'

'Willie, 'cos he and Sylvia are giving a hand at sitting in when the rector has to go out.'

'I wouldn't be sur . . .'

The door burst open and in came Vera's Don. 'Guess what?' he panted. 'Them two's released pending trial.'

'What two?'

'Gwen and Beryl.'

'Released? Never.'

The news flashed round the bar in a trice.

'Disgusting.'

'Whatever next?'

'Them courts have a lot to answer for.'

'We shan't be safe in our beds.'

'We don't want 'em 'ere.'

'Definitely not.'

'They should be locked up forever.'

'That's right, locked up till they're dead and gone.'

144

'The nasty wicked beggars that they are.'

'Have you ever been in their house? Willie says it's disgusting.'

'I bet it is.'

'We don't want them in Turnham Malpas with their dirty ways.'

'We should get rid of 'em.'

'That's right we should.'

And their voices rose to a crescendo, filling the bar with clamour.

Bryn and Georgie tried to lighten the atmosphere but the customers wouldn't listen.

'Now ladies and gentlemen let's take this calmly please. We'll all have a drink on the house and settle down. The two of them do belong here and they haven't been proved guilty yet.'

'Not been proved guilty? It doesn't need a trial, we were all there when they brought little Flick out. Double whisky for me.'

Bryn and Georgie regretted offering drinks all round. The whole bar was inflamed at the news, and the extra alcohol only made matters worse.

The more hotheaded among the regulars came to the conclusion that the police wouldn't do a thing to make sure Gwen and Beryl didn't do worse than hiding Flick in the cupboard. 'Murder it'll be next,' they said. 'Let's clear 'em out ourselves,' they said. 'Right come on then! We'll soon see off two old bats like them. Let's be rid of them. We want our village to be safe.'

There was a concerted dash for the door and the bar emptied. Bryn and Georgie decided to ring the Sergeant. The crowd surged down Stocks Row and into Culworth Road. They stood outside Gwen and Beryl's cottage chanting, 'Out out out. Out Out Out. OUT OUT OUT.' Someone found a stone on the road and threw it at the house. By chance it hit a downstairs window and broke it. Someone else found a bigger stone and aimed it deliberately at another window which shattered with a resounding crack. Incensed by the injustice of Gwen and Beryl's release and inflamed by the sound of the breaking glass the crowd began throwing stones in earnest. Being so close to the road the windows were an easy target. The chanting began again, 'Child molesters. Filthy women you are. Get out get out get out.' The sound of their chanting rose to a crescendo.

The Sergeant, summoned by Bryn's phone call, pushed his way to the front of the crowd, but they shouted to him to get out of the way.

'Your lot have let 'em out. It's no use you coming, you're on their side, go on shove off before you get hit. Out out out.'

The Sergeant shouted above their noise, 'I shall charge you all with a breach of the peace! Now please go away to your homes before you do something you regret. Move along there please. Come along now, go to your homes. Justice will be done but leave it to the law.'

'We've done that and look what's happened. Move away Sergeant. Out out out.'

Peter came across from the Rectory and pushed his way through. Standing in front of the cottage door he faced the angry crowd. 'Please, please, everyone have you forgotten who you are? This *must* stop. You must *not* take the law into your own hands. Tomorrow morning, in the clear light of day, you will be ashamed of what you are doing tonight. What will your children think of you when they hear what you have done? Shame, that's what they will feel. Absolute shame. And I am ashamed, that you are part of my flock and you behave in this way. In the name of God go home, before something more terrible befalls this village.'

The steady quietness of Peter's voice and the strength of his argument cooled their tempers, and after some muttering and resistance the demonstrators gradually began to thin out and make their way home.

The Sergeant was shaken but relieved that the trouble had been resolved and he thanked Peter for his help.

'Let's go inside and see how they are,' Peter suggested.

The two of them went round to the back of the house. Peter knocked on the door and tried to push it open but it was bolted and he couldn't move it.

He shouted through a broken front window, 'This is Peter from the Rectory. Are you all right in there?'

Gwen came to the window. 'Yes.'

'Can I help in any way at all?'

'No, we shall manage.'

'Very well, but if you need help you know where I am don't you?'

'Yes.'

Gwen turned away from the window and the Sergeant asked Peter what on earth he could do with people like them who wouldn't allow themselves to be helped.

'I honestly don't know. But I'll tell you one thing Sergeant, you must see to it that they are not attacked in this way again. Law and order is your responsibility, and the safety of these two women is essential if justice is to have any credence at all. If I think for one minute that you have neglected your duties to these two people, I shall not hesitate to make it known. They deserve your protection, and turning a blind eye will not do.'

'No sir. I'll see to it.'

'Indeed you will.'

The next morning the village woke to the sound of hammering. Gwen was boarding up the windows. Only the window at which Gwen used to sit watching the comings and goings of the village was left intact. The Sergeant went round later in the morning to check they were all right, but Gwen came to the one remaining intact window and signalled to him to go away.

Later that morning she went as usual to the village store to buy her newspaper and get the groceries.

Jimbo and Harriet had already talked about what they should do.

'If they can't get their food here, Jimbo, they will starve to death.'

'Peter would certainly give me a hard time if I refused to serve them. On the other hand, it isn't his child they nearly suffocated.'

'In all conscience we can't refuse to serve them.'

'I can't serve her.'

'No, and neither can I.'

They consulted Linda and she said she would come out from behind the Post Office counter and take Gwen's money if they wished.

Jimbo thanked her. 'I feel very un-Christian behaving like this, but they threatened Flick's life.'

Gwen's arrival was greeted with silence. There were only two other customers in and they were from Penny Fawcett so they weren't aware of any problem. When she had collected her shopping Linda came to the cash desk and took her money. Gwen never spoke, and neither did Jimbo or Harriet.

Peter came in later that morning. 'I'm truly sorry about all this trouble with Gwen and Beryl, Jimbo. It must be very distressing for you, I'm sure.'

'It is, Peter. If we don't allow them to shop here they will starve, but it's very hard to be Christian about it in the circumstances.'

'I'm quite certain it is. If it was a child of mine who'd been threatened I don't know how I would react. But the fact remains we cannot take the law into our own hands. The two of them came within an ace of being lynched last night. I was appalled by the hatred everyone felt. It was mob rule and no mistake. I feel this morning as if I am a complete beginner as a judge of character. The behaviour

148

last night was positively mediaeval. I couldn't believe it. It's a wonder they didn't put them in the stocks and stone them to death.'

'It's hard for us, Peter, to condemn them. They were doing it in outrage at what happened to Flick.'

'I know, but you wouldn't want anything but justice for them would you?'

'No, we wouldn't.'

Peter's sermon the following Sunday had as its text 'Let he who is without sin amongst you cast the first stone.' There was coffee for everyone in the church hall afterwards and Peter set about rebuilding the bridges he had so painstakingly constructed during the last year.

Chapter 13

The morning following Peter's sermon was the first day of Ron and Sheila's membership of the Turnham House Health Club. In preparation for this day Sheila had bought a plush tracksuit, not the same pink as Venetia's but very similar. She'd toned down her choice of colours since her conversion to more refined dressing, brought about so insistently by Ron. Joining the Health Club was a move in the right direction she was sure. One had to move in the right circles and have the opportunity to meet the right people. You never knew where it might lead. When Sheila counted up how long it was since she'd worn a bathing costume, no, she musn't say that, a swimsuit, she discovered it was thirty years. The one she'd bought was in pink to match her tracksuit. Ron had made sure she bought the correct size. She knew he was right, she always bought her clothes too small. She didn't like to admit she needed a sixteen whereas before she'd worn size twelve.

It was a fine, warm morning so Sheila wondered whether they should run up to the Health Club or take the car. Ron shook his head.

'I think we should go in the car. No sense in arriving dead beat. Better wait till we get fit, and then run up there.'

The reception hall was cool and elegant. The girl at the

desk checked their membership cards, handed them fresh, pale pink towels with Turnham House Health Club emblazoned on them and was directing them to the pool when Venetia came across the hall to greet them.

'Hi there, come for your first dip have you? Glad to welcome you to the Club. I'm sure you'll get great benefit from coming here.'

'I'm sure we shall.'

'Give me a knock on that door over there when you're ready to try the gym. I like to plan your personal exercise routine myself. I make sure you take things easy to start with and gradually build up to maximum. Have a nice day.'

Ron and Sheila met at the poolside. There were huge, plastic palm trees arranged in gargantuan pots along the perimeter of the pool, interspersed with white plastic chairs and loungers for relaxing in. The enormous glass windows were closed but could be opened wide on really hot days. There was a terrace outside with another batch of white plastic chairs for people to sun themselves.

Sheila lowered herself into the jacuzzi. The warm pulsating rhythm of the water throbbed around her bottom and she suddenly understood why they came so highly recommended. Oh my word, she thought, there's more to this than meets the eye.

Ron was swimming backwards and forwards slowly and somewhat painfully. She had to admit that no one seeing him stripped off in public could describe him as athletic. Lumbering might be a more appropriate description. She hoped that Venetia wouldn't get designs on him. She was getting too old to fight off opposition. But someone like Venetia wouldn't be interested in an overweight man of mature years would she? Though come to think of it, that was exactly what Jeremy was. Overweight and lacking sex appeal. Like Ron.

Ron suggested they had a sandwich lunch from the

151

pool bar. They'd just settled themselves nicely in two of
the plastic loungers by the pool when Venetia appeared,
wearing quite the smallest bikini it was possible to
imagine. It was a sharp, bold purple colour which gave
Sheila spots before the eyes. She watched Venetia poised
on the edge of the pool, giving them the maximum
opportunity to admire her slim, taut body and then
she dived sleekly into the azure water. Sheila turned to
make a sneering remark to Ron about exhibitionism, but
she looked at his face and bit back the words. Ron was
avidly watching the bronzed and purple blur which was
Venetia racing back and forth down the pool. Sheila
tapped him on his thigh and said, 'Ron? Ron?' But he
ignored her. Venetia finished her swim and came over to
them, tossing her thick dark hair from her face and
shaking her limbs to rid them of water. Her well-toned
flesh trembled as she did so. She reminded Sheila of a cat
which had got wet in the rain. Feline. That was it.

'When I've got dry would you like to come to the
gym, Ron, and we'll plan your schedule?'

Sheila answered on his behalf, 'When we're ready we'll
come and give you a knock.'

She watched Ron's face as Venetia jogged off to the
changing rooms. He was positively relishing the sight of
that woman's behind.

Ron was about to knock on the door marked 'Private'
to ask Venetia to come to the gym, when Sheila stopped
him. The door was partly open and they could hear
voices inside.

'Look here, Sid, you said you'd got it in the bag.'

'I know I did. They promised twenty staff for each of
six weekends starting this coming weekend. They wrote
and promised it, there's the letter. Now this has come
saying that due to the recession they're having to lay
people off and make economies wherever they can. One
of their economies is cutting out these special weekend

incentives.'

'But that means we've no one here for the next six weekends now.'

'Don't state the obvious, Marge. It doesn't take much of a brain to come to that conclusion.'

'Don't call me Marge here. You might do it in front of the clients.'

'What clients?'

'What the hell are we going to do? You'll have to get out on the road and look up some of your old contacts. Offer them weekends at special introductory rates or something. You know, to give them a taste of the fabulous opportunities for body health or whatever.'

'Hell, what a mess.'

There was a pause and Ron took this opportunity to knock on the door. Venetia came out and headed with enthusiasm to the gym.

She got Ron and Sheila onto the exercise bikes. It seemed to require a lot of stroking of Ron's legs and extra special placing of hands on his thighs as he made the pedals go round. She didn't help Sheila at all. Sheila was told she was performing excellently and she must have been on an exercise bike before. She protested she hadn't, but noticed that Ron needed an awful lot of attention considering all he had to do was make his feet go round. The worst of it was, he was lapping up the attention with a silly grin on his face.

Later that day, Sheila went to the Store to get something special for their evening meal. Jimbo was in there entertaining his customers with his usual gusto.

'Hello there, Sheila, you're looking sprightly today. Been up to the health club, have you?'

'Yes, for the very first time. It's very nice up there. Have you been yet?'

'Harriet and I go quite regularly. We've both taken out

membership. I like the gym and the running track, but I'm not too keen on the pool. It's not very big, is it?'

'No, it isn't, but then you don't need it with having a pool of your own. I tried the jacuzzi and found it most enjoyable. We had lunch there as well which was very pleasant.'

'All supplied by Turnham Malpas Store, you know, so it should be.' Jimbo raised his boater and took a bow.

'There was only us there this morning. I expect it will be busier in the evenings.'

'Let's hope so for their sakes. They've got groups coming for the next six weekends so that will help. We've just been planning the menus for them.'

'Oh . . . I don't know if I should tell you this, but by mistake we overheard Venetia and Jeremy talking, and they've had a cancellation and those people aren't coming. We heard them say that they had no one now for the next six weekends.'

'They haven't told us.'

'Well, that's what they were saying. I think they only heard this morning.'

'I'll give them a ring and ask a few questions about the food and see if they tell me anything. Thanks for letting me know, Sheila.'

'There's something else as well. Her name's not Venetia.'

'What is it then?'

'It's Marge.'

Sheila and Jimbo burst into hysterical laughter. Sadie came through, asking what the joke was. When they told her she had to lean on the counter for support. She got her handkerchief out and wiped her eyes.

'Never. I don't believe it. Oh my word what a laugh.'

Sheila, enjoying centre stage said, 'That's not all. You'll never guess what Jeremy's real name is.'

Jimbo hazarded a few guesses but in the end Sheila had

to tell him, 'Its Sid.'

Sadie laughed till she had a pain in her side. 'Marge and Sid. Sid and Marge. Oh help, wait till Harriet hears this.' And she went off in search of her daughter.

After Jimbo had calmed down he asked Sheila what she wanted and when she pointed to some fresh salmon, he cut her two generous steaks and gave them to her as a gift.

'You and I haven't always seen eye to eye Sheila, but I'm very grateful for your warning. Accept these as a peace offering.'

'That's extremely kind of you, Jimbo, Ronald loves fresh salmon. So much nicer than those nasty tins.' She chose vegetables and a homemade blackcurrant cheese-cake from the freezer and went home.

Jimbo rang the Health Club number with his list in his hand of the meals he'd planned. Jeremy answered the phone. 'Turnham House Health Club, how may I help you?'

'Good afternoon . . . Jeremy. It's Jimbo here from the Village Store. Got some menus worked out. Could I run a few ideas past you? I'd fax them but the dratted thing has gone on the blink and I can't make it transmit.' He crossed his fingers because of the whopping lie he'd just told.

'Ah, right. I'm listening.'

'I know it's only Monday but I'll need to get the food ordered you see and I don't want to find I've asked for things which aren't suitable. Can't afford waste in these hard times, as you well know.'

'Indeed, indeed. Fire away.'

Jimbo read out his list, trying to decipher from Jeremy's response whether or not the man was bluffing or whether Sheila Bissett had got it wrong.

Jeremy's voice came back down the line confidently agreeing to Jimbo's menus, 'Excellent, Jimbo, excellent.

Just what we want.'

'In that case then we'll go ahead and order?'

'Yes, do that please.'

'I'll deliver very first thing Friday morning. Give your cook time to sort himself out.'

'Of course. We're lucky to have such excellent service so close at hand.'

'Payment on delivery as agreed?'

'Of course, of course.'

Jimbo put down the phone, took off his boater and stood looking out over the green. Either the man was a very convincing liar or Sheila had made a mistake. Only time would tell. All the salad stuff would be a pain, he'd have most of that to throw away. And he'd never sell the ten litres of carrot juice. Such waste. He couldn't bear it. However, when the Friday came he delivered the food, received his payment, and came to the conclusion that Sheila Bissett had misunderstood what she had overheard.

Harriet planned to go up on the Saturday with the children and see for herself what was happening. Jimbo was still sticking to his decision about her being with the children whenever they weren't at school, and she'd found herself enjoying their company more than she had expected. Sometimes when she saw Caroline's pram she almost fancied having another baby herself.

At the Health Club the receptionist checked their membership card, gave them the appropriate number of pink towels and they finally got to the pool. The children all swam like fishes so Harriet gave herself the luxury of lounging in the jacuzzi while they swam and played with the floating toys provided by the management.

She was soon joined by two couples. They began chatting to each other and Harriet lay listening with her eyes closed, enjoying the warm water and the feeling of relaxation it engendered. They chattered on about how much they were enjoying the club and one of the women said, 'Nigel, how come we got invited for free? Do you know this Jeremy chap well?'

'Not that well. Met him a couple of times in our local hostelry and he gave me the chance to come for nothing so I suggested I brought friends as well, and he was well chuffed. In fact, everyone here this weekend is here for free. Shan't be taking out membership though, too far away from my usual haunts. No doubt the sales pressure will be administered before we're much older.'

That was Jimbo's answer then. The guests were all there on a freebie.

She told her news on her return and Jimbo's mouth went down at the corners. 'They won't last long at that rate then. Better watch our backs where they're concerned. Blast it! I was hoping the income from the health club would balance the lack of earnings from the restaurant. Something will have to go. We can't keep Henderson's open when it's such a drain on our resources. I can't tolerate failure. Damn and blast it.'

Ron and Sheila went four times that week to the Health Club. Sheila was not nearly as keen as she had been but couldn't permit Ron to go up there on his own. Heaven alone knew what might take place in the sauna. Ron had taken a great liking to them.

'Help me to lose weight you know Sheila, which is just what we want isn't it?'

'Yes it is.' Privately she wondered if she would be better off keeping Ron overweight.

The crunch came when Sheila lost Ron one afternoon. They'd both been for a swim and done their scheduled exercise plan which was taking longer now they were getting better at it. Then Sheila had got changed and they'd arranged to meet in the pool bar for a drink before they went home.

Sheila ordered her gin and orange and sat perched on one of the high stools watching some children swimming and waiting for Ron. She assumed he'd be along soon. After twenty minutes she went in search of him. She tried to appear casual, not wanting to have to admit to losing him. She opened the door of the men's changing room and called in a loud stage whisper, 'Ron, Ron are you there?' There was no reply. She wandered around for a little longer, looking here and looking there until besides the treatment rooms, there was only the gym left to check. Sheila looked through the glass panel in the door. Ron was laid on his back working hard on a weights machine, pushing up and down, up and down under the close supervision of Venetia. She was alternately holding his hands and helping him push and then holding his legs to stop him lifting his knees. Ron was working away as though he was a young man of twenty not an old man of sixty-six. The stupidist grin imaginable was creasing his face. She marched in and stood beside them. They were so preoccupied that at first they didn't notice her.

'What are you trying to do to him? Kill him?'

Ron let go of the handles and sat up abruptly. Venetia stood up and said, 'You've got a much better movement now Sir Ronald. You just needed a little help.'

'Let's get home. I've been waiting twenty minutes for you Ron.'

By the time Sheila had made their bedtime cup of tea, Ron wished he hadn't been born. It was all so innocent he kept telling Sheila, but she wouldn't listen.

'It was an excuse for getting her to paw you all over. And what's more you were enjoying it. I wasn't born yesterday Ron. She's a nympho . . . whatever it is. Look how she pursued the rector. Disgusting that was. She's man mad and anyone will do.'

'That's not very flattering to me.'

'One more word out of you and I shall tell the world and then where will your political career be? Down the pan that's what. And what's more I don't care. And another thing, first thing tomorrow I'm getting my leopard skin coat out of store and wearing it as soon as it's cold enough, so you can put that in your pipe and smoke it.'

'No, Sheila don't do that.'

'You're in no position to tell me what to do Ron Bissett. I listened to you about going up in the world and dressing like Sadie Beauchamp. Well I'm not listening any more. In fact I think I shall ring the *Sun* tomorrow and let them know, anonymously of course, what really goes on up there.'

'If you did that, membership would rocket. It would really take off.'

'You're right it would.' Sheila caught Ron's eye and they both started laughing. 'Honestly Ron, what were you thinking of?'

'Just an old man flattered by her attentions. At bottom I knew it was all a sham. I couldn't have done anything about it if I'd wanted to, could I?'

'I doubt it, though if you got fitter you might.' Sheila sat up and looked down at him. 'That's it Ron, get fitter and perhaps we could resume diplomatic relations.'

'Right then old girl.'

'Not too much of the old girl Ron, I'm not drawing my old age pension yet. Shall we keep going and both of us get fit? You hear about these pensioners who have an exciting sex life. Let's have a try shall we Ron? There's not much else on the horizon is there? You get fit and me as well and I won't get my leopard skin out of storage and then we'll go for a second honeymoon. We'll have to hope you don't have a heart attack that's all. And

remember no getting Venetia to pay you undue attention, 'cos you'll have me to answer to if you do. I'll maim
her for life . . . right where it hurts.'

Chapter 14

Sylvia broke the news to Caroline on her return from her holiday with Willie.

'Have you a moment Dr Harris?'

'Of course Sylvia, if you don't mind me burping Alex while we talk.'

'No that's all right. I've managed to find somewhere else to live.'

'Oh Sylvia, you don't mean you're leaving me?'

'Oh no, well, that is if you still want me to work here.'

'Well, of course I do. We get on so well together. Peter and I really appreciate your help, you know that. Where will you be living? Is it in the village?'

'Well, yes, it is.'

'Oh where? I didn't know there were any cottages empty.'

'There aren't. I don't know how to say this, but I'm going to live next door, with Willie.'

To give herself time to think, Caroline carefully wiped Alex's mouth where some food had spilled out when he burped. Sylvia, stacking the diswasher, cast sidelong glances at her while she worked.

'It's no one's business is it, but mine and Willie's?'

'No, that's quite right. Have you thought this out properl . . . Sorry. Sorry, Sylvia, of course you have, you're not a child, you've a perfect right to do as you wish.'

'I can't contemplate marriage yet, you see.'

'Why not?'

'Because I got such a rotten deal the first time round. My first husband was a womaniser. The pain I suffered was intolerable. I put up with his unfaithfulness for fifteen years and when he got killed, I had all on not to cheer. No woman should be asked to put up with what I did. They wouldn't nowadays, you know Dr Harris. They'd divorce them straight off. I wish I'd divorced him years back. But marriage is marriage and I stuck to what I'd promised.'

'I'm sorry you had such a hard time of it.'

'That's why I can't marry Willie, not yet anyway. When I said those marriage vows before, I meant it and I stuck to 'em. I daren't make them again until I'm really sure.'

'Willie's not like that though Sylvia.'

'No, but I've yet to be convinced. Trouble is, he daren't tell the rector.'

'He's no need to, I shall. Your private lives are your own. We can't avoid him knowing but I don't know what he'll feel about it. He's old fashioned where things like that are concerned. Church's teaching and all that.'

'He might not want me to work for you then?'

'He will, because I can't manage without you. Leave it to me.'

Caroline suggested Sylvia went out for the evening. She wanted her out of the way while she tackled Peter.

He loved treacle pudding and she'd made an especially good one for him. He sat back after his second helping and complimented her on the sheer perfection of it.

'That was splendid Caroline. How you manage such delights with so much to do I don't know.'

'I wouldn't if I didn't have Sylvia to help me. You'd be

162

making your own treacle pudding if I didn't have her.'

'If she looks like leaving give her a rise. We can't afford to lose her.'

'I know. Do you want to finish the wine?'

'I'll have another drop, do you want some more?'

'No thanks. You finish it. Have you seen Willie today?'

'Yes, of course. Why?'

'I just wondered. Was he all right?'

'Bit quiet, but he seemed OK. Why are you so concerned about Willie?'

'I'm not. You couldn't manage without him could you, just like I can't manage without Sylvia.'

'Caroline, is this leading up to something?'

'Well, I have to be truthful. Yes it is.'

'He isn't leaving is he?'

'No, he's taking in a lodger.'

'A lodger. In that little cottage? Who is it?'

'Sylvia.'

Peter put down his wine glass, stood up and went to look out of the dining room window.

'Can you tell me why? Are they getting married?'

She explained what Sylvia had told her.

'I see. Well, they sound like good reasons.'

'They are.'

'But I can't be seen to condone it. It's quite against my principles.'

'I promised myself some time ago that I would never use what I am going to say next in any discussion we had. I made that a sacred vow to myself. But on behalf of your reputation in this village I have to remind you that where marriage vows are concerned the rector must be seen to tread extremely warily. After firing that particular salvo I shall retire to stack the dishwasher and empty the drier.'

Caroline had set the dishwasher going and was folding nappies onto the top of the tumble drier when Peter finally came to find her.

'I can't accept that what they are doing is right, because it isn't. Willie is the verger here and as such should be showing some example to the parish. However, as you so rightly and tenderly reminded me I am in no position to comment. Forgive me Caroline.' Peter stood waiting for her reply. She finished folding the nappies, held the last one to her cheek, relishing the soft warmth of it and then turned to him.

'My darling, you know I forgave you months ago. I may not forget, I have two constant reminders day and night and I can't avoid the memories, but I have forgiven you. Lock stock and barrel forgiven you.'

Peter held out his arms and drew her to him.

When Willie met Peter in the churchyard a few days later, he knew he had to say something about Sylvia. They'd both kept silent about it and Willie didn't enjoy being estranged from the rector. It made life very difficult; the air needed clearing.

He leaned against the side of the shed, took out his pipe and when he'd got it going to his satisfaction he looked at Peter and began his apology, 'I know, sir, that as rector you won't agree with what Sylvia and I have arranged.'

'That's right Willie.'

'I also know that as the verger I ought to set an example, but it's like this. When I was a boy I fancied girls like all boys do, but the years went by and I never met one I wanted to share the rest of my life with. A quick roll in the hay, begging yer pardon sir, and goodbye was my philosophy. Then I clapped eyes on Sylvia and wished both she and I were thirty years younger. But we're not. We haven't got a right lot of time left, well not enough anyways. She's the first one I've met I'd really want to share my life with, not temporary but permanent like. She's told me all about 'er first, and I can understand why she can't make 'er mind up. She's got to be sure and she isn't yet. So I've had to compromise, as you might say. I can't face spending the rest of my life without her, so at the moment its second best as far as I'm concerned. As soon as she's sure we shall be up that aisle.'

'I'm glad to hear it, Willie. Let me know when she decides and we'll regularise things. Meanwhile, we won't discuss it any more. You're both grown people and know full well what you're doing. I do know this, she's a tremendous help to my wife and lovely to have around. You've got good taste.'

'There'll be a lot of gossip in the village and I shan't like it but I expect it'll be a nine days' wonder and then they'll get something else to talk about. I'd be glad if you didn't say anything about me hoping to get married. It might make Sylvia feel obliged when she isn't.'

'I shan't say a word Willie. And if, when the time comes, you want to keep the wedding a secret, then so be it.'

'I'll be round tomorrow to dig that border for yer sir. Yer know your good lady guessed all along it had been me and not you doing your garden, but she never said a word did she?'

'No, she didn't, not to me anyhow.'

'She's a lovely lady sir. You're well blessed and so am I with my Sylvia.'

'Indeed we are both well blessed. By the way Willie I've asked several times about you giving me a lift down with that tin trunk in the boiler house store room, but we haven't got round to it yet. How about it?'

'Can't find the key sir.'

'Well, then we shall have to saw through the padlock.'

'I'll be round like I said to do the plants.' Willie spun on his heel and disappeared into the shed.

*

Two days after Sylvia had moved into Willie's cottage, she went shopping for the rectory and bumped into Gwen collecting her groceries. Gwen's coat button caught on her basket. As she tried to disentangle them she said, 'I'm sorry Miss Baxter.'

'Not sorry enough, you slut.'

'I beg your pardon?'

Gwen raised her voice. 'Slut, I said.'

'What do you mean?'

'You know very well. Listened to Willie's sweet talk have you? Let yourself get persuaded eh? Not even his ring on your finger.'

'I think you need to mind your own business.'

'We've got eyes. We see what you're up to. Tainted, that's what you are, TAINTED. A scarlet woman.'

Gwen's voice grew louder and brought Jimbo out from behind the meat counter.

'Miss Baxter would you please pay for your groceries and leave.'

'Leave? Oh yes, I'll leave. I wouldn't want to be consorting with women like her. Harlots and sluts. Toys for men's pleasure, that's what you all are, toys. You'll all end in hell.' She glared around at the customers who were all staring at her, wagged her finger at them and then went to pay Linda who stood waiting by the till to take her money. Sylvia blushed bright red, put down her wire basket and fled from the Store to the safety of the rectory.

By the time Gwen had left, those who hadn't known about Willie and Sylvia now certainly did. The hubbub in the Store was raised several decibels.

'Wonder where that Gwen thinks she'll end up, considering what she's done?'

'Lucifer 'ull have it nice and hot for her I bet.'

'Nasty old besom she is. Open that door, Mr Charter-Plackett, and let some fresh air in. After what she's done I

166

don't know how you can let 'er in 'ere to shop. If it was me I'd refuse.'

'Can't do that, they'd both starve.'

'Serve 'em right for what they did to your Flick. Mind you she was right about them two.' The speaker nodded her head in the direction of Willie's cottage. 'And 'im the verger too.'

'Like rector like verger,' someone at the back said and laughed rather too loudly.

Pat Duckett waiting in the Post Office queue interrupted. 'No cause for you to say that Bet, he's lovely is our rector and 'is wife is too.'

'Oh yes he certainly is, too lovely if you ask me,' Bet said, nudging the woman next to her and winking.

'Nobody asked you, it's no business of yours, seeing as you come from Penny Fawcett.'

'He's our rector as well yer know.'

'Not like 'e is ours.'

'No, but I can offer an opinion.'

'Oh no you can't, you old cow.' Pat left her place in the queue, marched to the back and swung her handbag resoundingly round the head of the woman from Penny Fawcett.

Before Jimbo knew where he was he had a fight on his hands.

'Ladies, ladies, if you please.' He waded into the mêlée intending to extricate Pat, but his boater was knocked off and he came close to getting a black eye. Peace eventually restored, he retired to the mail order office and sat, considerably shaken, on Sadie's stool.

'There are times when I wonder if it's all worthwhile trying to make a living. Those women were at it tooth and claw. That Gwen has a lot to answer for.'

'I heard the skirmish and saw you disappear into the fray. Masterly it was, Jimbo.'

'All right Sadie, enough of your sarcasm. The sooner

167

those two women are in prison the better.'

'I think they'll get off due to their age or something.'

'Surely not?'

'Wouldn't surprise me. The law is such an ass nowadays. I'd get prison for a motoring offence, but I bet they don't for kidnapping Flick.'

'Heaven alone knows what will happen if they do get off.'

Chapter 15

That week Harriet and Jimbo got notification of the date for the court case. What they had dreaded confronting was about to become reality. They decided not to tell Flick until nearer the time. There seemed no point in her worrying for days before there was any need. The letter revived all their hatred of Gwen and Beryl.

The following day Harriet noticed that Gwen seemed very confused when she came in for her regular shop. Harriet got Gwen's newspaper out for her and put it ready on the counter. She watched Gwen move vaguely along the shelves and pick up a loaf of brown bread and two Chelsea buns. Then she went to the greengrocery and chose some parsnips. All the time Harriet had been in the Store she'd never seen Gwen buy parsnips. Carrots and swede yes, but not parsnips. Then Gwen went to the meat counter and selected a small pack of braising steak and a piece of pork fillet. She went back to the greengrocery and took a long time choosing two apples and two pears. Then she went to collect their two pensions. Linda came out from behind the Post Office counter and took her money and she wandered distractedly out of the store.

Harriet was very busy that day and dismissed the incident from her mind. The next day Jimbo was serving when Gwen slid into the shop and wandered around. She made completely different purchases from those she'd made the previous day. When Jimbo offered her her newspaper she shook her head. She paid for a portion of cheesecake, a tin of corned beef and a packet of tea and went out.

On the Monday Flick was in there after school sorting out the birthday cards. Jimbo paid her one pound a week for keeping the card display tidy. She loved doing it. The boys plagued her about the extra pound but she knew they only did so because they were jealous.

Her job that Monday was to put out loads of new cards with ages on them. They'd got really low. As she bent down to slot in the 50, 60, 70, and 80 birthday cards she smelt that peculiar smell which surrounded Gwen and Beryl. To Flick it smelt like a mixture of the boys' old football socks when they'd forgotten to ask Mummy to wash them, that awful French cheese Daddy said was like nectar and of unwashed clothes. Plus for Beryl the smell of garlic. Flick crouched down by the card displays and stayed as still as a mouse. Her breathing became rapid and that same terrible fear she had experienced in their cupboard came back and washed all over her and nearly made her wet herself. She couldn't get out without being seen so she stayed curled up, hiding her face, praying for her to go.

After she'd paid and left the shop Harriet spoke to Jimbo, 'Do you know Jimbo, Gwen is going peculiar.'

'Going peculiar? Don't you mean even more peculiar?'

'Well, yes. She has always bought exactly the same things each day of the week. But she hasn't had a tin of that dreadful Spam we keep in for her for nearly a week. Two days last week she never came in at all and now when she does she buys unusual things. I think she's finally lost her marbles.' Harriet felt Flick clutch hold of her skirt. 'Flick, you're pulling my skirt off! Oh, darling, I'm so sorry. I didn't think. Here, hold my hand tightly and we'll get out of here and go rustle up some food for the ravening hordes we call our menfolk.'

Harriet settled Flick on a kitchen stool and gave her the job of cutting up the cherries for a pudding she was making.

'Feeling better now, darling? I'm sorry I didn't realise you were there. You must have felt dreadful.'

'That wasn't Gwen.'

'When we go out on Satur........ What do you mean that wasn't Gwen? They're twins, you can't tell the difference.'

'It wasn't, it was Beryl.'

'Beryl never shops.'

'She does now, that was Beryl.'

'How do you know?'

'She smells different from Gwen.'

'That's not very polite, Flick.'

'No, but she does.'

'Is that how you tell the difference?'

'Yes. Gwen is old football socks and Daddy's French cheese with unwashed clothes and Beryl is the same but with garlic as well.'

'Well, of all things! What an awful way to tell which is which.'

'I thought everybody knew them by their smell.'

'We all know they smell but no one has said anything about the smells being different. Are you absolutely sure it was Beryl?'

'Oh yes. Is that enough cherries?'

'Yes, that's plenty. In fact you can eat a few if you like.'

'I'm going to watch children's telly now.'

The following day when Beryl, or was it Gwen? went to the till to pay for her purchases, Harriet deliberately didn't ask Linda to come to take her money. Harriet asked innocently, 'Is your sister keeping well?'

Beryl looked at her, nodded and began to back out of

the Store.

Harriet was determined to find out what was going on. 'And how are you today Miss Baxter. Keeping well?'

The dark brown eyes stared nervously at her.

'Yes.'

'It will be winter before we know where we are, won't it?'

'Yes.'

Harriet watched her hesitate and almost begin to say something but she changed her mind and fled from the shop leaving half her purchases on the counter.

'This is my moment Jimbo, I'm going after her with these things.'

'You're doing no such thing. If she wants them she can jolly well come back for them.'

'Someone's got to find out what's going on. Gwen could be lying seriously ill in there and Beryl too frightened to do anything about it. You and I pick up the phone as easy as we comb our hair, but to Beryl it's a major undertaking.'

'Have you heard what I've said Harriet? You are not going to their house!'

'You are getting far too dictatorial James Charter-Plackett, do you know that? Do this, Harriet, don't do that, Harriet, I shan't allow et cetera, et cetera. Well it won't do. I'm going.'

'Then I shall come with you. Linda can you manage for five minutes while I escort my bossy wife across the green?'

'Yes, of course I can. If you're not back in ten minutes I shall send for Inspector Proctor.'

'You do just that. Come on, Harriet, put it in one of our carriers and we'll be off, though what you expect to find I don't know.'

They set off at Jimbo's usual brisk pace. He dreaded going to their cottage, but wouldn't admit it for the

172

world. His memories of that awful day when Flick was missing rose in his throat as they neared the house, and almost choked him. He found he could hardly breathe.

As they passed the front of the cottage they saw Gwen sitting bolt upright on a chair by the one window which hadn't had to be boarded up, her head resting against the high back of her chair. They waved and signalled to her to come to the door but she ignored them.

They knocked and knocked but got no reply.

'We'll put the carrier by the back door and then go,' Jimbo decided.

They went back to the Store and faced the morning rush, but at the back of Harriet's mind she kept seeing Gwen sitting so still by the window. It was all very odd.

'Half a pound of braising steak and two pork chops? Right you are Mrs Goddard. How's life in Little Derehams nowadays? Still as lively as ever?'

'We leave all the lively happenings to you in Turnham Malpas, Mr Charter-Plackett. That's why we all shop here, so we can learn the latest gossip. Apart from the fact your food's the nicest of any hereabouts, of course!'

'Thank you for that kind compliment.' Jimbo raised his boater in acknowledgement.

Mrs Goddard went out of the shop and returned immediately. 'Quick! Ring for the fire brigade, there's a cottage on fire. Look! Over there! The other side of the green!'

'It's the Baxters' cottage. Oh Look! Clouds of smoke there is.'

The customers rushed outside to see. Smoke was curling steadily up from the thatched roof and beginning to collect in a huge pall above the thatch. Harriet dashed inside to the phone and Jimbo rushed out across the green. Ron and Sheila were coming out of their house as he passed. Jimbo banged on the door of the sisters' cottage. Surely to God that wasn't Gwen still sitting in her chair? He peered in through the one remaining window. Oh God she was. Then he realised with horror that Gwen looked as if she might be dead. There was no smoke in that room yet, so she must have been dead before the fire. Where the hell was Beryl? Willie, Jimmy, and Peter along with Bryn from The Royal Oak had all arrived.

'We'll have to break in round the back and get them out,' Peter said urgently.

'It's too late for Gwen. She's already dead. Look.'

'Oh dear Lord, whatever next.' Peter took charge. 'Willie go and get my hose pipe from the rectory and get Caroline to fasten it to our kitchen tap. Bryn see if Sir Ralph is in and get him to fix his up too. We'll have to move quickly, at best the fire brigade won't be here for twenty minutes.' In no time at all they had two hoses struggling to keep the fire under control. 'Play it on the thatch there Bryn. That's right. Jimbo and I will go in round the back. Willie and Jimmy you come with us. That's right Ralph, pour it in through the windows. Plenty of water onto those flames.'

They pushed open the back gate and threw their combined weight into opening the door. It burst open and clouds of smoke billowed out.

'You're not going in there sir,' Willie shouted. 'The smoke'll get you before you've gone two strides. Don't let him Jimbo.'

'Do as we say Peter, you don't go in there.'

'We must save them.'

'Gwen's already dead . . .'

'Already dead?' Willie couldn't believe what he'd heard.

'We'll pull down the boarding from one of the front windows and get in that way,' Peter shouted. They rushed round to the front of the house, getting drenched by the water from the hoses. By now a crowd had

174

gathered and Bryn had organised a chain of buckets which they were filling from Jimmy and Vera's kitchen taps.

'She's sat in the window, get her out. Overcome by smoke that's what.'

'It's Beryl we're looking for. Has anyone seen her today?' They all began shouting 'Beryl. Beryl.'

Peter pulled a piece of boarding from the window. As it came away the outside air rushing in caused flames to belch out. Gwen could no longer be seen from the window.

'I'm going in.'

Willie grabbed Peter. 'Oh no, you're not, sir. Here stop him somebody.' Jimbo held Peter's other arm and refused to let go.

'You're not going in there Peter. Thank God here's the fire brigade. They'll go in with breathing apparatus.'

The firemen sized up the situation and began releasing the hoses and getting out their breathing apparatus.

'How many are we looking for?'

'Well, one sister is already dead sitting in a chair in the front room here and there should be one other sister.' Peter wiped the sweat from his forehead and took over the hose pipe from Ralph.

Two firemen named Barry and Mike were soon kitted out. They entered the blazing cottage. Those onlookers not fully occupied with the chain of buckets waited with bated breath to see who they brought out. Within moments Barry emerged carrying the body of Gwen. He laid her on the green. Peter took off his cassock and covered her with it. 'We can't find anyone else in there, are you sure they were both in?'

'Well, they hardly ever go out.'

'There's mountains of paper smouldering in there. It makes searching very difficult. One more try Mike, eh?'

'Right.' Barry and Mike disappeared again. The other

firemen were playing their hoses into the upper windows, from which they had dragged Gwen's boards.

'There's only the old lady we've already brought out,' Mike announced when he emerged through the smoke.

The Sergeant arrived on his bike, having been contacted on his radio at a farm he was visiting.

'This is a right do this is,' he grunted. 'Have you got both of 'em out?'

'We can only find one old lady and she's dead.'

'Which one is it?'

'She's under the Rector's cassock on the grass there.'

The flames had died down now but the piles of newspapers were still smouldering and clouds of smoke were pushing up into the sky. The entire village was out on the green watching. It must surely have been the most interesting day they'd had for years.

'I shall have to send for the Inspector. Can I borrow your phone, Rector?'

'Certainly.' The Sergeant bustled off across the road.

Georgie came across from The Royal Oak carrying a tray filled with mugs of tea. Behind her trotted Muriel, also holding a tray filled with mugs.

'You firemen get first call on the tea, and then the bucket brigade, and after that anyone else who helped,' Georgie shouted.

'Peter?'

'Caroline! What are you doing?'

'Helping. She's been dead for a few days, I'd say.'

'I suspected as much. Beryl's left her sitting in the chair. Why on earth didn't she get help.'

'Too frightened, I expect. I'm glad Jimbo stopped any heroics on your part.'

'You heard.'

'I did. The smoke would have killed you.'

'Wish we could find the other one.'

'She's not inside, by all accounts. Do the fire brigade

176

know how it started?'

'Not yet.'

Caroline stayed till the ambulance came to take Gwen away. They all assumed it was Gwen because it was always she who watched the comings and goings of the village from the windows. Caroline spared a thought for how Beryl must be feeling. It all looked decidedly disturbing.

The fire brigade stayed for nearly four hours before they were satisfied there was no chance of the fire restarting. But there was still no sign of Beryl. Muriel, mindful of her obligations to Pericles, had abandoned her ministrations behind The Royal Oak teapot and gone home to take him out.

They went on his favourite walk, down Jacks Lane, across Shepherds Hill and onto the spare land behind the chapel and then down by Turnham Beck. The rabbiting opportunities were legion around here. He raced from one hole to another his tail wagging furiously whenever he got the drift of rabbit. Then he began yelping in earnest. Muriel smiled, 'One day you'll catch one Pericles and then you won't know what to do with it.'

As Muriel stood watching Pericles searching for more rabbits, she felt a tug at her sleeve. She jumped with the surprise of it, unaware thanks to the hullabaloo Pericles was making, that someone else was down by the beck.

Standing behind her, bowed and distraught, was Beryl. Never looking particularly clean, Beryl looked even worse than usual. She had been crying and there were streaks of dirt and tears all down her face. Her hands were dirty as though she had been digging in the earth with them.

'Why Beryl, we've all been so worried about you,' Muriel said kindly. 'Where have you been my dear?'

Beryl rolled her eyes and then hid her face in her hands

and stood trembling and mute. Then she pulled her oversized cardigan over her head as though she thought, childlike, that if she couldn't see the world the world couldn't see her.

'Beryl can you tell me what happened at the cottage? Were you there when the fire started?'

At this Beryl sat down and tried to hide the whole of her body inside her cardigan. Her desperate writhings put Muriel in mind of a sick animal burrowing to find a place to die.

'My dear, let's go and find Peter from the Rectory. You know Peter don't you, he's tried to help you before. Get up and we'll go there together. He'll be sure to help us. Come along.'

It was all so beautiful there in the field, with the sound of the beck trickling its way along as it had done for centuries. The willows were bending their graceful twigs down to the water's edge, the grass almost emerald green with all the rain they'd had and the sun getting low in the sky. The contrast of that peaceful scene with Beryl's agony was almost more than Muriel could bear.

'Please, Beryl, get up. Let's go and find Peter. He's so kind, you can tell him everything that's happened. We'll ask Caroline to make us a cup of tea and we'll get warm by her stove. It's so comfortable in the Rectory kitchen.' Muriel called Pericles and clipped on his lead.

She bent over, put her hand under Beryl's elbow and heaved her up. The two of them began a slow walk towards the Rectory. Beryl's head stayed hidden in her cardigan. Muriel didn't even know if Peter was in but Caroline seemed the best person to find. Harriet and Jimbo could hardly be asked to help. No, Caroline was best with her being a doctor. Yes, that was it. Caroline and Peter.

'We'll have a nice hot cup of tea and then we'll talk,' Muriel promised. 'Come along, keep going.'

178

More police had arrived at the scene of the fire and were in deep consultation with several of the firemen. They all looked at Muriel as she guided Beryl across to the Rectory. Muriel signalled to them to leave Beryl alone, and pointed to the Rectory saying, 'We'll see you in there.'

Inspector Proctor and Sergeant Cooper followed them across the green. Cooper knocked at the Rectory door, while Muriel tied Pericles to the old boot-scraper still standing sentry duty on the Rectory step. Caroline answered the door, holding little Alex in her arms.

'Ah, hello,' she said, surprised to find this curious collection of people on her doorstep.

Inspector Proctor was the first to speak. 'Can we bring Miss Baxter in Dr Harris? As you can see she's very distressed and we can't take her to her own home.'

Muriel said, 'I've told her Peter will listen and understand.'

'Of course, of course. I think we'd better go into the kitchen. There's too many of us for Peter's little study. I'll put the kettle on and we'll all have a cup of tea.' Caroline led the way and settled Alex on Sergeant Cooper's knee, while she put the kettle on and went to find Peter.

Muriel sat Beryl down in Caroline's rocking chair by the stove. Beryl was still holding her cardigan over her head.

Inspector Proctor asked Muriel where she'd found Miss Baxter.

'Down by the beck, Inspector. She won't speak. She's like an animal who has lost all reason.'

'I'm afraid we've made a rather unpleasant discovery at their cottage.' Peter came in and the Inspector stood. 'Ah good afternoon sir, sorry for intruding, but we didn't seem to have anywhere we could take Miss Baxter.'

'That's quite all right, Inspector. Where else but the

Rectory for such a problem as this?'

Peter went to Beryl and rested his hand on her head and patted it.

'God bless you Beryl, you're quite safe here, my dear. My wife Caroline is making a cup of tea for you. I'm sure you must be ready for it. It's been a very tiring day for you, hasn't it?'

Peter pulled up a chair, Caroline gave him a mug of tea for Beryl and he handed it to her under the canopy of her cardigan.

'Do you take sugar?'

From inside her cardigan she whispered, 'Gwen says no.'

'Well, she isn't here at the moment so we'll put some in. It will do you good. I like to have a biscuit with my tea, do you?'

'Can't.'

'Why not?'

'They make you fat, Gwen says.'

'I'm sure she won't mind you having one out of my special tin just this once. Here you are, it's got chocolate on one side.' Beryl grabbed the biscuit and hurriedly crammed it into her mouth. Then she took a second one and ate that more slowly. The Inspector began to fidget. He looked at his watch and coughed pointedly.

Without taking his attention from Beryl Peter said, 'I can't hurry this, at least she's started talking. There we are Beryl, I'm sure that feels better.' He took the empty mug from her hand and then held her dirty hands in his and asked, 'Now what were we saying, oh yes, I know, about when you started the fire.'

'I didn't.'

'I know you didn't do it on purpose.'

'Wanted candles for Gwen. Couldn't put her in church. He'd never done us a good turn in all our lives, so why should we bother with Him she said. She didn't

180

believe.'

'I know she didn't.'

'I wanted to light candles for her . . . hands shaking, she shouldn't have gone. She should have waited for me. Where is she? Dropped the candles you see and the rug caught fire and then the newspapers. She would keep the newspapers.'

'Why did she keep the newspapers?'

'To hide it. Make a wall.'

'Ah I see, she stacked the newspapers up to hide it.'

'Don't tell that bobby. Don't want him to know.'

'I realise that Beryl. But I need to know don't I?'

Caroline quietly took the sleeping Alex from Sergeant Cooper and left the kitchen. Muriel and the Inspector sat completely still, their minds racing to guess what Beryl was trying to tell them.

Beryl was shuffling and twisting about under her cardigan and then the rush of words began to come, stumbling over each other in Beryl's urgent need to tell.

'Gwen smothered it you know. It was her. When it came I wanted to keep it but Gwen said no. The shame she kept saying, the shame. It won't take a minute to smother, not a minute. I cried. I cried, but she wouldn't listen. It's a bastard twice over she kept saying, twice over. Its an abomination, that's what it is. An abomination. But it wasn't, it was lovely and I wanted to keep it.' Under her cardigan Beryl shaped her arms as though cradling a baby. 'She said, this way it will never grow up, it will never need to leave this house. So that was when she did it. Then she put . . . it . . . it . . . in the tin trunk and we hid it with the newspapers.'

Muriel wished she was anywhere but here. All these terrible happenings and no one knew. What a frightful secret. When Caroline came back Peter asked her to get a brandy for Beryl.

'No one found out though did they Beryl?'

'No. We were clever. I never left the house once I got fat. She made me stay upstairs. Gone to a sanatorium for TB she told the people at the factory where we worked. But that wasn't it really. She called me a slut and a harlot. But he'd done the same to her, hadn't he?'

'Oh. I didn't realise that.' Peter gave her a glass of brandy. 'Drink this Beryl, I think you need it. It's not easy telling me all this is it?'

Muriel was beginning to feel very faint but held on for everyone's sake. This story had to come out now or it might never be told. Her collapsing would break Beryl's thread. The inspector, keeping well back, was taking notes as Beryl spoke. Caroline sat perched on the edge of the table, both absorbed and horrified by what she was hearing.

Still under her cardigan Beryl blurted out, 'I haven't told a soul. She said I mustn't. All those years it went on. That was why Mother was always scrubbing and cleaning and washing our clothes. She thought she'd wash away the sin, but you can't do it as easily as that. She could have helped us. As soon as Mother died in nineteen forty seven Gwen decided it would be Father next. She said he deserved to die slowly, but in the end we smothered him the next time he came to our room. "This'll be the last time," she said. "The very last time. You'll do it no more to us." And we both pressed hard on the pillow and he struggled for a while but we won in the end. Then we carried him back to his own bed and covered him up and told the doctor next day that we'd found him dead. We got away with it because he'd been ill on and off for a while, and they thought he'd died in his sleep.'

Muriel was feeling distinctly ill, and wished Ralph would come to rescue her. Beryl had come out from under her cardigan and was staring Peter full in the face.

'We couldn't help it, you see. Father started coming in

our bedroom when we were in our early teens. We tried to stop him but we couldn't. I knew Mother knew because she wouldn't look at us the next day. That was why Gwen said the baby was an abomination, because it was his. So I've had nothing and no one to love all these years. We couldn't let anyone in the house in case they found . . . you know . . . that . . . thing in the trunk. Then when we got the letter about the court case Gwen took ill and I found her dead in the chair. I didn't know what to do.'

Peter looked in on the twins before he went to bed. He touched their smooth cheeks and smelt their lovely sweet cleanliness. How true what someone said about the sweet innocence of a child's sleep. They neither of them knew anything about what had happened, nothing of the pain and horror in that cottage over the way. Please God they would never need to know of such things in all their lives. No, that was unrealistic, please God they would have the strength to cope with such evil, and come through it.

He lay in bed unable to sleep. It had taken all his skills to get Beryl to go quietly to the hospital. Caroline had volunteered her help and Muriel, feeling that moral support would be needed, had gone with them. The Inspector had wanted her to go directly to the police station and give a formal statement, but eventually even he realised that he was never going to get that from Beryl. A permanent bed in a secure mental hospital was the likely option. It was when Beryl had decided she would be safe with Peter that his worst fears were realised. Hell, what a situation to be in. As a Christian he ought to have said, 'Yes, of course.' But how the hell could one invite a known murderer to share one's home when it contained two precious children besides his darling girl? She would more than likely have become obsessed with the twins and none of them would ever have known a moment's peace. No, it had to be somewhere secure where she could get help. At least she would be kept clean and well fed which was more than had been the case for a very long time.

He heard Caroline at the door.

He ran down the stairs and she almost fell into his arms.

'Peter, I am so tired I can hardly stand up.'

'My darling, it's so late. Whatever happened?'

'I'll tell you everything when I'm in bed.'

'I'll help you.'

Once he had got her settled in bed and his arms were round her she said, 'She'll never be free again, you know. They've put her in the psychiatric ward but she'll have to be moved somewhere more permanent. She has absolutely cracked now. When we got her out of the ambulance she was so meek and mild, but as soon as we stepped into the hospital she ran amok trying to escape. Fortunately Terry was on duty, he's the nurse I told you about who's built like an ox and is very fleet of foot. They always call him when there's trouble. Anyway he managed to catch her and restrain her. Muriel was terribly upset and I didn't know which one of them to comfort first. However, we calmed her down and I had the inspiration to give her a bag of dolly mixtures I had in my bag. She's like a child; it took her interest and she sat calmly munching them, while I filled the registrar in on what had happened. Then when Muriel and I tried to leave she decided she was coming with us. So we had another set to. She clung to Muriel and they had to pull her off. There's no Gwen, you see, to tell her what to do. What an awful mess. How did we not realise what was going on?'

'We knew things weren't right, but how could we possibly have guessed how terribly wrong they really

184

were? This has taught me a profound lesson, I shall not give up so easily next time I sense something is not as it should be. Thank you for all your help, darling. What did it feel like being back at the hospital?'

'It's nice being able to pull strings because of who you are, but I'll tell you something and then I'm going to sleep. I much prefer my life as it is now, thank you very much, and you were wonderful today.'

Peter kissed her and gave her a hug then found she was already fast asleep.

Chapter 16

Peter laid his morning post on his desk without even a glance. Dressed in his oldest clothes he had plans for clearing out the old trunk in the boiler house store room, the one which Willie had so adamantly refused to attend to. Today was Willie's day off and Peter was taking his chance whilst he could.

'You never know, Caroline, I might find documents in there which are of no use to the church but could be sold and the money used towards the new heating system.'

'Well, you're certainly dressed for it. I threw out that pullover about six months ago. How come you're wearing it?'

'I found it in the bin and rescued it. Sylvia washed it for me and now it's being put to some use.'

'Sometimes you do cling to your old things. Is it your security blanket?'

Peter kissed her and declared she was his security blanket thank you very much. He played for a few minutes with the twins who were rolling about on a rug on the kitchen floor. 'Before we know where we are these two will be walking . . .'

'And then your troubles will begin.'

Peter laughed. 'Right, I'm away. I'll open the post when I get back.'

The trunk was far heavier than he had expected and it took all his strength to lift it down from the shelf. Thick, grimy dust lay all over it. Peter rooted about in the cupboard where Willie kept his cleaning materials and found a brush and a cloth which he used to clean the outside. The padlock on it was stoutly made and as he had no key available, Peter had to saw through it to get it off. He had difficulty in forcing up the lid, and it creaked stiffly as he pushed it fully open. Inside were dozens of papers and files filling the trunk right to the top. Some of the papers were minutes of parish meetings from years long gone. Some were old letters belonging to Victorian rectors, even one from a bishop telling the Reverend Samuel Witherspoon that he would be visiting the parish on the 15th May 1867 at precisely two thirty. All very commendable but scarcely of much use as saleable objects. At the very bottom of the box was a thick, leather-bound book. In copper plate handwriting on the inside page were the words Turnham Malpas Parish Charity Fund. The first entry was dated December 1st 1761. After the date it was recorded that James Paradise had received the sum of ten shillings for food for his family.

Each subsequent December the names of villagers who had received money from the Fund were recorded. Names of families Peter recognised as still living in and around Turnham Malpas. The last recorded distribution was 1st December 1916. The sum of £1 had been given to each of four Glover brothers; Cecil, Arnold, Herbert and Sidney. Since then there had been no further distributions. Why had the distributions stopped and why had the book been so carefully hidden beneath all the other much older papers?

Peter put all the papers back in the trunk. He brushed the dust and dirt from his trousers and sweater, rubbed as much as he could from his hands, took the Charity Fund book with him and placed it on his study desk.

Caroline took his coffee into him and he drank it while he opened his post. There were several letters, three items of junk mail, his credit card statement and a letter from the County and Provincial Bank. Puzzled as to why he should be receiving a letter from a bank he didn't use Peter opened it first. Inside was a statement saying that the Turnham Malpas Parish Charity Fund had twenty three thousand four hundred and thirty three pounds thirty four pence to its credit. The bank manager had enclosed a letter suggesting Peter visit the bank to discuss more advantageous investment of the money.

Peter opened the study door and called out, 'Caroline, come here a minute.' She came into the study with a baby wriggling under each arm.

'Yes?'

'I've opened this letter and it says we have all this money in the bank, in a Charity Fund. Curiously enough I've found an old book in that trunk, here look, with the words Turnham Malpas Parish Charity Fund on it. Distributions went on right up until December 1916 but there's no further record in it after that. Isn't it odd that we've never heard of this fund before and yet on the same day the book turns up and the bank make contact? And why has there been no further money given out? I can't believe there has been no one in need of help for the last eighty years, can you?'

'How very odd. Look, I'm putting these two to bed for a sleep before lunch. I'll be back in a while and have a proper look. Twenty three thousand pounds! Just think what the church could do with that!'

'Exactly. This could be the answer to a prayer.'

The bank manager gave Peter an appointment for that afternoon and he set off straight after lunch. Caroline used to comment derisively on the speed he drove at, but since becoming a father he'd reduced it by at least fifteen miles an hour and drove far more cautiously. He was familiar with the little cross roads three miles from the village, heaven knows he'd crossed it often enough, though there was always that bend in the road which blocked a driver's vision. It did make one hesitate and check carefully before driving on. Suddenly, out of nowhere, a tractor crossed in front of him. He braked, and swerved viciously to the right to avoid an impact. The car lurched and juddered as it shot across the road, straight towards the ditch. Peter braked even harder but couldn't prevent the car from going down into it where it lay tipped at a crazy angle, front end right down in the nettles, the back wheels spinning in the air. The tractor driver, apparently oblivious to other road users, appeared to melt into thin air. Peter waited a moment to collect his thoughts before attempting to climb out. His knees had come sharply into contact with the edge of the dashboard and both felt amazingly painful. He managed to force open his door and climb out onto the road.

The first Caroline knew about it was Peter arriving home in a breakdown truck.

'What's happened? Are you all right'? Where's the car?'

'Thanks for the lift Brian, I'll ring you tomorrow about the car.'

'That's fine, sir, we'll do our best.'

Peter came limping into the rectory. 'Don't panic, I'm only bruised.'

'Show me, show me.'

'The car went into a ditch, I managed to struggle out, hailed a passing lorry and got a lift into Culworth.'

'You didn't go straight to the bank?'

'Yes.'

'You should have gone to casualty.'

'I thought perhaps I'd come home instead.'

Peter undid his trousers and pulled them down so Caroline could examine his knees. 'Not much problem there I think. I guess you'll have massive bruises by tomorrow. They are already swelling. I'll make you a cup of tea with plenty of sugar in it. Explain how it all happened.' Peter dressed himself and told her the story of the phantom tractor.

'That tractor driver is an absolute pig for not stopping.'

'Well, never mind, I'm not badly hurt.'

'And the car?'

'Well, that's another story. The front end is badly damaged, headlights gone, radiator stoved in, bumper badly damaged, bonnet buckled and that's what you can see before it's been examined inside. I think I'll get it repaired and then sell it. Cars never feel right once they've been involved in an accident.'

'What did the bank have to say?'

Peter sipped his tea. 'That tastes good. They are as surprised as I am about the bank account. They've got a new manager and in the way of new managers he's something of a new broom. They're having a massive face lift and really bringing the bank into the twentieth century, so every nook and cranny is being cleared out. He found a file pushed down the back of a cupboard which hadn't been moved since the year dot. In it were details of the Charity Fund. None of the money was on their computerised system and no one can understand why not. They've done all the necessary with calculating the interest over the years, which must have been very complicated, and that's what it amounts to. He recommends that I write to the Charity Commissioners and get things sorted out.'

'It's all very odd. How could a bank have money hidden like that and no current record of it?'

'He doesn't know either. What amazes him is the fact that we both unearthed evidence of its existence in the same week. It's all very strange.'

*

When Willie realised that the rector had got the trunk down and broken in to it, he was very upset and indignant.

'I did say, sir, I'd look for the key.'

'Yes, Willie, I know you did, but you didn't actually bother did you?'

'No, sir. But there was no call to go investigating it though. That trunk's been on that shelf for years, there's nothing in it of any use. It was best left where it was, untouched. You 'aven't taken anything out of it 'ave you, Rector?'

'Yes, I have as a matter of fact. A book with entries in it to do with a Parish Charity Fund.' Peter could have sworn that Willie blanched, but he dismissed the idea as ridiculous.

'Right, well, I'll be off.'

'Don't you want to hear the rest of the story, Willie?'

'No.' He walked off without so much as a good morning, leaving Peter feeling affronted by his attitude. It was so unlike Willie to be bad mannered.

In The Royal Oak that night Willie was very quiet.

Jimmy asked him if he wasn't well.

'I'm OK, but the Rector soon won't be.'

'Clairvoyant are yer then? Or 'ave yer been poisoning 'is soup?'

'No. 'Nother drink Sylvia?'

'Yes, please love.' While Willie waited at the bar for the drinks Sylvia told Jimmy she was quite worried. 'He keeps going on about a trunk the Rector's opened up, says he's no business bringing up the Charity Fund again. Says no good will come of it.'

Jimmy looked pensive and then offered his opinion. 'Ah, well, he could be right at that. How's the Rector going on about 'is car?'

'They've lent him one from the garage while his gets repaired. Though I don't know if he'll be well enough to

191

drive. He's looking real poorly tonight. Dr Harris is quite worried about him. She's sent him to bed. Flushed and coughing a lot he is. When I told Willie he said, "and no wonder" whatever that might mean.'

Willie came back with the drinks and they began talking about other matters, in particular what Jimmy would do when he got this massive win he expected from the pools.

'You've been filling in the pools for twenty years that I know of. Whatever you get you'll deserve it, you've spent a fortune on them pools.' Willie laughed and Jimmy snorted his annoyance. 'You wait and see.'

'I will.'

Peter was diagnosed as having a virus. For a week he lay in bed with a high temperature unable to eat and scarcely able to get to the bathroom unaided. He lost a great deal of weight and caused Caroline and their GP serious anxiety. Then he developed a secondary bacterial infection and a patch of fluid on his lung. The curate from Culworth came to conduct his services and he prayed with the congregation for Peter's recovery. There was a continuous stream of parishioners at the Rectory door, some inquiring after the latest news, others bringing gifts for the invalid. Calves foot jelly and beef tea had to go down the waste disposal. Caroline said to the jelly and the tea, 'Sorry about doing this to you. I know you have the best of intentions, but he can't eat you.'

She was having the most harrowing time of her life. She rather wished she wasn't a doctor as ignorance of the true state of affairs would have been bliss. The specialist who had come to the house felt that Peter would be better left at home, especially after Peter became very distressed when he realised there was a possibility of going to hospital. And Caroline was, after all, medically quali-fied. One evening, when it had taken Peter three hours to decide he couldn't eat a small piece of grilled trout,

Caroline asked Sylvia to keep an eye on the twins and Peter for a while, took Peter's keys and let herself into the church to pray. She turned on the small lights by the altar and went to kneel in the rectory pew. Gazing up at the beams of light illuminating the brass candlesticks and ornaments and the huge, ancient cross hanging above the altar, so beloved by Muriel, Caroline prayed for Peter's safe deliverance, reminding God that she didn't often ask for things, but that this time she really meant what she asked.

She recollected sitting in this very pew with Peter when he told her about the twins. The desolation she felt then was as overwhelming as what she was feeling now. If I lose him whatever shall I do? Keep going for the sake of his children, that's what I would have to do. She thought of them being fatherless and she a widow and then shook herself. This morbid dwelling on death would have to stop. She allowed her commonsense to get the uppermost of her thoughts and finished her prayers with the words, 'Your will be done.'

In The Royal Oak, Jimmy told Bryn that nothing, not even prayers, would cure the rector. Bryn, recognising the curious village persona which existed and to which he wouldn't belong even if he lived there fifty years, asked him, 'Now, why Jimmy, I mean why? People come in here, ask how he is and then wisely nod their heads and say, "Well, there's no wonder he's so ill, is there?" What has the rector done to deserve whatever it is?'

'Interfered where 'e shouldn't that's what. Interfered 'e 'as. Like Dr Harris did over me and my snares. Stuck 'er nose in where she shouldn't, and so's he. 'Cept this time it's more serious.'

'Interfered with what? He seems a charming, enthusiastic and very genuine chap to me. Just what the village needs in the church.'

'He is, but this time he's over stepped the mark.'

Jimmy tapped the side of his nose with his forefinger and took his drink to his seat opposite the settle to await Pat and Vera and perhaps even Don; a bit of male company would be nice seeing as Willie appeared to have gone into a decline, and was refusing to socialise nowadays.

It was three weeks before Peter was well enough to venture outside. Ralph suggested he came to have coffee with him and Muriel for his first outing.

'Sit down here Peter in this big chair. It's more suited to your frame. I must say though, you've lost a lot of weight.'

'A stone and a half actually Ralph. Caroline is busy feeding me with suet puddings and meat pies trying to build me up, but I've very little appetite for them I'm afraid. I have never been so ill in my life. Never. I've walked from the Rectory to here and feel exhausted.'

Muriel came in with the tray of coffee. 'Here we are Peter, and I've brought some shortbread too, do you think you can manage a piece of it?'

'I think so.' Muriel handed him his coffee. 'Thank you, you're very kind.' He sipped his coffee and said, 'This is lovely Muriel.'

'How are your legs after the accident?'

'Fine thank you. I've been so ill, a couple of very bruised knees paled into insignificance!'

When he'd drunk his coffee and finished the short-bread, Peter asked Ralph if he knew anything about the Charity Fund.

'I'd heard that was what you'd been meddling with.'

'Meddling with?'

'Yes, meddling with. Best leave well alone, Peter.'

'How can I leave twenty-three thousand pounds alone? Just think what we could do with that money. The new heating system, the pointing which needs doing, the organ serviced. It would help us out of a big hole wouldn't it? And Neville Neal would be smiling for once.'

'Even Neville as Treasurer wouldn't want you to use it.'

'So he knows why, half the village knows why, you know why, but I don't.'

'No, Neville doesn't know why. But I've told him he mustn't use it even if he gets permission from the Charity Commissioners, because the village will come out in open revolt. Your accident and illness have only served to confirm their fears. If you used it for repairs they would expect the church to fall down on their heads, literally. Make no mistake about that.'

'Will you tell me what it's all about?'

Ralph hesitated and then said, 'No. Partly because I don't know the full story and partly because I can remember my father saying, "The village won't stand for it, so it's best to leave well alone."'

'Is there anyone who *will* tell me?'

'Go see Grandma Gotobed in Little Derehams. She's well into her nineties, but don't imagine for one minute that means she's soft in the head. She rules her two unmarried daughters with a rod of iron and won't even allow them to bake the bread, because she reckons they're too young to get it right. And believe me neither of them will see seventy again!'

Muriel laughed and then said, 'Oh Ralph, how can she know about the Charity Fund? The Gotobeds lived in Little Derehams when we were children.'

'If Peter looks in the old records he'll see that the Gotobeds were originally a Turnham Malpas family. They only moved to Little Derehams towards the end of the First World War.'

Peter asked Muriel if she knew anything about the Fund.

'Nothing at all. My parents protected me from anything and everything, and the nuns told me nothing. I didn't even know how babies came till I was sixteen, and even then it wasn't my parents but a girl in my class at the secretarial college who told me.'

'Quite right too. Children know far too much, far too soon nowadays,' Ralph retorted. Muriel reached across and kissed Ralph's cheek. 'You're behind the times, dear, I'm afraid.'

Peter stood up to go. 'My new car is being delivered this week, so as soon as I'm feeling up to it I'll drive out to Grandma Gotobed's and see what she has to say. Thanks for the coffee, hopefully I shall be back to work next week.'

Chapter 17

That same week Sheila called in at the Store to speak to Jimbo.

'Is he in, Linda?'

'Oh yes, I'll give him a call.' Linda left the post office counter and called through into the store room, 'Mr Charter-Plackett, Lady Bissett would like a word.'

Jimbo came bustling through into the Store, raised his boater to Sheila and asked her if she liked the new, scarlet ribbon Harriet had put round it.

'Very smart I must say, Jimbo. You always keep things so stylish here. I like that new display area for the meat. Very "olde world" isn't it?'

'Strikes you like that does it?'

'Mmm, very tempting. You're a good salesman. I've come with another snippet of news for you about the health club.'

'Thought you weren't going there any more?'

'Who told you that?'

'You know how news gets around.'

'Were you told why?'

'No,' Jimbo declared innocently.

'That Venetia was trying it on with Ron in the gym. I soon gave her short shrift.'

Jimbo drew closer, looked around the Store to ascertain whether he was being overheard and repeated,

'Trying it on? What was she doing then?'

'Making ten times too much fuss helping him with the weights machine, holding his hands and pressing his legs down. Making him work like a maniac at his age, too. I was really angry about it. Anyway, what I came in to say was that this weekend, all the people there were having it free again.'

'Venetia's very liberal with her favours isn't she?' Jimbo laughed.

Sheila giggled, 'Really! You know full well what I mean, Jimbo. I meant they were *staying* there for free.'

'This can't go on, can it? I'll go up there myself tonight and nosy around a bit.'

True to his word Jimbo went to Turnham House with Harriet. Besides them there were only three other clients. The two of them plunged into the pool and swam vigorously back and forth and then went into the jacuzzi. Venetia appeared wearing another of her miniature bikinis. 'I shall be joining you soon. I'll have a swim first.'

She poised on the edge of the pool and then dived in, scarcely rippling the water.

'Give her her due she can dive.'

'Jimbo, shall I go for a sauna and leave you to her mercies?'

'What a good idea.'

'Find out all you can, won't you?'

'And some.'

'Remember Mother's garden shears though won't you, darling?'

'Ouch, don't remind me.'

Harriet climbed out of the jacuzzi and made her way to the sauna, while Jimbo lazed with his eyes shut waiting for Venetia to strike. When she slid into the water and sat opposite him with her feet touching his, he pretended to be surprised.

'Why Venetia, hello. Harriet was just saying how beautifully you dive. Quite spectacular.'

'Thank you Jimbo.' Venetia smiled at his compliment. 'I thought with having a pool of your own you wouldn't be interested in swimming here. The gymnasium would be really useful to you though. Have you got an exercise programme?'

'No, I haven't. Are you the one to give it to me?'

'Yes, I will. We do have a gymnast but it's his night off tonight. When you're ready, we'll go in to the gym and I'll take your pulse and things and show you how to pace yourself.'

'In that case I'll get my gear on right now. Harriet's in the sauna so she'll be a while.'

'Let's stay here a little longer Jimbo.' Venetia slid along the seat and sat very near to him. Jimbo nestled close.

Jimbo took his chance. 'How's business then? Looks as if things are going well. I wish I could say the same of Henderson's.'

'Isn't it going well?'

'Comme ci, comme ça. Not bad, but not good enough unfortunately. You're a businesswoman, Venetia, have you any advice?' Jimbo's leg came in for some sympathetic patting from Venetia who then said, 'I'd no idea things weren't too good. Jeremy could advise you I'm sure.'

'What I need is some sensational happening to create a lot of interest. A customer of mine, who's a member of a health club up in town, was telling me that membership was none too buoyant, until one of the girls in the gym began giving "extra mural" tuition to the men in the sauna, then membership soared. News like that travels fast. The owners were feeling well chuffed and rubbing their hands with glee, till they got a visit from the police and the girl had to be sacked. They came close to being accused of running a brothel.'

'That's something one has to be very careful of in this business. It's so easy for clients to get the wrong impression.'

'What is really happening here? Membership wise I mean?'

'It's building up and will soon be a roaring success. Jeremy is very confident, and so am I. These things take time, that's all.'

'That's OK so long as the money doesn't run out.'

'It won't run out believe me. Anyway, you get paid on delivery for what you supply, so you should worry.'

'Cheques are fine so long as there's something in the bank to back them up. I might need to ask for cash soon if I get edgy.'

'You must do that if you wish. Here's Harriet. Bye, I've got things to do.'

Harriet joined Jimbo as Venetia left.

'She is a liar I'm afraid. They are in grave difficulties.'

'That's not what she said.'

'No, I know it isn't, but I haven't worked in the City for years without getting a sixth sense about money. They are mortgaged up to the hilt I bet. No more food Harriet, unless they pay cash. Remember.'

After she'd dried and changed Venetia went to the private office to find Jeremy. He was seated at a desk covered with well fingered files, his latest cheap bodice ripper novel spreadeagled on top, ash trays stacked with cigar stubs and a pile of Snickers, Jeremy's latest craze. He unwrapped his third since tea and sat gloomily reading a letter he'd already looked at innumerable times that day.

'It's no good reading the same thing time after time, Jeremy, action is what's needed.'

'I can't believe that things have gone so badly wrong. I mean, old Arnie having to call in the receivers. He and I have known each other for years. If anybody was to go down I wouldn't have thought it would be him. I can remember watching him getting a huge roll of banknotes out of his back pocket and peeling off a few to give his son to go to the cinema with. Generous to a fault, he was. Now look what's happened.'

'Well, he won't be peeling any banknotes off for us will he? He was our last hope.'

'You know, Venetia, we have got to stop these free weekends, all this entertaining trying to persuade the punters to part with their money. There quite simply isn't the cash for it any more.'

'What the hell are we going to do? We've got so much on HP and a bloody gigantic overdraft. I feel sick, absolutely sick.'

Jeremy buried his head in his hands and groaned. 'When I think how much time and money I spent greasing the palms of pathetic councillors to get planning permission for this place, God I could weep. They're all sitting pretty, safe as houses grinning all over their faces while we're in queer street and no mistake. All the time it took convincing people to lend us the money too. They'll be after me like rockets once I stop paying the interest. There must be a way out.'

'And there was me going round telling everyone you were rich.'

'You shouldn't have done that. Most of it was borrowed. Added to which the alterations all cost far more than we thought they would.'

'I only did it to give everyone confidence you know. Well, you're supposed to be the business brain, get thinking.'

'My brains have dried up completely. All I can see is us being saddled with a massive debt for the rest of our lives.'

'You'll be saddled with it, Jeremy. Not me. It was

your idea.'

'We went into it together.'

'I know we did. But you borrowed the money, I didn't.'

'I did it for you.'

'Yes, but none of it is in my name is it? Remember? It had to be all Jeremy. The big I am. "Look what I can do for the little woman." I can walk out of here tomorrow and no one can touch me.'

'Look, Venetia . . .'

'Don't you Venetia me. You signed all the papers, you talked to the bank. Second class citizen that was me. It's all yours lock stock and barrel.'

Jeremy leant forward and lowering his voice said one word.

'Fire.'

'Fire?'

'Shush, don't talk so loud.'

'What do you mean?'

Jeremy beckoned her closer. 'I mean, we'll start a fire. Burn the place down and then collect on the insurance.'

'Jeremy you wouldn't.' Venetia peered closely into his face. 'You would, I can see it in your eyes. You can't do that to this lovely place it would be sacrilege. To say nothing of the risk you'd be taking.'

'*We'd* be taking. We'd have to be very clever. Being a listed building there'd be an awful lot of investigation. Look at the chap who came a couple of weeks ago. Went through the place with a fine tooth comb to ensure we were attending to the upkeep as we should. He spent ages poking about at that west corner. His report should be here soon, let's hope he found nothing too serious. It's not a question of setting fire to this place and doing a runner, then they'd know it was on purpose. We've got to be around and need to be rescued or even to ring the fire brigade when it's all too late. No staff here, us out for the evening, back about two in the morning to find the place in flames.'

'Surely it won't come to that?'

'We'll keep it in mind anyway.'

'How do you start a fire?'

'They're so clever nowadays, a pile of rags near the curtains and petrol poured on won't do at all. They'd soon tipple to that little scheme. We've got to be more subtle. Much more.'

'Let's hope it won't come to that. Surely the recession won't last much longer.'

'It will. Our game is a luxury not a necessity and businesses like ours go under first.'

'Oh God! Whatever are we going to do?'

'Like I said, put a match to it. Well, not literally but almost.'

'If we get found out you'll go to prison.'

'Oh, will I? And what about you?'

'They wouldn't send someone like me to prison, now would they?'

'Yes.'

'Would they?'

'Of course. Why not? This whole thing was your ridiculous idea in the first place. I should never have listened to you. You aren't in the right class for this kind of enterprise. Turnham House is a far cry from 'Let Pam Pamper You' unisex salon in Soho. If the police had had anything about them it would have been closed down.'

'They couldn't very well, half the clientele were senior police officers. That was the reason we didn't get shut down.'

'I'll do some thinking and see what I come up with.'

Jeremy and Venetia's regular food order at the Store for the following weekend had to be cancelled now that freebies were out. Jimbo had to come to some decisions of his own.

'Harriet. Council of War, my darling, if you please.'

'When the children are in bed, Jimbo. We don't want them worrying their heads about money, that's our problem.'

'Fine. Eight thirty sharp then, in Sadie's office, then we'll be well out of hearing.'

A little before time he carried a tray in. There on it were Harriet's usual gin and tonic and a whisky and water for himself. He began his drink while he waited for Harriet to come in. He'd done his figures and he knew what he was suggesting was the only valid solution.

'There's no other way Harriet. Last month we lost nearly a thousand pounds in Henderson's, and now the health club is apparently on its way out. Jeremy says it's only a blip and things will come right but you and I know different, so we've lost that income which did help a bit to offset the losses. The areas where we are actually making money are with the mail order, with the catering side and to a lesser extent with the Store. Rather than bleed those areas to death supporting a restaurant which is failing, I propose we close it. Much as I hate admitting defeat it will sink us if we don't. What do you think?'

'As a director of Charter-Plackett Enterprises I agree. But what the blazes do we do with the building?'

'I very much doubt we could sell it as a going concern. I propose we sell the kitchen equipment and the tables and chairs and, hold your breath here, re-vamp it into a house again and move in. That would give us more living space there and more room for the catering side and the mail order business here. You would be the first to admit we are very cramped in here anyway, we've always said that.'

'You mean use the whole of this building for the business and live separately over in Henderson's?'

'Yes, what do you think?'

'I think that's brilliant. In fact it fits in very nicely with some news I have for you.'

'News for me? What news?'

'I feel like one of those blushingly coy wives in a Victorian melodrama. We shall need that larger house fairly soon.'

'Blushingly coy? What do you mean?'

'I don't mean I'm really blushing, I thought it might do your ego good in these difficult times to know you are good at something. I think I must be expecting again.'

'Harriet!'

'Well, I'm a week late so it's early days, but I'm sure I'm right.'

Jimbo leapt out of his chair. 'Darling I'm so thrilled. That's wonderful. Are you sure it's all right with you?'

'Absolutely. I'm completely delighted, you've no idea how thrilled I am. It will be such fun, we had the other three so close together there was hardly time to enjoy them being babies. With this one we shall all be able to enjoy it. Having a house completely for our own will be marvellous.'

'Does your mother know?'

'No, she doesn't and I'm not telling anyone till we're sure and it's been confirmed. It can be our secret.'

'Come and sit on my knee. I don't mind nearly so much about the restaurant now. We'll expand on the catering side, which I'm sure I can do when I haven't the worry of Henderson's and we shall do fine. Well I never, I can't believe it. It's all come right hasn't it?'

'Yes, Jimbo, I knew you'd be pleased.'

'I couldn't be more pleased. I found out what the children meant to me when we thought we'd lost Flick. Another one is wonderful.'

'Early days Jimbo, we'll keep our fingers crossed.'

'It'll be all right you'll see, it was meant to be. There's life in the old dog yet. I feel positively frisky.'

*

In the middle of the night Jimbo, planning where he could sell the kitchen equipment, had the inspiration that Bryn and Georgie Fields might like some of the stuff in The Royal Oak. This could be their chance to open up their food side. With this in mind he drifted over there the following day and when there was a quiet moment he broached the idea to Bryn.

'Settled in now are you Bryn?'

'Yes, thank you, we could do to be making more money but I expect that will come slowly as we get known. I don't think the previous licencee encouraged new customers. Trade was very low when we took over.'

'Well, they did have problems you know. They made a lot of enemies and then their daughter was killed and it about finished them. You've improved the bar no end. It's much brighter and more inviting now. What's the food side like?'

'I get too much competition from a certain person sitting not too far from me. But it's picking up.'

'What if the certain person told you he was giving up with the restaurant and tea room? What would you say?'

Bryn stroked his moustache into order while he thought of the implications of Jimbo's question. 'Do you mean that? Really?'

'Yes, I do.'

'Well, of course that would make a tremendous difference to us. All the tourists and the locals would have to come here wouldn't they?'

'You know the barn down the side at the back? Wouldn't that make a good food area if you knocked through into it from that wall at the end of the bar?'

'We thought about that but with you open it wouldn't have been worthwhile. Now it would be. Georgie, have you a minute? Come and listen to this.' Georgie listened and her eyes lit up at the prospect.

'Wonderful, that's good news Jimbo. Well, sorry, not for you, but it is for us! It would be a big investment though, they're such sticklers for everything being absolutely hygienic nowadays with all these new regulations.'

'Not many miles from where you are now, is someone with nearly new equipment for sale.'

'Of course,' Georgie grinned. 'That's the answer. We could go in for meals in a big way then couldn't we? Would the chairs and tables be for sale too, Jimbo?'

'They wouldn't come cheap, but, yes, I'm sure we could come to some arrangement beneficial to both sides.'

'We'll keep quiet about our plans till we've reached a proper financial agreement, then the sky's the limit. Thank you Jimbo for letting us know.'

'OK then, I'll be in touch when I've worked something out.' Alan Crimble, under the pretence of needing more clean glasses, had been listening to their conversation. He grinned at Jimbo and tapped the side of his nose knowingly. Jimbo didn't acknowledge the gesture, thinking it was none of a barman's business listening in on his employer's private conversations, but Bryn and Georgie didn't seem to mind.

Harriet had misgivings about Jimbo's arrangement.

'If we can't make a go of it why should they? I'd feel awfully guilty if they failed.'

'The business decision to start proper meals is theirs Harriet, not ours. They have been wanting to do meals but realised our enterprise prevented them. I simply suggested they purchased our equipment, they didn't have to go for it. Anyway they'll do much better. They won't be making it into a top class restaurant as I tried to do. It'll have wider appeal.'

'We'll close this Saturday shall we?'

'Yes, I've written the notice out for the doors and we'll

207

put a message on the answer machine in the restaurant for when clients ring up to book. Good riddance is all I can say.'

Chapter 18

The villagers saw the notices and many of them made a point of needing to buy something in the Store in order to find out more.

'Sorry you're having to close the tea room and the restaurant Mrs Charter-Plackett, too much for yer was it?'

'Not making money Vera, that's the top and bottom of it. Glad to be rid of it.'

'I see, well it was a bit ambitious wasn't it? Don't know where they'll all go for their cups of tea and that when they've looked round the church and had their photo taken in the stocks. Do you?'

'No, I don't. Is there anything else?'

'No thanks, that's all for now.'

Vera complained in The Royal Oak that night.

'She told me nothing, shut up like a clam she did. 'Ave you heard anything Jimmy?'

'Can't say as I have. Been out all day with Sykes. Walked to Penny Fawcett and then over by Turnham Rocks and then home. Best part o' fifteen miles I reckon.'

'Have you got that smelly dog in here with yer?'

'Keep yer voice down. He's under the table. Bryn'll turn him out if he knows.'

'Well, take 'im home then, you haven't far to go.'

'I will in a minute. He's me friend yer know Vera, I

don't like to leave him on his own too much.'

'Been setting yer snares then?'

'Not yet, thought I'd have a drink first and then pop into Sykes Wood before I go to bed. What's it to you?'

'Nothing, I don't mind, but plenty do.'

'Well, that's up to them. I mind mi own business and they should mind theirs.' Jimmy took a long drink of his beer, and then glancing round to make sure he wasn't being watched he placed the glass under the table. Sharp ears could have heard Sykes quietly lapping the remains of the drink.

Vera launched into a story about a woman from Penny Fawcett who'd been seen with a man other than her husband in the cinema in Culworth. 'Back row in them double seats they were, he was nearly eating 'er. Her cousin Lily told his Aunt Polly and there's been a right row. Are you listening?'

'No. I'm off now. Set mi snares before it gets dark. If I get one do you want it or have *you* gone all soft as well as everyone else?'

'Yes, I'll 'ave one thanks.'

'I'll skin it for yer.'

'Right, thanks.'

Sykes, having business of his own in Little Derehams with a Westie bitch on heat, left Jimmy to set the snares. When Jimmy was ready to leave, no amount of calling brought Sykes to heel, so he reluctantly set off for home. He made himself a cocoa, took the last of the 'Mr Kipling' almond slices out of his cake tin, switched on his ancient black and white TV and watched till nearly midnight. Before he went to bed he opened the back door and called again but his little white and black shadow, the best friend he had in the world, wasn't home yet. 'Damn 'im for being so randy, it'll be that Westie bitch again. I don't know where 'e gets it from, the little beggar. If all 'is wives meet up one day there'll be a right

210

show down. Well, 'e might as well enjoy 'imself, life's short enough.'

Early the following morning Jimmy rolled out of bed, dressed, drank a pint pot of extremely strong tea and went off to inspect his snares. He missed Sykes running along in front of him. If he didn't come home by lunchtime he'd walk along to Little Derchams and see if he could find him. There were times when he wished he'd had him 'done' but his scruples wouldn't allow it, after all he couldn't ask Sykes' permission could he?

As Jimmy climbed the stile in the fence which divided the field in front of the Big House from Sykes Wood, he thought he could hear crying. His astute countryman's ears picked up that it was the crying of a dog or a fox in pain. His heart, with a tremendous lurch, somehow found its way into his throat. He began running. There was nothing in the first snare and it wasn't until he reached the third one that his worst fears were realised. Sykes was caught round the neck in the wire. He tried to greet Jimmy and his little white tail wagged faintly but then he began yelping again. Very gently, trying not to hurt him more than necessary, Jimmy slowly loosened the wire, and slipped Sykes head out of the noose. The dog slid slowly to the ground and lay panting with relief. He tried to lick Jimmy's hand as though thanking him for his rescue. All round his neck, where the wire had been pulling tighter, as he struggled to free himself, the flesh was gouged open and hung around his throat almost like a necklace. There was plenty of congealed blood around the wound but releasing the wire had caused more bleeding and it was dripping onto the grass. For one dreadful moment Jimmy thought he could see his neck bones.

Off came Jimmy's old poaching jacket. He laid it on the ground and, picking up Sykes as gently as he could, he laid him on it. Sykes appeared to have fainted, if dogs did such a thing. The journey home almost broke Jimmy's heart, Sykes lay so still. How he could get into Culworth to that vet he'd used once, he didn't know.

When they got home Jimmy warmed some water in the kettle, poured it into a saucer and added some honey and a teaspoon of brandy. Sykes obliged by trying to drink but he was too weak to make the effort. Jimmy sat down trying to think of a plan of campaign. Ralph, that was it, Ralph. He'd ask him to drive him in. He'd do it. He understood about country ways.

But Ralph wasn't in. 'I'm sorry, Jimmy,' Muriel said, 'Ralph's gone to London on business. He left about half past six to miss the worst of the traffic. Why not ask Peter, he'll just be finishing prayers, it's almost seven.'

'No, no I can't ask him.'

'Yes you can, if I was dressed I'd ask him myself. He's always willing to help anyone in trouble. I'm so sorry about Sykes, he's such a nice little dog.'

'I'll go ask then. There's no one else up and I can't delay he's that poorly.' Jimmy left Muriel and went up the church path. As luck would have it Peter was just locking the church door.

'Why, good morning Jimmy, you're up and about early.'

Jimmy took off his old cap and stood twisting it in his hands. Being of an independent mind, asking favours didn't come easily. 'Rector, I know you and I are not best friends at the moment . . .'

'Don't say that Jimmy, please. We are always friends.'

'Well, we've 'ad our differences, but it's Sykes, he's injured and he needs the vet real urgent like. It's all the way to Culworth sir, I don't really like to ask. Ralph's already gone to London or I'd 'ave asked 'im, so Muriel said why not ask you, sir.'

'I'll get the car out straight away. Let's ring the vet first and let him know we're coming in.'

'Will you do that sir? I 'aven't a phone.'

'Of course, come in the Rectory.'

'No, I'll get back to Sykes. The one I went to years ago was Forsythe and Blair, the one at the bottom of Abbots Row.'

'See you in a couple of minutes then.' Peter returned to the Rectory to find Caroline just going into the kitchen to start the breakfast.

'Jimmy's Sykes has been involved in an accident and he needs to get to the vet's so I'm going to take him.'

'Oh poor thing, what's he done?'

'I don't know, but Jimmy's very upset. It sounds serious. I'll ring the vet and go straight away. Don't know how long I'll be.'

Around lunchtime Caroline heard knocking at the door. Peter had returned from Culworth hours ago, leaving Jimmy to return on the lunchtime bus. It was he standing on the doorstep. His normally ruddy brown complexion was pale with anxiety, his thin cheeks were more hollow, and his stoop more pronounced; all told he was a sorry figure. They hadn't spoken since the night of the rabbit incident, but when she saw how strained his face was, she could feel nothing but compassion.

'Oh, sorry. Thought it would be the rector. It's 'im I need to speak to.'

'The Rector isn't in Jimmy, he's sick visiting today. But tell me how Sykes is. Look, please come in.' She opened the door wider and waited for him to enter.

'No, no, it wouldn't be right.'

'Yes it would, come in and tell me all about it.'

Jimmy stood on the doormat, cap in hand. 'I don't know how to tell yer. It's the judgement of the Almighty, that's what it is. The Almighty, yes, that's right.'

'What is?'

'Well yer see Dr Harris, I'm afraid . . .'

213

'He hasn't died has he?'

'No, but it wasn't an accident, well, it was I suppose, but it was my fault. All my fault, 'e got caught round 'is neck in one of mi own snares. 'E ran off last night yer see when we went to set the snares, 'e right fancies a b . . . a lady dog down Little Derehams way and I expect he came back to find me after I'd gone and that was when he got caught.'

Caroline put her hand on his arm. 'Oh Jimmy! I'm so sorry, so very sorry. Look, the twins are having a nap, I'm about to have lunch, come in the kitchen and at least have a drink of tea or something.'

He followed her in and sat in her rocking chair by the Aga. She busied herself boiling the kettle and making sandwiches, leaving Jimmy to pull himself together.

'Yer see Dr Harris, it's a punishment isn't it? You wanted me to stop, I didn't stop and now look what's happened.'

'Vets can perform miracles nowadays, you know, with all these new drugs they have. He'll probably be up and about in no time, you'll see. Peter said you went to the Abbots Row Clinic. I use them for the cats, they're very good.'

'Septicaemia is the worry. The wire wasn't clean yer see.'

'Ah right. Yes, I see. Here's a sandwich and your tea, it's turned out rather strong. Is that all right?'

He left after lunch with Caroline's words of reassurance ringing in his ears. 'While there's life there's hope.'

But by the weekend the vet held out little hope. Jimmy had had Sykes eleven years and he was already fully grown when he got him, so his age was against recovery. Septicaemia set in and by Saturday evening Jimmy was begging a lift from Peter to get to the surgery before Sykes died.

Jimmy stood stroking Sykes as his life slowly ebbed

away. All Jimmy could do was wait for the end and comfort him as he lay motionless on his sheepskin bed. Suddenly Sykes shuddered and let out a long sigh. "As he gone, vetnary?'

Mr Forsythe listened with his stethoscope and gently nodded his agreement. Jimmy bent down to place a kiss on Sykes' head and then turned away to look out of the window. He surreptitiously took out his handkerchief and wiped his eyes. In a moment he said in a curiously thickened voice, 'Do yer reckon dogs go to 'eaven?' Mr Forsythe said he was sure there was a heaven for dogs where the sun always shines and the rabbits all run slowly.

Jimmy turned from the window and gave a slight smile. 'That's a grand idea, what a grand idea, that's very comforting. Well 'e was always randy, lets 'ope there's plenty of bitches there too, then 'e'll be well content.' Jimmy nodded his head, 'Yes, well content.' No one saw Jimmy for a few days, then he came out of his cottage door, with a huge bunch of flowers he'd picked from his garden, and was seen walking across to the rectory. Caroline answered his knock.

'Morning Dr Harris.'

'Good morning, Jimmy, do come in.' Jimmy stepped inside and said, 'You'll know, of course, about poor Sykes. I've come with these flowers to thank you for being so kind to me, you and the rector, when you'd every right to be annoyed and say "Serves you right."'

'I wouldn't ever say that, Jimmy, of course not.'

'Well, thank you for everything, and these are for you and I'd like yer to know I shan't be setting mi snares again. Ever. I've given it up. When I saw 'ow frightened my Sykes was, and 'ow much pain 'e suffered it made me think. I've bundled 'em all up and buried 'em in the wood near where I used to set 'em, deep down where they'll never be found.'

215

'Well, I'm sorry it took Sykes dying to make you stop, but I'm glad you're not going to kill rabbits in that way anymore.'

'Aye well, that's that then. Good afternoon, Dr Harris.' Caroline stood at the door watching Jimmy walk back to his cottage. He looked so woebegone. Her victory, won at such a price, seemed very hollow.

Chapter 19

Muriel, despite being Lady Templeton, still cleaned the church brass once a fortnight. This time it was three weeks since she'd done the polishing because she and Ralph had been to the south of France for a week. She'd loved Cannes and Monte Carlo and Monaco and had come back with renewed zest to her quiet, country life. She was standing on a chair cleaning the big brass cross above the altar when she saw the sun had come out from behind a cloud and it was shining through the stained glass window covering her with curiously shaped streaks of colour. Her delight in the rich colours made her rub even harder and the old cross gleamed. No one knew how long the cross had hung there but Muriel liked to think it had been there since the Middle Ages and had seen the village through wars and calamities, joys and celebrations, for hundreds of years.

Only the noise of her cloth, rub rub rubbing on the cross disturbed the silence. Satisfied there was no more room for improvement she held onto the altar and stepped down. The chair, given by an ancestor of Ralph's in memory of a young and much loved husband who had died in a hunting accident, belonged at the side of the altar for Peter to use when the choir sang an anthem or a visiting preacher or a parishioner was reading the lesson. She gave it a pat as she replaced it. There was such comfort to be had from familiar things. Muriel collected her cloths and the tin of polish and went to clean the brass work on the lectern. It was then she heard the sound of weeping. Seated in the pew in front of the tomb Willie always insisted was haunted, was Venetia Mayer, her head bent, her shoulders shaking with sobs.

For a few more minutes Muriel continued to clean the lectern. Venetia Mayer was not her kind of person and she'd hardly spoken to her in all the time she'd been in the village. What really stuck in Muriel's throat was the damage done by the modernisation of the Big House. She couldn't quite forgive her for that. Eventually her soft heart could ignore the crying no longer. Muriel went to sit beside her. To Muriel's conservative outlook Venetia's apparel seemed hardly appropriate for church. She wore her brightest pink, plush velvet tracksuit with a purple headband and purple slouch socks. Because she was bent over as she cried, Muriel could see the words 'Turnham House Health Club' emblazoned across the back and they caused Muriel pain; it was such an insult to that lovely gracious old house.

Holding Venetia's hand Muriel said, 'Now, my dear, is there any way in which I could help?'

Muriel's sympathetic voice made Venetia sob even louder, so Muriel put her arm around her and rocked her gently saying, 'Hush, hush, nothing can be so bad that it can't be solved. Come, come, my dear.'

The crying lessened and Venetia lifted her head and looked at Muriel. The false eyelashes on her right eye were coming unstuck, her thick black mascara was running down her face in tiny black rivulets. Where the tears had run down her cheeks there were light coloured trickles amongst her tan makeup. Where had the super confident Venetia gone?

'Whatever is the matter? You can tell me, or if not, I'm sure the rector would be only too pleased to help.'

'Oh no, not him, not Peter, that wouldn't do. No, I don't want him to know.'

Muriel took Venetia's handkerchief from her and tried to wipe her face dry for her, but the streaks became even more pronounced, 'Here, my dear, I have these two clean tissues in my bag, use them.'

Venetia wiped her face as clean as she could without the aid of a mirror, and said, 'Lady Templeton isn't it?' Muriel nodded, 'I'm sorry for making such a fool of myself, but we're in such trouble, you've no idea.' Venetia sniffed into the tissues.

'I am sorry about that.'

'We can't pretend any longer.'

'Can't pretend what?'

'That everything's all right.'

'All right?'

'With the Health Club I mean. We've been pretending for weeks that the clientele was slowly building up, but sod it, it isn't. We're going to have to close. We were so full of excitement, this was really going to be the big deal, the big opportunity and this bloody recession has killed it.' Muriel's embarrassment at her swearing in church showed in her face and Venetia apologised, 'Sorry, sorry for that.'

'I see, so it isn't Mr Mayer that's the problem then?'

'Well, it is, and it isn't. I tell people I married him for his money, well now he hasn't *got* any money, well not much. He borrowed it all and . . . and . . . and . . . ' Venetia broke down again. Muriel hugged her again, puzzled as to what the problem really was. 'Now, now dear, pull yourself together. It's something else besides the business isn't it? You can tell me. A problem shared is a problem halved.'

Between her sobs Venetia said, 'I don't know what I'm doing sitting in a church. I've done something terrible and you'll think it's terrible too and that I don't belong

219

here at all.'

'That's not so. Don't let Peter hear you say that. He would say no one is outside God's love.'

'Well, when I tell you what I've done you might think I am.' She hesitated for a moment and then said, 'I've just had an . . . well, I've just had an affair you see.'

Muriel sat speechless while she absorbed what she'd just heard then she said, 'Oh dear, oh dear, no wonder you're upset.'

'I've been the biggest fool, you've no idea.'

'No, I haven't.'

'He came to the Health Club and I fell for his charm, hook, line and sinker. He was so good looking and I did need cheering up. He gave me a wonderful time, treated me like a queen and then dropped me like a red hot brick. Men can be cruel. Now Jeremy's found out and well, we've had a terrible row.'

'I'm not surprised.'

'Anyway it's over with and I've said I'm sorry, but Jeremy's really cut up about it. I do like excitement in my life you see and with everything going wrong at the Club and Jeremy being so worried I got carried away. I've been such an idiot.' The tears began falling again and Muriel searched in her bag for another tissue. 'Here you are Venetia, another clean tissue. Wipe your eyes, my dear, and cheer up. Hopefully Jeremy will come round.'

'Oh he will, he's such a kind man really. I could kill that man for egging me on like he did. He's a slimeball.'

Muriel flinched at the word. Taking a deep breath she said, 'We all make mistakes at some time or another, so you must learn from your experience and resolve not to make the same mistake again.'

'Yes, you're right, but he was so lovely and so well off. I shall miss him.'

Muriel smiled wistfully at her. 'Time is a great healer you know.'

Venetia sniffed loudly. 'Still let's face it, he wouldn't really have wanted to take someone like me seriously would he? On top of all that upset and the Health Club failing I don't know what to do anymore. We don't know which way to turn.'

'Mr Mayer must be very upset too, with this . . . well with your problem and then the business failing. Oh dear, I am sorry, so sorry.'

It was Venetia's turn to comfort Muriel. 'Please don't upset yourself, I'm fairly tough you know, I'll get over it I expect. If I could just come up with a solution, you know, find a buyer or something. But what hope is there of that in these times? No one has money, no one at all.' Inspiration came to her and her eyes lit up. 'I don't suppose Sir Ralph would . . . '

'No, definitely not, he hasn't that kind of money.'

'Oh I see, just a thought.'

'Come with me to the house and we'll have a coffee and a good think.'

Venetia shook her head. 'I shouldn't really you know. Anyway, I look such a mess.'

'You can have a wash and brush up while I put the kettle on.'

'Righteo then.'

Ralph, who'd been in the bedroom changing into some old clothes in readiness for cleaning his car, emerged to find Venetia coming out of the bathroom. He couldn't hide the shock he felt. To find her in his house at all came as a surprise, more so as it was hard to recognise this drained looking version of the colourful Venetia.

'Oh, beg pardon Sir Ralph, I'm sure.'

'That's quite all right . . . Venetia isn't it?'

'Yes, Lady Templeton asked me in. We're just having a coffee. Are you going to join us?' She flicked her hand up to her hair and rearranged her head band. Something of the old Venetia was coming through despite her

221

problems.

Ralph hastily declined. 'Thank you, no, I won't. I'm going to clean the car, so I'll leave you ladies to enjoy a good chat on your own.'

Muriel made three cups of coffee and took one out to Ralph as he hosed down the car.

He thanked her and then in a stage whisper said, 'Muriel, what the blazes have you asked that dreadful woman in for? You know I don't like her. She looks terrible this morning. What a sight to find on one's landing!'

'Yes, she does look terrible, but it's because she has a lot of problems and needs help.'

'Whatever you do, *don't offer money!*'

'Of course not. I'll explain later. When she's ready to go would you drive her back to the Big House?'

Reluctantly Ralph agreed, 'Very well, but you're far too soft hearted Muriel.'

When he returned from taking Venetia home Ralph asked Muriel for an explanation.

'So you see Ralph I couldn't leave her there could I?' Muriel concluded.

'No, in all honesty you couldn't, but there is no way that you and I could buy it back. It makes me very sad to see my old home receiving such cavalier treatment. I expect really it's ruined forever. Wars have repercussions one doesn't always bargain for don't they? If my father hadn't been killed in Malaya the Big House would have been as it always was. Ah well, much as I should like to live there it is quite impossible, my dear. Still, thank you for being kind to her. I don't like the woman but she obviously needed your help. Now, afternoon tea in Culworth I think. I have a mind to buy my wife, my one and only wife something special to celebrate her kind heart.'

'Ralph, you indulge me far too much.'

'Why not? I love you. It was the best day's work I ever did coming back here to live and finding you.'

'Thank you, dear. I think you can buy me that suit I saw in Fisk's. It's terribly expensive but I do love it and it's my size. Let's go now Ralph, buy the suit and then have lunch at the George. I have a feeling it might be sold if I don't hurry.'

Venetia had waved an exaggerated farewell to Ralph as he swung the Mercedes round and headed back to the village. Now *he* really was something despite his years, and so charming. She found Jeremy seated at his desk, head resting on his arms fast asleep. He'd obviously been working at some figures as his calculator was still switched on, his glasses carelessly flung aside and a pen lay between his fingers. His pudgy fingers, his thick wrists, his balding head, his fat ears, his solid shoulders, his suit with flakes of dandruff scattered on the collar, revolted her; whatever had made her fancy him in the first place? Was there any point in staying with him? The debts were all his, her name was on nothing at all. He'd lost all his capital. All he had was the home he'd used as collateral for some of the borrowings. Even that was rented out so they couldn't live in it. Get a job in a beauty salon, or a leisure centre? Only trouble with getting a job was it wouldn't keep her in the manner to which she had become accustomed since she'd teamed up with Jeremy. It would have to be the fire idea after all. But how dangerous. Found out, and she'd be in prison. In any case you couldn't do that to such a lovely old house.

He stirred, opened his eyes and stared vaguely round. He patted amongst the clutter on the desk, found his glasses and put them on. 'Oh, Venetia, you're still here. I dreamt you'd left me. It was a terrible shock. I wept, in my dream, I really wept. You wouldn't leave me would you? I love you, ducky. I know I don't show it, but I do.'

'I know you do.'

'Feeling better now old girl?'

'Better?' Venetia looked up questioningly. 'Oh, yes.'

'You don't look it, in fact, you look quite odd.'

'Thanks. I've been having coffee with Lady Temple . . .'

'Lady Templeton! She didn't offer . . .'

'No. Neither did he.'

'Oh well.' Jeremy hesitated and then said, 'I've let you down badly.'

Venetia looked shamefaced for a moment and then patted his hand. 'I've let you down badly too, and I'm sorry. I shall go see Jimbo. Maybe he might have some bright ideas, he's the only business man hereabouts.'

'It's my place to go.'

'No, I'll go. Jimbo is very susceptible to feminine charm.'

'So am I.'

'Yes, but you haven't the money, have you Jeremy dear?'

Chapter 20

Peter drove to Little Derehams not expecting to hear a very accurate recollection of the story behind the Charity Fund. One couldn't expect an old lady in her nineties to be able to recall all the details. Nevertheless he'd no alternative. He wasn't sure where she lived as the Gotobeds didn't come to church and he'd never had the opportunity to meet them before. Along the Turnham Road he saw a girl playing with some children in the garden of a neglected cottage. He realised he knew her. Peter got out of his car and went to speak to her.

'Good morning Mrs Paradise, how are you?'

Simone stopped pushing the home made swing and lifted the baby from the seat.

'Don't be polite Peter, get round it by calling me Simone.'

'Right, Simone then. Young Valentine is looking better than when I saw him last.' Simone pushed back her long brown hair from her eyes and agreed. 'Valentine's coming on fine now, Peter, thanks. The operation's been a complete success. Say "Hello" to the rector, Valentine.' Simone held his plump brown arm and waved it up and down, then grinned engagingly at Peter. 'How are your two coming along?'

'They're both doing fine, thank you.'

'Good. Mrs Gotobed lives at Weavers Cottage, last

one on the right before the T-junction.'

'How did you know that was what I was going to ask?'

'I'm a mind reader didn't you know?'

Simone laughed and popped Valentine back on the swing. Peter said goodbye and returned to his car. He shook his head in disbelief, one really couldn't catch a cold in this parish but they all knew before you did.

The door knocker at Weavers Cottage was a bright brass Cockington elf rubbed almost smooth with years of polishing. A sprightly woman in her seventies opened the door. She was like an elf herself, so tiny was she, with bright, shining brown eyes and a mass of snow white hair.

'Oh good afternoon, Rector, how nice to see you, do come in.'

Peter shook hands, 'Good afternoon to you Miss Gotobed.'

'I'm Primrose and this is my sister Lavender just coming from the kitchen.'

Though older by some years, Miss Lavender Gotobed was very like her sister, a round chubby woman with round chubby cheeks, sparkling brown eyes and a mass of curly, undisciplined, snow white hair.

'Mother's having a cup of tea, she will be pleased to see you. Would you like a cup too?'

'Yes, please, I would. I'm sorry for calling unexpectedly.'

'That's quite all right, we're always ready for visitors.'

The tiny cottage sitting room was furnished as it must have been some eighty years ago. Clean to within an inch of it's life the room was welcoming with, despite the warmth of the day, a fire blazing in the hearth.

Mrs Gotobed, with her apple cheeked face, looked the epitome of a lovely ancient country woman. Her fine white hair now grew so sparsely, her pink scalp could be seen through the well washed strands. She struggled to rise from her chair to greet him.

'Please, please, stay where you are Mrs Gotobed. Don't get up on my account.'

She ignored him and stood to shake hands. 'In my day the rector was given great respect in this parish and you still are as far as I'm concerned, sir. I don't hold with all this Christian name business for the rector, it's not right. Now sit down. I hear you haven't been well.'

'I have had a bad dose of something or another, but I'm much better now thank you.'

'Lavender, where's the rector's cup?' Mrs Gotobed's thin piping voice penetrated every corner of the tiny sitting room. 'That girl is just as slow as she's always been. I don't suppose I can expect any improvement now, it's much too late. Now, sir, have you a special reason for coming to see me.'

He knew by the intonation of her voice that she was aware of his mission. He explained the curious coincidence of both the book and the bank statement turning up on the same day and how Sir Ralph had suggested she would be able to tell him the whole story. Mrs Gotobed interrupted him, 'And as soon as you found them you had your accident and then you've been very poorly. No wonder they're all getting in such a state.'

'Can you explain what it's all about?'

'Well, I will, because I'm old and if I popped my clogs tomorrow it would be a blessing for all concerned. So I'm not afraid you see. Now drink that tea and have a piece of Primrose's parkin, it's about the only decent thing she bakes, while I tell you what happened.'

'It all started with those Glover boys. They didn't want to know about hard work. A bit of labouring here and there, poaching, helping put up the roundabouts when the fair came, helping at harvest time, working in Culworth at Christmas, anything and everything so long as it wasn't sensible work needing application six days a week. Well, of course, the war was on, that's the first one you know, and not one of 'em was in the army. Caused a lot of ill feeling that did, but they didn't care. Somehow they'd managed to avoid it even though they were all fit as lops.

'They were that handsome, those boys. I quite fancied Cecil myself except Jonathan Gotobed had decided I was marrying him. Sixteen, that's all I was, but he was determined. I used to laugh, I was much too young to be settling down and those Glover boys did have a lot of dash especially Cecil.'

She paused for a moment and smiled secretly to herself. Then recollecting her story she went on, 'Then late in 1916 they got their call up papers. They were always short of money and when the time came for parishioners to apply to the rector for some help for Christmas from the fund, they applied. Said they needed it to set themselves up with stuff for when they went off to war. Well, of course, it wasn't for young men who could fend for themselves and the rector told them so. But one night after they'd been in The Royal Oak and drunk far more than was good for them, they called at the rectory, all four of them, and threatened the rector and made him give them the money. The verger was there too. Now what it was the Glover boys knew I can only guess at, like all the rest of the village did. But they must have had some sort of hold over the two of them, because they didn't harm the rector nor the verger, but before you could say knife the four of them emerged from the rectory each with a pound in their hand.

'It might seem a small thing in itself, but it was as though the results of their badness were never ending, like the ripples on a pond when you throw a stone in.

'The verger was a widower and his only child died of diptheria on Christmas Day that year. He saw her buried decent and then gassed himself in his kitchen, where

228

Willie Biggs lives now. Then, would you believe it, on New Year's Eve the rector, what was his name? my memory isn't what it was, was coming home from Penny Fawcett. In those days of course he rode in a carriage, little it was, just big enough for a lone bachelor. Just by Havers Lake Woods his horse took fright at some gun shots and it bolted. He was thrown out and killed. No one put two and two together then, it all just seemed like dreadful coincidences and after all we had so much else to worry about, what with the war and the food shortages and young men dying right left and centre. There seemed no end to the horror.' Mrs Gotobed stopped for a moment lost in thought.

Peter sat patiently waiting, wondering if she'd fallen asleep.

'Where was I, oh yes, so the worst was yet to come. All four of the Glover boys were at the front by the following summer. Within the space of three weeks their parents received telegrams, one by one, informing them that they had all been killed. Went down like ninepins they did. Terrible. Terrible. Turnham Malpas almost died too. It was a dreadful blow. None of us could hardly lift our heads to the light of day for months. Then as people talked about it, all the tragedies seemed to come together and everyone became convinced that the deaths were caused by the Glover boys getting money from the rector by force. Since that Christmas of 1916 not a single person hereabouts has dared to ask for a penny from the Fund, for fear of what might happen. Blighted it is, blighted. Christmas 1917 the new rector tried to distribute some money but no one applied and it's been like that ever since.'

'If all the Glover boys died who was Jimmy Glover's father?'

'Ah well, there were the four boys who died, they were the eldest, and then came three girls and then

229

Jimmy's dad. He was only eight when it all happened. How they all squeezed into that little cottage of Jimmy's I'll never know.'

'Thank you for telling me all that. I don't know how you remembered so clearly. I won't stay any longer, I don't want to tire you.'

'You won't try to use the money for the church will you? The village won't tolerate it, you know. Heaven alone knows what might happen if you do. You're a grand young man with a lot of good work still to do, and we don't want anything to happen to you. It nearly did you know, you've come very close to it killing you.'

Somewhat shaken by Mrs Gotobed's warning Peter laid his hand on her head and gave her his blessing. As he finished making the sign of the cross on her forehead, she smiled up at him and took hold of his hand. 'And when my time comes, you make sure my funeral service is a happy one, don't want everyone sat there looking glum, they've to sing Hallelujah! After all, I've gone to my reward.'

'I'll remember, I promise.' Peter turned at the door and said, 'So why did the Gotobeds come to live in Little Derehams?'

'Because my Jonathan was too frightened to live in Turnham Malpas any more, so we moved here when we married, and I've never been in Turnham Malpas since that day. What's more I shan't, so you'll have to hold my service in Culworth, and I want you to do the service, not that young whippersnapper of a curate they've got there now, all microphones and guitars. And I'm to be buried there too, alongside my Jonathan. Right!'

'Right!'

When Peter got home for lunch he told Caroline the full story.

'In that case then Peter, leave well alone.'

'You're as bad as Mrs Gotobed, threatening dire

consequences if I so much as mention the Fund.'

'Have you seen the local paper today?'

'No, I haven't had the time.'

Caroline put the Culworth Gazette on the kitchen table. She pointed out a news item with the headline *LOCAL BANK MANAGER DIES*. Peter went very quiet. *'The new manager of the Culworth Branch of the County and Provincial Bank collapsed and died of a heart attack in his office, early yesterday . . .'* he read.

'The poor chap, such a nice man too. This is pure coincidence though and you know it. It's quite preposterous to imagine there is any connection. How you, level headed and thoroughly sensible, can imagine that there is anything . . .'

'Peter! Take note. Please take note. I *know* it's silly but . . . well, anyway, I don't often insist about matters which are rightly your own concern, but just this once do as I say, please, and be thankful you've been spared. I know I am.' She reached across the table to kiss him.

Chapter 21

Muriel was still worrying about Venetia. Ralph felt that hers and Jeremy's affairs were quite outside their concern.

'I fail to see why you should worry about her.'

'I know Ralph, but I can't help feeling that beneath all that dazzle she is sad and it hurts me that she has no one to sympathise with her.'

'She's got Jeremy.'

'In the circumstances he won't feel like comforting her will he? Should I tell Peter? Oh no, I can't because she doesn't want him to know. So you see, she has some scruples.'

'Not enough by the sound of it!'

'Ralph!' Muriel picked up her purse and a Liberty shopping bag Ralph had bought her when he last went to London. 'I'm going to the Store, is there anything you want?'

'Order me some cigars will you, my dear? Jimbo knows the kind I smoke.'

'Very well. I shan't be long. Are you going into Culworth today as you said?'

'Yes, come with me Muriel, I hate going alone.'

'Very well, on the understanding that we have lunch at the George to celebrate.'

'Celebrate?'

'Yes, this week it's one whole year since you came back to Turnham Malpas.'

'A year? It doesn't feel like that it feels more like tw . . .'

'Twenty. I know. I know. You're a tease Ralph Templeton.'

Muriel laughed as she escaped Ralph's embrace and headed for the Store. Only one whole year yet her life had been transformed. She couldn't believe that there was a time when she didn't know how to love. Her heart leapt with joy as she heard the birds singing, and saw the flowers blowing in the breeze, and to cap it all, she was going out to lunch with her best beloved.

Jimbo's adored brass bell jingled fussily as she entered the Store. Unusually at that time in the morning Muriel found the Store quite empty. Linda always had her coffee break about now. Fifteen minutes and no matter how busy it was, she always, much to Jimbo's annoyance, took her full time. Muriel collected a basket and began to consult her list. She decided that if they were going into Culworth she wouldn't have much time for cooking so she went to the freezer and chose gourmet fish pie and two of Harriet's delicious individual sherry trifles. When she'd collected milk and bread too she went to stand by the till. She waited a few moments and when no one came to take her money, went into the back to find Jimbo or Harriet or even Linda, if she could be prised away from her coffee break.

Muriel went hot all over with embarrassment when she looked in the storeroom. Standing close, very close together were Jimbo and Venetia. His boater abandoned on a nearby shelf, he was holding her tightly and hugging her, and she was hugging him, her arms around his neck, her cheek laid against his. Neither of them noticed her horror-struck presence. She hurriedly retreated back to the Store. Confused and upset, Muriel left her wire basket near the till and fled for the security of Ralph, bumping into Bet from Penny Fawcett in the doorway of the Store who was just coming in. 'Oh oh-h-h-h,' Muriel said unable to find anything else to say. 'Good morning Lady Temple . . .' Muriel didn't hear the rest, she was rushing on flying feet for home. Her own door was open to catch the sun and she burst into the hall shouting, 'Ralph, Ralph, where are you?'

'In the study, my dear,' Ralph called out. She stood just inside the door of his study and began weeping. Ralph rose to his feet. 'Why, whatever's the matter?'

'Oh Ralph, I don't know what to do.' She got out her handkerchief and wept into that.

'Muriel, my dear, have you been attacked or something? What's happened, please tell me?'

'It's Jimbo . . . and . . . and Venetia.'

'Yes?'

'They're embracing in the storeroom.'

'Embracing? You must be mistaken.'

'No, I'm not Ralph, I know what embracing is.'

'Of course you do, my dear, I'm not doubting your word. I'm just amazed. There must be some very good reason for it, though one doesn't spring to mind very easily.'

'I couldn't pay for my shopping, so it's still there on the counter. I can't go back it's so embarrassing.'

'I'll go. Make yourself a cup of tea while I see what's happening.'

'You don't normally go shopping Ralph, I always go.'

'Well, we'll break with tradition shall we? Shan't be long.'

'No, I'll come too.'

When Ralph and Muriel entered the Store, Jimbo was standing by the till, puzzling over Muriel's abandoned basket. He raised his boater in greeting.

'Good morning Muriel, good morning Ralph. What

234

can I do for you this fine day?'

'This is Muriel's basket she left it because there was no one here to take her money, so I've come back with her in case there was anything wrong.'

'Wrong? No, just busy in the back, and Linda's got half a day for a rather nasty dental appointment. Sorry about that Muriel, I'll check your shopping for you then.'

As he was putting Muriel's things into one of his smart green carrier bags the bell jangled madly and in stormed Harriet.

'Back from the antenatal clinic and feeling on top of the world and who's just stopped to speak as I got out of the car? Bet Whatsername from Penny Fawcett.' Harriet imitated Bet's high pitched voice. '"Oh," she says with a malicious glint in her eye, "I think you ought to know Mrs Charter-Plackett, I've been to have a word with your husband about the bread rolls for the Village Centre Fair, and found him and that floosie from the Health Club hugging and kissing in the back. So embarrassing it was, really." I was so astounded by this juicy piece of information I actually thanked her for it, though I can't think why. Well, what the hell's going on?' She glared furiously at Jimbo who looked flustered but innocent.

'Now look Harriet, she's completely exaggerating the situation. Venetia was very upset and I took her in the back to give her a chance to calm down. You know perfectly well I wouldn't dream of hugging and kissing her.'

'Do I? You're a sight too friendly with some of our women customers Jimbo, I've spoken to you about it before.'

'My dear Harriet, it's all good for trade. You're well aware that's why I do it; a smile here, a chuckle there, here a nudge, there a wink. Muriel knows I wouldn't put myself in a compromising situation, don't you Muriel?'

There had been many times in her life when Muriel had wished the ground would open up and swallow her and never more so than now. 'Well, it's like this you see I . . .'

Jimbo jumped in with the assumption that Muriel was about to agree with him. 'There you are, Harriet, I couldn't have a better testimonial than one from Lady Templeton could I?'

Muriel held onto Ralph's arm as she replied, 'I didn't say what you think I said.'

'What did you say?' said Harriet hopping with temper, and clutching at any straw that might justify her suspicions.

Ralph spoke on Muriel's behalf. 'This is all very difficult but the truth of the matter is . . .'

The door opened and in came Jeremy. 'Good afternoon all.' He looked round the assembled company and nodded to them in turn. They all stood in stunned silence. 'I've come to see you Jimbo. Venetia's just found me in the pub and told me all about it, so I've come straight round.'

Muriel went deathly white and grabbed Ralph's arm. 'I'll take Muriel outside for some air, she's feeling faint,' he decided.

The two of them went to sit on the bench thoughtfully provided by Jimbo.

'Whatever am I going to do?'

'Nothing, my dear, nothing at all. Leave them to sort it out. Jimbo's quite capable of taking care of himself.'

'Oh Ralph, I forgot to order your cigars, and I still haven't got my shopping.'

'Never mind. We'll get it all in Culworth. We're best out of the Store for a while.'

'I would hate anything to go wrong between Jimbo and Harriet, especially now when she's expecting their baby. Oh dear, life is so complicated sometimes isn't it?'

'None of this is your fault is it, so don't fret about it.'

'You see, Peter and Caroline have a much stronger marriage than Jimbo. They could withstand, and have withstood, serious trouble and still come through, but I'm not as sure about these two. I do hope Harriet doesn't get too upset.'

'Don't worry. They'll sort it out.' Ralph patted her hand and then said, 'You look a better colour now, so do you feel able to walk gently home?'

'Oh yes, I shall be glad to get out of Turnham Malpas today. I'll take Pericles . . .'

'No, I'll take him for a walk. When I get back with him we'll set off. Put your new suit on Muriel. I like you in that.'

'But we're only going out to lunch.'

'Yes, but we're celebrating aren't we? Had you forgotten?'

Harriet lay in bed that night with tears rolling down her face. Jimbo was sitting beside her drinking a medicinal whisky. 'It's all right you laughing now Harriet, at the time you were livid.'

'Livid? I could have throttled you. I don't know when I've been more angry. It'll be all over the village and then some. You'll never live it down.'

'Poor Ralph, he just didn't know how to cope.' Jimbo held his side to alleviate the pain he had there with laughing so much.

'I really thought Muriel was going to faint. She went deathly white when Jeremy walked in. You do realise that Muriel had seen you, don't you?'

'Oh God, no. Really? Are you sure?'

'Pretty sure.'

'So that was why she abandoned her shopping, of course.' Jimbo began laughing again. 'And then when he said, "Told me all about it and I've come straight round."

237

Oh God, I thought she'll be killing me with one of my butcher's knives.'

'Or he would. I certainly nearly *did*.' Harriet started laughing again. 'Tomorrow I shall go round to see Muriel and apologise. I wonder what they had for dinner tonight? It certainly wasn't individual sherry trifle preceded by gourmet fish pie!' They looked at each other and Jimbo laughed uproariously.

'Harriet, darling, I do love you.' He bent over and gave her a kiss.

'Good, because you came very close to the garden shears this morning Jimbo. I won't tolerate unfaithfulness you know. That's one of the rules I live by and one of the rules we agreed upon when we married. I know lots of our friends in Wimbledon thought nothing of spreading it around but that isn't for you and me.'

'I know that. I enjoy women's company, Harriet, I can't deny that, but it is only harmless flirting and absolutely nothing more. I can swear that on the Bible, please believe me.'

'Well, I've calmed down now, and of course I do know that darling.' Harriet began to giggle. 'Venetia must have thought it was her birthday!'

'She was *so* grateful! She clung on really hard. She's done that once too often though, if what she told me is true.'

Harriet sat up. 'What did she tell you?'

'She told me in confidence, and I can't reveal a confidence can I?' Harriet began tickling him. 'Tell me, tell me.'

'Stop it Harriet I can't bear it, stop it and then I'll tell you. I don't suppose she'll mind me telling you. She told me,' Jimbo glanced round the bedroom as though making sure no one was listening, 'she told me she'd had a tempestuous affair with a chap called Nigel who came to the health club on a freebie. He's an acquaintance of

Jeremy's.'

'No o o o o. I met him one Saturday when I went up there with the children.'

'Added to which . . .'

'Go on then.'

'She isn't married to Jeremy at all. He picked her up in some kind of massage parlour in Soho. He's borrowed thousands, she's not sure how much. In addition they have a sleeping partner and so he's going down with them too.'

'A massage parlour? Whatever next! Hell, what a mess. So why was she weeping in *your* arms?'

'She came to me for advice seeing, as she said, I was the only one around with a business head on my shoulders.'

'Was it your head she was interested in?' At this Harriet started laughing again, till Jimbo said, 'You must calm down Harriet, just remember you're pregnant, you've had enough excitement for one day. You're not as young as you were and we don't want anything going wrong because you've got overwrought.'

Harriet picked up a paperback from her bedside table and beat Jimbo over the head with it. 'And how old does that make you then?'

After he and Harriet had settled down with their arms around each other, they talked about Jimbo's plans for the Big House. 'This business of a staff training house somewhere away from the bustle of the City is quite the thing with lots of the big companies now. The Big House has the extra filip of having the sports and leisure facilities already there. I could try Drew Turnbull, he's chief on the personnel side at my old firm, he might be able to put me in touch with someone, or, I know! There's always Declan O'Rourke, property manager of Reilly, Buckton and Shears. Now he might be a very good lead. He's a terrible gossip and knows everyone and everything. I'll try him first.'

'When you think about it, establishments for staff training purposes won't need a full catering staff all year long will they? Times like August and Christmas and weekends there won't be any staff there to train, so the domestic people will be twiddling their thumbs. Being on the spot so to speak you could put staff in as and when.'

'Of course, of course. Having put A in contact with B and got a sale I shall then be able to tender from a strong position. At least they will know that with my City background they're not dealing with a complete country bumpkin.'

'I always knew I'd married a brilliant brain.'

'Thank you and good night.'

'I wonder if they could find a job for Venetia?'

'Now that really is magnanimous of you.'

Chapter 22

Sylvia was taking advantage of the twins having gone visiting with their mother, and the rector being out at a meeting in Culworth, to get some housework done without interruptions. She began by cleaning the bathroom Peter and Caroline used. She'd tidied up Caroline's bottles and jars, changed the towels for fresh pale green ones and given the taps an extra polish. Standing back to admire the sparkling bathroom Sylvia noticed the curtains needed a wash, so she took them down and opened a window to let in some air. It was late September but still quite mild. The Rectory garden, since Willie had worked on it, was looking splendid. Beyond it she saw a car wandering down Pipe and Nook Lane, and watched it till it disappeared behind Sir Ralph's hedge. Her little car was still going strong. Pity Willie had never learned to drive. She really preferred to see the man driving the car. That was just what Willie was. A MAN. A tender loving man. That fool she'd married in the first flush of her youth hadn't as much tenderness in the whole of him as Willie had in his little finger.

She picked up the used towels and put them in the linen basket on the landing. It seemed an age since breakfast so she went downstairs for a drink. The kitchen felt warm and welcoming and when she'd made a coffee she decided to sit down and read the newspaper. With her elbows resting on the table she sipped from her mug. It had some unknown tropical flower decorating it and Sylvia smoothed her fingers over the pinkness of the petals and thought about Willie and his garden. There couldn't be much wrong with a man who had green fingers. Sylvia added up Willie's qualities. Since she'd gone to live with him she'd found he was kind, considerate, tender, sensitive, thoughtful, a good laugh, and, surprisingly, she'd found him passionate. He did have a sense of humour, you needed that in a relation-ship. A loud hammering at the door made her jump and she spilled her coffee. That'll be Willie.

She heard his footsteps coming down the hall and him shouting, 'It's me Sylvia, where are you?'

'In the kitchen wiping coffee off my blouse.'

'What made you spill your coffee?'

'You, banging on the door like that. Is there a fire?'

'Fire? No.'

'You should really have waited for me to answer the door you know.'

'Well, I knew they were both out, so I thought I'd come and cadge a coffee with my Sylvia.'

'Nevertheless, I work here, Willie, it's not my house, and you should wait. It's only right.'

'Give us a kiss and then I'll remember next time.' He grabbed her round the waist and pulled her to him. 'By Jove, Sylvia, but you're grand. You always taste so sweet.'

'Willie.' Sylvia struggled to get free. 'At your time of life! Kissing in the middle of the morning. Really. Anyone would think you were in your teens.'

'I am. Where's that drink, I'm a working man and I need it.'

Willie sat at the other side of the table from Sylvia, stirring his coffee. He glanced at her from under his

242

eyebrows and relished what he saw. Sylvia became conscious of his penetrating eyes and looked up. For a moment, with not a word said, they spoke directly to each other from their souls. Time stayed its hand. Then Sylvia heard the kitchen clock begin ticking again and her heart righted itself. Willie's spoon rattled against the side of the mug because the hand that held it was trembling.

Their silence was broken by the sound of Caroline's voice. 'Sylvia! Can you take Alex for me please?' Sylvia jumped up guiltily. 'Willie, you shouldn't be here.' Caroline was holding Alex and keeping the front door open with her foot to stop the wind banging it shut on her. 'You take him and I'll get Beth. Thanks.'

Sylvia propped open the door with the wedge and stood watching Caroline getting Beth out of her car seat. She'd have to apologise. She felt her face. It was still hot from the aftermath of that stare of Willie's.

'I hope you don't mind Dr Harris but Willie came in for a coffee. We thought you wouldn't be back just yet.'

Caroline looked at Sylvia's flushed face, with a twinkle in her eye she said, 'I hope I haven't interrupted something?'

'Oh no, no, not at all.' They took the twins into the kitchen. Willie stood as she entered. 'Good morning Dr Harris.'

'Good morning Willie. My friend had left a note pinned to the door. "Sorry gone to casualty, Piers has fallen and I think he's broken his arm." So I've come straight back home. I think these two could manage a drink, Sylvia, please and I'd like the coffee I missed. No, no, Willie you stay and finish yours.'

Willie sat down again embarrassed by the tumultuous feelings he'd experienced when he'd looked into Sylvia's eyes and by the fact he'd been caught out doing his courting in the Rectory kitchen.

With Alex and Beth seated in their high chairs each

with their feeding beakers and a biscuit, Caroline took time to speak to Willie. But he hadn't much to say and as quickly as he could he finished his drink and left.

Caroline, bending down to the floor to pick up Alex's biscuit which he'd knocked off the tray said, 'You know, Sylvia, your face was the colour of a beetroot when I came in and the atmosphere in here was electric. You're going to have to capitulate and marry that man.'

'I can't make up my mind.'

'It seems to me the chemistry is right, oh so right. What's holding you back?'

'I don't know.'

'Neither do I. Don't break his heart, Sylvia. He's a good, kind man and he feels it quite badly you not being properly married, you know. Sometimes I see him look at you very wistfully. He doesn't just want his socks washing with no commitment on his part. Have courage.'

'I know. I can't believe he's fallen in love like a young man would do. I'm so afraid he'll wake up one day and find he's been fooling himself.'

'Have *you* fallen in love? That's the other half of the equation you know. Only time will tell. Now I must press on.' But the door bell rang and it was Muriel on the step.

'Good morning Caroline, I've come about the fund raising for the refurbishing of the small hall.'

'Come right in Muriel. Isn't it a lovely day?'

'It certainly is.'

Caroline showed Muriel to a chair in the sitting room and settled herself in another close by. 'I've been meaning to tell you Muriel, I've been to visit Beryl Baxter.'

'No! You make me feel very guilty. I never gave her another thought. How is she and where is she?'

'She's in a secure mental hospital in Brackley. Rather a grim place but they've done their best to make it bright and homely. At first apparently, Beryl simply sat motionless and they had to do everything for her. Feed her, wash her, dress her, put her to bed. Then one day she disappeared from the ward and they couldn't find her. She'd wandered into the occupational therapy area and joined a class of people learning to paint watercolours. They gave her a brush but she sat staring at the paper and didn't paint. This went on for days, going in there, holding the brush staring at the paper. Sometimes she sat there for two hours without moving and then wandered off back to her bed again.'

'Oh the poor thing.'

'Then miracle of miracles one day she dipped the brush in some paint and painted like a small child would, just hectic brush strokes all over the paper. But the significant thing was that she smiled at it. It was the first emotion she'd shown.'

'How wonderful.'

'Now she goes in there every day and paints. There's no therapy at the weekends but it's doing her so much good and as it's the only way she can express herself, they allow her to sit in there unsupervised at the weekends. Gradually her painting is improving and one can see what she's trying to paint now, and they have great hopes that she is going to cure herself through it. Normally she doesn't speak to anyone at all, but when she paints she talks to herself, so there is a ray of hope there. Isn't that wonderful?'

'Oh, it is Caroline. I don't think I'd be brave enough to go see her myself but, when you go again, would you let me know and I'll send her a present.'

'Of course. I won't be going till next month but I'll let you know when I am.'

'Harriet came round to see me you know.' Caroline looked questioningly at Muriel because the tone of her voice seemed strange. 'Yes, she came to apologise. It was

245

all a misunderstanding.'

'Was it?' Caroline was nonplussed.

'Oh, don't you know? I thought you would have heard. Yes, you see Venetia was very upset because the Health Club has failed and Jimbo was comforting her.'

'Oh I see. How do you know all this?'

'Because I found them in the storeroom. I was so embarrassed I left my shopping and fled home to Ralph.'

'Oh, Muriel.' Caroline collapsed with laughter. 'What a fix to be in! What's happening about the health club?'

'I don't know. Jimbo's trying to rescue it but I don't know how. Venetia's not too bad when you get to know her. In fact I have developed quite a soft spot for her. She confided in me one day you see.'

'You have been a busy person Muriel.'

'I have, very busy in fact. You'll never guess what I've done this morning.'

'No, tell me.'

'Well, I met Michael Palmer in the Store and he asked me if I would play the piano for him at the school for a while as I used to do before I married. Doesn't that sound wonderful? "Before I married." I am glad I did what you said. Where was I? Oh yes. So we got talking, he's such a lovely man and so alone. However, I asked him if he ever heard from Suzy Meadows.' The moment the name was out of her mouth Muriel regretted it. 'Oh Caroline, I'm so sorry, I'd completely forgotten, how thoughtless of me. I'll leave and come back another time. I'm so sorry.'

Caroline, knowing Muriel could never be guilty of duplicity, nor intentionally take any action which would cause distress, smiled painfully. She and Peter had an unspoken rule about not mentioning Suzy's name. To hear her name spoken in her own sitting room was shocking to her and Caroline had to struggle to keep control of her feelings. She covered the stress by taking time to remove an imaginary piece of thread from the hem of her skirt. Having done that she looked up and said, 'That's all right, Muriel. I can talk about her and wish her well. After all, in one sense I owe her so much. But I never mention her name in front of the children, it's ridiculous but it feels almost indecent. I know when they are older we shall have to speak the truth, because Peter has promised he will, but for now her name is never mentioned in front of them.'

'I see, well, I must apologise for causing you such distress. I just didn't think. I won't say any more.'

'Please do. They're with Sylvia and not within earshot. I don't wish her harm you know, I do want her to be happy.'

Her lovely piece of news had been spoiled for her but Muriel decided she would look silly if she didn't carry on telling it. 'Well, apparently he is in touch with her mother, you know the twins' grandmother, all because her mother wrote to him wanting to have news of her twins, because after all they are her grandchildren aren't they? So she would wouldn't she?'

'Yes, she would.'

Muriel cleared her throat. This was so difficult, why ever had she launched herself on this story. 'So I told Michael Palmer that they'd always got on well and that if he liked the idea why didn't he go ahead and begin courting her. He went red and said she had started writing to him occasionally, you know, putting little messages on the bottom of her mother's letters, so I said, take life by the scruff Michael. We only have one life to lead why not plunge in and grasp the nettle. Oh dear, I seem to have got things mixed up but you know what I mean?'

'Yes, I do and thank you for telling me. What did he say?'

'Well, he said that was just what he was going to do and winked. So, yes, I am going to play the piano for him until he gets a new permanent teacher who can play, which will be straight after Christmas, and it does look as if he is going to do something positive about . . . Suzy. Which will be lovely won't it?'

'Yes, it will.'

'Only what I've told you is in complete confidence, except of course you wouldn't want to talk to anyone about Suzy would you seeing as things are? Oh dear, I am sorry, that came out all wrong too. I'm so confused.'

'No, I won't divulge it to a soul. Thank you for telling me. Now about the fund raising. I have been giving it a lot of thought and I wondered what you . . .'

'I really think I'm too exhausted to think about it now, and you're very busy, can I come back another time please?'

'Of course. It truly is all right Muriel, honestly.'

'Yes, well, I still think I will go. Ralph will be wondering where I am. I'll come back another day. Don't worry I'll see myself out.' Muriel let herself out thankful to have escaped. What a stupid silly thing to have done. So thoughtless. She shut the front door, stepped off the stone step into the road and bumped into Sir Ronald and Lady Bissett.

'Oh I'm so sorry, I didn't see you there.'

'Are you all right Lady Templeton?' Sir Ronald took her elbow and steadied her.

'Why, yes, of course. My goodness Sir Ronald you look to me as if you've lost weight.'

Lady Bissett answered on his behalf, 'He has, a whole stone and a quarter *and* our best bit of news is we're off to the States, aren't we Ron..ald. We've been married forty years this year so it's a kind of second honeymoon.'

Muriel blushed. 'Oh, how lovely. It certainly suits you being slimmer Sir Ronald. How long will you be gone?'

'Four weeks, coast to coast we're going.'

'How lovely. I've never been to the United States.

Would it be helpful if I have Pom for you?'

Sheila looked grateful. 'Oh it would! I was dreading him going into kennels, he's not used to it you see, and I didn't like to ask.'

'Of course I'll have him. Pericles will be delighted.'

Sheila patted Muriel's arm. 'I've been thinking, how would it be if you called us Ron and Sheila? We're not really titled in the proper sense of the word and it would be much more friendly wouldn't it?'

'Well, yes, it would, in that case you call me Muriel.'

'Very well we will. Bye bye Muriel. Be seeing you.'

'Bye bye Sheila, and bye bye . . . Ron.' At home Muriel sank gratefully into her favourite armchair and consoled herself with a cup of tea and a biscuit. She'd had just about all she could take this morning. There were times when she wished she was a hermit.

Chapter 23

'Good afternon, Turnham House Health Club. Venetia speaking. How may I help you?' Venetia gripped the receiver between her jaw and her shoulder while she hitched herself onto Jeremy's desk.

'Hi Venetia. Jimbo Charter-Plackett here. How are you this fine bright day?'

'Bloody awful.'

'You don't sound too perky.'

'I'm not and neither is Jeremy. We are completely at the end of our tether.'

'Hold on Venetia, surely things can't be as bad as that?'

'You know full well they are. I wish I was in Timbuktoo, anywhere but here.'

'I jolly well hope you won't be in Timbuktoo on Monday.'

'On Monday? Why?'

'Because I have been incurring a huge phone bill beavering away on your behalf.'

'Yes?'

'Ann-n-n-d on Monday of this week, at precisely eleven thirty a certain company chairman in the City will be coming to give the Big House the once over.'

'The once over?'

'Venetia, you're not very bright eyed and bushy tailed this morning.'

'Run it past me again and then it might sink in.'

'A person by the name of Craddock Fitch is coming to look over Turnham House with a view to purchasing it for his company. He'll be arriving at eleven thirty on Monday morning.' His announcement was met with total silence. 'Hello. Hello. Venetia are you there? Hello. Hello.' It sounded as though the receiver had crashed to the floor. After a moment Jimbo could hear a voice quite unlike Venetia's screaming, 'Sid, Sid.' He heard footsteps and then faintly, 'Sid, get up and come down.' The footsteps returned.

'Are you still there Jimbo? Oh God, I can't believe it. A buyer at last. Thank you, thank you, thank you. I don't know what else to say.'

'Now see here, I only said he was coming to *look*. There are no promises at all. A sale depends on the impression he gets. Can I be brutally frank?'

'Of course.'

'He is a very important person, Venetia, really important. He's coming because he is *seriously* interested. I happened to speak to him on the right day at the right moment, and he happens to be in the area at a weekend house party and is calling on his way back to London. You must, absolutely *must* give a good impression. On no account wear your screamingly dazzling track suit or bikini. Get out your darkest suit, your whitest blouse, tone down the old makeup, hide the gold jewellery in the drawer and wear only one small well chosen piece. In other words behave like a nun. Right? Get Jeremy togged to the nines in a dark suit, white shirt, restrained tie, well polished shoes. Have everywhere totally spick and span. Clear Jeremy's desk and in particular make sure there are no Snickers bars evident. Lots of flowers about, cushions plumped et cetera, create a kind of country house atmosphere. Get the picture?'

'Oh yes, oh yes. I'll start clearing up now. Right away.

I can't thank you enough. Jeremy's right beside me and he's dancing up and down.'

Privately, Jimbo thought that wouldn't be a pretty sight. 'Don't build your hopes too high, just play it cool. Most important don't pretend you've someone else interested. He'll see through that immediately. He's not an idiot.'

'Will you be coming up?'

'No, I'm quite certain you can manage the whole thing without me holding your hand. Got the date and time?'

'It's engraved on my heart. Thank you Jimbo.'

'Anytime. The ball's in your court, let's hope you win the match. Bye.'

Jimbo banged down the receiver. 'Well, Harriet, I've done all I can. The rest is up to them.'

Jimbo was having a quick lunch with Sadie in her mail order office on the Monday when the phone rang. Sadie answered it. Jimbo heard her saying, 'I'm sorry I can't tell what you're saying. Yes. Yes. Oh Jimbo. Oh yes, he's here. Hold the line.' Sadie put her hand over the mouth piece and said, 'Some incoherent idiot wants darling, darling, Jimbo.'

'Jimbo is that you?'

'As ever.'

'Jimbo, it's Venetia, he's just gone and he's very, very keen. We did exactly as you said, and he is very enthusiastic. He'll let us know by the end of the week. Jeremy and I can't thank you enough. We're just having a toast to good fortune. We're so thrilled.'

'Hold on a minute, nothing and I mean nothing, as Jeremy well knows, is definite until you've got his signature on a piece of paper. Don't believe your troubles are over until then. Please. Do you understand?'

'Yes, of course, Jimbo I'm not a fool. Oh, he really was dishy. Have you met him?'

'Only at business receptions, haven't spoken to him much.'

'He's one of those older men who still has that indefinable something. He's so handsome in an aristocratic kind of a way. I quite took to him.' Jimbo groaned. 'I did most of the talking.' Jimbo groaned again. 'Jeremy's so devastated by what's happened he can hardly speak. So I took charge.'

Jimbo interrupted her, 'Put Jeremy on the phone please.' He waited a few minutes while Venetia found him. He heard Jeremy's heavy footfalls nearing the telephone.

'Good morning Jimbo, things do seem to be working out don't they? Just opening the champagne.'

'Look here, I know in this day and age women no longer take a back seat and quite rightly so, but, men like Craddock Fitch still don't subscribe to that view. Please in future *you* must take the lead. You're the business man not Venetia. I know you've had a body blow, but please stand up and be counted. I know these kind of people and I know I'm right.'

'Righteo, yes, righteo. I'll do that. Thanks again.'

'Anyway, glad things are looking more hopeful. Keep me informed. Bye.'

Knowing Peter was out and that Caroline had gone to the dentist's, Willie called at the Rectory. He hammered on the door like he always did but dutifully waited for Sylvia to open it.'

'Come in, I expect you're wanting your coffee?'

'Yes, please.' He followed her into the kitchen. He hadn't been in many kitchens so he hadn't much experience to judge by, but this rectory kitchen always took his fancy. It glowed with comfort, yes, that was it, glowed. This morning the twins were playing on a big rug spread out on the kitchen floor. Their brightly coloured toys added to the welcoming feel of the kitchen. There were some gold chrysanthemums in a creamy vase on the window sill and the sun, the warm, autumn sun was shining in, casting a lovely colour on his Sylvia as she stood at the table stirring his coffee. Wholesome she was, downright wholesome. He bent down to give Alex back a ball which had rolled out of his reach. The sun picked up the reddish glints of the baby's hair. It was Peter's smile that he gave Willie when he got the ball. For a moment Willie felt sad that he would never see his own smile on the face of a child. Too late for that, but not too late for joy.

He took his mug from Sylvia and their fingers touched as she relaxed her grip on the handle. There was that thrill again, the sheer physical shock of touching her. They might live together and share the same bed, and you'd think the excitement of her presence would have waned a little by now, but for Willie the vibrance was as rich as ever and he wanted to claim it for his own.

Sylvia cleared her throat. 'I've been thinking Willie, it might be nice to get away for a few days.'

'I've got some holiday due to me, so I suppose we could. Where do you fancy?'

'I've always had a liking for Cornwall. I went there once when I was a little girl. My grandmother took me. Land's End we saw and I really thought it must be.'

'Must be what?'

'Land's End of course.'

'Oh, I see.'

Willie took a sip of his coffee, contemplating Cornwall. They could walk along the cliffs hand in hand, now that would be a romantic place for a proposal. She'd have a scarf on which blew loose in the wind and wrapped around his face, he'd have to tuck it in her coat for her and she'd smile and touch his cheek. He could hear the violins in the background and in his mind's eye he could see him taking her into his arms, the wind blowing wildly and their passion mounting as she . . .

'Willie, did you hear what I said?'

'Pardon? No I didn't.'

'I said a friend of mine went to Cornwall on honeymoon.'

'Nice place for a honeymoon, Cornwall.'

'Yes, it would be.'

Beth began to cry. Alex was dragging her toy from her. Sylvia sorted them out by taking Alex onto her knee.

Smiling, Willie chucked Alex under his chin. 'That's one of my great regrets that is Sylvia, that we can't have children together. I'd have liked a nipper or two.'

'Bit late for that.'

'But of course, I wouldn't have wanted them to be bastards.'

'Willie! What a word to use in front of the children. Dr Harris won't allow them to hear bad language or anything about killing and guns and things. Good job she isn't here.'

'Sorry, but I wouldn't. It would have to be all legal like.'

'That's what pains you isn't it? Us not being married?'

'I'm willing to wait.' His head was bent and he was studying the table top as if he'd never seen one before in his life. Alex reached out to grab Willie's mug and had hold of it before either of them could stop him. The contents streamed across the table and onto Willie's lap. He leapt up. Sylvia put Alex back on the rug and went to get the kitchen roll.

She pulled off a good length and handed it to him to wipe his jumper and trousers with. He made only a half hearted attempt to mop himself so Sylvia took charge and vigorously set about cleaing him up. He took hold of her hand removed the sodden paper from it and put his arms around her waist.

'I hardly dare to ask this, because I don't want to hear you say no. But I'm going to say it. Would *you* like to go to Cornwall on your honeymoon with me?'

She laughed. 'Oh yes, Willie, I would.'

'Sylvia, do you mean that? Are you sure?'

'Oh yes, I am, I am.'

Willie kissed his precious Sylvia, his heart bursting with joy. 'Cornwall it is then. Right? We'll talk about this later, I don't want Dr Harris catching me in here again. I'll do my very best to make you happy Sylvia. We may be getting married late in life but the next thirty years will be the best believe me.'

'I know that, Willie, and I'm sorry I couldn't make up my mind sooner, but I had to be sure this time.' Sylvia kissed his cheek and smiled.

Willie had to get away to give himself time to assimilate what had happened. He almost skipped his way back to the churchyard. As he went through the lychgate he suffered a massive explosion of energy, he leapt up and punched the air with his fist. He'd have the mower out and cut the grass for the last time this year. Next time he got it out he would be a married man. Married to his Sylvia, the light of his life. By Jove, but life was good and not half.

Which was just what Jeremy was thinking when he dialled Jimbo's number the following Friday.

'Hello, Jimbo that you? Jeremy here. Well we've done it. Craddock Fitch has taken the bait, he's buying.'

'Brilliant, brilliant. I'm so glad for you. Price right?'

'Oh yes, I had to bargain a bit with him but yes we are very satisfied. He came himself you know. Been here most of the day which was a bit unexpected. The little woman had to hurry off upstairs to titivate herself and leave the men to conduct the business. But yes, a very satisfactory conclusion I must say.'

'Good, good.' Jimbo's curiosity got the better of him. 'Been able to negotiate terms for staying on to manage?'

'That's in the melting pot, but I'm pretty certain I shall be able to organise that to our mutual satisfaction. Altogether a very successful day's work.'

Jimbo smild wryly, 'I'm glad. It's certainly saved your bacon hasn't it?'

'Well, I was pretty confident we'd clinch it.'

'Oh yes, that was very obvious.'

'When you've been in business as long as I have it doesn't take long to negotiate a deal does it? If you're holding all the best cards it's a matter of standing your ground. They soon come round when they realise you aren't going to budge.'

'Exactly. Well, busy, busy, got to get moving. Keep in touch Jeremy won't you?'

'Of course.'

Jimbo quietly put down the receiver and said. 'Well, thank you very much Jimbo for all your hard work. We really appreciate what you've done for us. You've pulled us right out of the mire, and we were in it up to our necks. How about a little dinner to celebrate?'

Harriet heard him. 'Talking to yourself are you, darling? It's the first sign you know.'

'Not a single word of thanks, I can't believe it. When he came that day he was on the floor, now he's bounced back up like a rubber ball, riding high and deceiving himself into thinking he's achieved it.'

'Let it go Jimbo, he isn't worth bothering about.'

'Dammit, I need cheering up. Let's ask Ralph and Muriel and Peter and Caroline for a meal tonight. Nothing fancy just something out of the freezer. What do you say?'

'What a good idea. I'll get onto that straight away.'

★

Harriet was still struggling in the kitchen when the first of the guests arrived. 'Jimbo,' Harriet shouted. 'Answer the door please. Flick don't overfill the jug. They won't be able to pour. Fergus! Don't you dare. You two boys upstairs and watch television for a while. Here's a tray with some goodies on and leave enough for Flick please. In bed eight thirty sharp, but you can read for a bit if you wish. Don't argue Finlay, please, I'm too busy for that. Where's the carving knife. Oh there. Now look, Flick I think you've done all you ca..'

Muriel put her head around the kitchen door and said, 'Good evening, sorry we're early.'

'Hello, Muriel. Just about ready. Shoo, shoo children. Off you go. Mind how you carry that tray Finlay, I don't want to have to shampoo the stairs carpet tonight.'

'Hello, children.'

Flick liked Muriel and slipped her hand in hers as she greeted her, 'Hello Miss Hip . . . oh no, hello, Lady Templeton. Mummy's got some lovely food ready for you. We're off upstairs now.'

'Hello Flick dear, I expect you've been a great help to your Mummy, haven't you?'

'Yes. I'm learning to cook like she does and then I'm going to be on TV when I get older, showing people how to cook.'

'And why not? That sounds like an excellent ambition.' Flick let go of Muriel's hand and went off after the boys. 'Harriet, we shouldn't really be allowing you to go to all this trouble when you're expecting a baby.'

'Nonsense, I'm perfectly fit and able. In any case Jimbo needed cheering up.'

'Did he?'

'Yes, it looks as if he's solved Jeremy and Venetia's problems and he's upset because they haven't even thanked him.'

'Oh dear, I expect they're so excited it's slipped their

minds. So is it still going to be a health club?'

Harriet put her finger to her lips. 'Can't divulge until it's all signed and sealed. As Jimbo's told them, nothing is definite until the money is in the bank, but they're so relieved to have found a buyer, they're behaving as if it's all gone through. Take these starters in for me will you Muriel?'

'Of course. Peter and Caroline are late.'

'Yes, perhaps got problems with those babies of theirs.'

It was ten minutes past eight when they arrived from the Rectory.

'Sorry we're late,' Peter said as he came up the stairs two at a time into the sitting room. 'Been celebrating.'

'Celebrating?' Muriel asked.

'For once I know something the entire village doesn't know first! Willie and Sylvia have become engaged to be married today.'

Muriel clapped her hands with delight. 'Oh I'm so pleased. I'm sure they'll be very happy.'

'I'm sure they will. We've left the happy couple drinking the remains of the champagne, sitting close together on our settee looking like a couple of teenagers.'

Caroline laughed. 'We'll cough loudly when we get back, so as not to catch them in a compromising position!'

'Caroline! If you please.'

'Oh Peter, don't be stuffy, darling. It's what makes the world go round isn't it Jimbo? And you should know from what I've heard.'

Jimbo groaned, 'Please be kind to me, don't mention that particular incident. Judging by the sly grins and innuendoes I've had to put up with, the story has been spread throughout the entire county. I wish someone would do something really wicked to deflect the flack from me. Here Ralph, your whisky, and for you Caroline?'

'Orange juice same as Harriet, please.'

They talked about plans for Christmas both at the church and for themselves and Ralph asked if anything more had been heard about the Charity Fund. Caroline shuddered when she heard the question. 'Please tell Ralph quickly and then we'll talk about something else.'

Peter gripped her shoulder and gently shook her. 'Don't let yourself get upset darling, I'm here OK?'

'I know, but it always makes me shudder when I think what a close shave you had. Please tell them and then we'll change the subject.'

'Briefly the Charity Commissioners have agreed that the parish can nominate a charity and the money can go to it. I suppose it would have been a good idea to share it out amongst several good causes but to be honest I just want rid of it. My greatest regret is that we can't use it here in Turnham Malpas.'

Ralph shook his head, 'Absolutely not. No.'

'I agree,' Jimbo said as he offered Muriel more sherry. 'This village persona business is so peculiar. You would think that the influence of TV and newspapers and films and videos would have wiped out such strange collective fears, but they do still exist.'

'Well, they haven't and they won't. Look what happened about Peter and Stocks Day. If he hadn't agreed to take part he'd have had no church left at all. Well, except for us here that is.' As she was speaking Harriet became aware of a strange noise out in Stocks Row. 'Someone celebrating!' The noise grew louder and sounded like children blowing on trumpets.

Ralph, being nearest to the window, got up to look. He drew back the curtains and looked out. Standing outside in the road in front of the Store were Jeremy and Venetia. He was dressed in a sweater and jeans so tight Ralph wondered how he managed to walk. On his head he had a huge tricorn shaped paper hat, giving him a

musical comedy Napoleonic look, in his mouth a toy
trumpet of the kind given to children at birthday parties
and he was blowing it for all he was worth. Venetia was
dressed in her purple velvet tracksuit, on her head she
had a huge shiny pink cardboard hat which sported a
large purple feather curving down around her chin. She
too was blowing a toy trumpet and was holding what
looked like presents in her hands. Both of them carried
bottles under their arms.

Venetia looked up as the light from the window
caught her attention. She waved enthusiastically and
shouted, 'Open the door, we're going to have a party.'
By this time they were all crowding to the window to see
who was there. Jimbo laughed and went to let them in.

They heard Venetia's light footsteps coming up the
stairs and she burst into the sitting room. 'We've come.
We've come. Get the champagne glasses out, we're
going to have a party all night. So glad you're all
here, thought there'd only be Jimbo and Harriet.'
Momentarily she remembered her manners. 'I do hope
you don't mind us gate crashing, but we had to come to
thank our good friends for their wonderful help didn't
we Sid?' Jeremy rolled in, obviously already the worse
for drink.

'We certainly did, didn't we Marge?' He hugged
Venetia and the two of them almost toppled over.
'Ooops sorry old girl. Now Harriet, a formal presenta-
tion. I expect you already have a watch but we've bought
you an extra special one, as a thank you for all you've
done for us.'

'I didn't do anything, Jerem . . . Sid. It was Jimbo.'

'I'm coming to him in a moment.' He lurched
unsteadily and grabbed the edge of the table. 'I hereby
present you with this gold watch in grateful thanks for
saving us from certain ruin.' He held out a jeweller's box.
Harriet took it from him, hesitated and then kissed his

plump cheek. He flung his arms around her and hugged her, almost crushing her ribs in his enthusiasm. Then he nudged Venetia. 'Your turn now, old girl.'

She gave Jimbo his present and when he opened it he found a beautiful gold pen engraved with his initials, and before he could thank her Venetia placed a big kiss full on his mouth. 'No need for thanks Jimbo, it's worth every penny for what you've done for us.' Jimbo gave her a hug, glancing out of the corner of his eye to check Harriet's mood. But she was laughing as she watched Jeremy going round shaking hands with Ralph and Peter and kissing Caroline and Muriel. Harriet giggled to herself, poor Muriel was looking horrified and dishevelled, Jeremy's hug had pulled up her dress and she was struggling to straighten it and at the same time smooth her hair which had somehow become entangled with the trumpet Jeremy still had in his hand.

When he'd finished kissing and shaking hands Jeremy shouted, 'Out with the glasses Jimbo, I've had the champagne in the fridge at the Club, so it's all ready for drinking.' He gave several blasts on his trumpet as Venetia opened up a roll of streamers and threw them across the room. The streamers caught Peter and Ralph so that the two of them stood entwined, with the curly coloured strands decorating their heads and shoulders. Muriel relaxed when she saw Ralph was catching the mood of the evening and was looking amused. While Jimbo opened the champagne Harriet thanked Venetia for her watch. Taking it from its box she said, 'This is absolutely lovely, there really was no need to be so generous.'

'Of course there was, you've saved our lives.'

'Look Venetia, why don't you and Jeremy stay for dinner? It's only a scratch one, but there's plenty. Do say you'll stay, we can soon lay two more places.'

Venetia couldn't hide the delight she felt at being

invited to stay.

'Oh Harriet we'd love to, really love to, thank you very much. Jeremy will be delighted.'

The sound of the sitting room door opening made Venetia look up. Standing in the doorway were the three children, blinking in the bright light, and looking puzzled by the noise and excitement.

'Drinkies for the children,' she shouted. Venetia asked Harriet for three more glasses and poured a small amount of champagne into each one. 'Here you are children, you can drink a toast as well.' She patted Flick's head and kissed the two boys, whereupon they blushed and vigorously rubbed their cheeks where her lips had touched.

Venetia climbed on a chair and raised her glass.

'Ladies and gentlemen and children drink a toast to the future of Turnham House and to all our very good friends.'

They all clinked their glasses with each other's and then drank.

Jimbo helped Venetia down from the chair and then said, 'May I propose a toast?'

'Everyone shouted, 'Yes!'

'To Venetia and Jeremy! Long may they be with us here in Turnham Malpas.'

'Hear! Hear!'